VENGEANCE

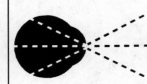

This Large Print Book carries the
Seal of Approval of N.A.V.H.

VENGEANCE

ZANE

THORNDIKE PRESS
A part of Gale, Cengage Learning

GALE
CENGAGE Learning®

Farmington Hills, Mich • San Francisco • New York • Waterville, Maine
Meriden, Conn • Mason, Ohio • Chicago

GALE
CENGAGE Learning®

LIBRARY OF CONGRESS CATALOGING-IN-PUBLICATION DATA

Names: Zane, author.
Title: Vengeance / by Zane.
Description: Large print edition. | Waterville, Maine : Thorndike Press, 2016. | Series: Thorndike Press large print African-American
Identifiers: LCCN 2016018597| ISBN 9781410491084 (hardcover) | ISBN 1410491080 (hardcover)
Subjects: LCSH: Revenge—Fiction. | Women singers—Fiction. | African Americans—Fiction. | Large type books. | GSAFD: Love stories. | Erotic fiction.
Classification: LCC PS3626.A63 V46 2016b | DDC 813/.6—dc23
LC record available at https://lccn.loc.gov/2016018597

Published in 2016 by arrangement with Atria Books, an imprint of Simon & Schuster, Inc.

Printed in Mexico
1 2 3 4 5 6 7 20 19 18 17 16

For my parents, Jim and Lib.
Thanks for showing me what it means
to be loved unconditionally simply for
waking up in the morning.

INTERMITTENT EXPLOSIVE DISORDER

Intermittent explosive disorder involves repeated episodes of impulsive, aggressive, violent behavior or angry verbal outbursts in which you react grossly out of proportion to the situation. Road rage, domestic abuse, throwing or breaking objects, or other temper tantrums may be signs of intermittent explosive disorder.

People with intermittent explosive disorder may attack others and their possessions, causing bodily injury and property damage. They may also injure themselves during an outburst. Later, people with intermittent explosive disorder may feel remorse, regret, or embarrassment.

Explosive eruptions, usually lasting less than thirty minutes, often result in verbal assaults, injuries, and the deliberate destruction of property. These episodes may occur in clusters or be separated by weeks or months of nonaggression. In between explosive outbursts, the person may be irritable, impulsive, aggressive, or angry.

Source: The Mayo Clinic
http://www.mayoclinic.org/diseases-conditions/intermittent-explosive-disorder/basics/definition/con-20024309

■ ■ ■ ■

PART ONE:
THE VERSE

■ ■ ■ ■

"Rape is a more heinous crime than murder since the rape victim dies throughout the period she lives."
— Amit Abraham

PROLOGUE

Saturday, September 18, 1993
10:18 p.m.
The Black Screw
Los Angeles, California

"Ladonna, get your little fast ass over here!"

Hannah was drunk as all get-out as she rubbed her hands up and down the chest of a dude who called himself Minister of Seduction. He was about six three and built like a truck. Not to mention the thirteen-to-fourteen-inch dick hanging in between his chiseled thighs. He was bouncing his dick up and down her behind as "Whoot, There It Is" by 95 South pumped through the speakers.

I was returning from the bar with two blow jobs — apparently the drink special of the night because a lot of the ladies were drinking them from shot glasses. I wasn't a fan of the taste of coffee but was willing to give the concoction of Baileys Irish Cream and Kahlúa, amaretto, and whipped cream a try. It was my twenty-first birthday and I had been waiting for the chance to do two things: drink some liquor legally, and drink it at a club. Hannah had made both dreams come true, albeit, it was not quite the kind of club that I had in mind.

I couldn't believe that she had taken me to a strip club — the Black Screw. There were at least two dozen half-naked men tickling the fancy of the ladies who ranged in ages, races, and levels of intoxication. Alcohol definitely made people loosen up, but I knew that already from all my concerts. Even though I was a superstar already by that age, no one recognized me in the club. I always wore a veil onstage. My physical scars were gone, and I was totally unrecognizable from the prior version of me. Yet, I still was not quite ready to embrace my beauty enough to put it on display in front of the world.

I had led a complicated life — a serious understatement — but I was finally happy with the family that I had always wanted. Daddy was back at the Beverly Wilshire on a business call with his partners in Japan. Part of "the conditions" for me to even pursue a music career was that Hannah had to always travel with me — a nanny of sorts.

12

Yes, I was "of age," but I still needed her. I realized that one day she would want to — and need to — go discover herself. She was already in her early forties but still trying to figure out what she truly wanted to do for a career *legally.* At least by Daddy paying her, she was able to stop stealing for a living. I loved Hannah so much. She was the only true friend that I had ever had. She had been there for me when no one else was. She had seen my first round of tears, caught my second round, and was helping to prevent a third. I would always love her for that.

"Whoot, There It Is" faded out and "Knockin' Da Boots" by H-Town came on as the sexy announcer / hype man introduced the next act. I reached Hannah and handed her a blow job as Minister of Seduction started gyrating his hips toward a woman old enough to be Hannah's mother at the next table. She straight up grabbed his dick through his G-string and started caressing it like the Holy Grail.

"Are you ladies ready for some serious dick action?" the announcer yelled out, and received a bunch of "hell yes," "damn right," and "bring on the dick" responses.

"I'm talking massive, enormous, long and strong, hard-as-nails dick!"

It sounded strange to hear one man describing another man's dick, but I giggled and guzzled down my shot. I expected to be drunk within seconds but that didn't happen. I was going to need quite a few blow jobs to feel something. At least, that is what I thought.

"Ladies, ladies, ladies! Coming to the floor here at the Black Screw are the set of twins who always bring on double delight!"

Hannah screamed out, "Twins? Oh, hellz yeah!" She nudged me with her elbow. "Don't you tell Richard I took you to a strip club," she added, referring to my father.

"Hannah, I'm grown," I replied. "Besides, this is fun. I thought we were going to a dance club, but this is a great way to break me into adulthood."

"You're a singer," she said as she grabbed at the six-pack abs of a male dancer named Daddy Longstroke walking through. "You're always around dancing, but not this kind of dancing."

We both laughed as the announcer went on. "Here they come, and I do mean come. The North Pole and the South Pole are about to make some panties wet up in here."

"Damn," was all I could say as two pieces of hunk slid out on the stage from opposite directions on their knees, with a single long-stemmed rose in each of their mouths. They were dark chocolate with hazel eyes and had on red silk boxers and black boots with Santa Claus jackets and hats. "Christmas has come early this year."

I was a bit tipsy after all from that one shot. I was talking crazy and totally unlike myself. I wasn't even impressed with fine men on that level. I was around them all the time because my backup dancers were no joke. Two of them were only checking for men, though, but they were still fine.

"Knockin' Da Boots" was the perfect song for the twins to show off their stuff. As they spun around on the stage and women tossed money at them, the announcer asked, "How many of you ladies think you can climb one of their poles?" as they both lowered the front of their boxers, revealing long-ass dicks covered in thin fabric. You could see the veins popping out of their dicks through it.

"I want to climb the North Pole!" Hannah yelled out. She chuckled and poked me in the arm. "She'll climb the South Pole!"

They got to the part of the song where they said it was the intermission and that women should go get their towels. Someone threw two red towels on the stage from the back and, by that time, the twins were down to their G-strings. They placed the towels in front of their groins and then stepped out of the G-strings, leaving all of us to imagine what was hanging behind the towels as "I Wanna Sex You Up" by Color Me Badd came on. That was all she wrote. The women in the audience completely lost it as the twins came down the steps into the crowd and let chicks take turns copping a feel under the towels.

"You having fun?" Hannah asked as she called over a waitress to get some more drinks. "I shouldn't have sent you to get drinks. We need something *harder,* pun definitely intended."

I had gone to the bar to get drinks only to see if I would get carded again. I was so excited about flashing my license at the front door, proving that I was twenty-one as of that day. I had wanted that feeling again but hadn't known what to order once the bartender asked what I was drinking, so I had gone with the flow.

"Give us two sea breezes," Hannah instructed the waitress. "And make those joints strong. Double up that liquor."

"That'll be two dollars extra per drink," the waitress informed her.

"Well, I guess it's a good thing Ladonna

here" — Hannah pointed to me — "is filthy rich."

The waitress looked offended and then started eyeing Hannah suspiciously. A few other women had thrown shade about Hannah's appearance earlier and I was ready to jump anyone who came out the side of their neck with any negative comments. I was hoping the cute little waitress with the dreads wouldn't be the one to end up getting my ass whooping that was on deck.

"I was just informing you," the waitress said sarcastically. "The manager insists on it. Some people start tripping when they get their tabs."

Hannah shrugged and turned her attention back to the stage, offending the waitress even more.

"The surcharge is cool," I said. "In fact, bring us four of them so we won't have to track you down for the next round."

The waitress smiled at me and actually looked like she wanted to jump my bones. "No problem, sweetie. I like that top," she yelled out over the music.

As she walked away, I asked Hannah, "What's in a sea breeze?"

"Cranberry juice, grapefruit juice, and vodka."

"Sounds delish."

"Speaking of delicious!" One of the twins was upon us, in all his glory and with all his dick. Hannah started feeling his chest, from the middle of his pecs down to the top of his pubic hair on his lower torso that was a tease of what was below.

His brother caught me off guard by picking me up from behind and damn near impaling me on his dick through my jeans. I found it amusing — at first — but then he got kind of rough with me. He tried to bend me over and pretend to fuck me from the back. That was when it all came rushing back and I exploded.

I started yelling and attempted to push him off me. "Get off me! Get the fuck off!"

Hannah didn't hear me apparently. She was still caught up with flirting with his brother.

The one behind me started moving his hips faster and faster and some of the other women were telling me to "take that dick," "get it, sister," and "work that billy over."

I started having a panic attack and grabbed for my purse on the table beside me, reaching inside to get my can of pepper spray. I didn't hesitate to pull the trigger over my shoulder and spray not only the beast trying to attack me but also anyone else within range.

He yelled out in pain and called me a bitch. His brother yelled, "What the fuck are you doing?"

Hannah immediately took me by the arm and started pulling me toward the exit. "Let's go!"

There was a panic in the club, but we rushed out before the bouncers at the door could be alerted that I had done anything. Hannah pushed me into the back of the limousine that was waiting out front for us.

"Back to the hotel," Hannah instructed the driver, who immediately took off as the twins and the waitress made it out the entrance to search for us.

"I'm so sorry," I whispered. "Please don't tell Daddy what happened."

"It's my fault," Hannah replied. "I wasn't thinking. I never should've taken you there in the first place."

I started crying. "Will I ever be normal, Hannah? How am I ever going to fall in love if I can't stand a man touching me?"

"That's what your therapy is for. It takes time."

"It's been six years!" I dried my tears with my sleeve. "This is never going to end."

"Everything ends eventually, or at least improves," she reassured me. "You're going to have to learn to forgive them. They were kids, like you, and made a huge mistake."

"A mistake? What they did to me wasn't a fucking mistake!" My chest tightened as memories of the past rushed through my mind. "They ruined my life!"

Hannah took my hand. "We've been through this. Your life is not ruined, Ladonna. You've been given an opportunity for a new beginning. Richard loves you and he'll never let anyone hurt you." She ran her fingers from her other hand across my cheek where my scar had been removed by several plastic surgeries. "You're stunning, you're talented, and you're famous. I only wish that you would let the world see the real Wicket. You shouldn't hide behind that veil onstage."

"But what if someone recognizes me?" I asked as tremors shot through my body.

"Think about it. Who on earth would put two and two together? As far as the world is concerned, Richard adopted you nearly a decade before it actually happened. You don't look the same. Money talks, and Richard has made sure that the truth will never come out."

"Maybe it should come out," I said. "Maybe I should go back and fuck up their lives like they fucked up mine."

"That's not truly on your heart."

"How do you know?"

"Because I know you. There's no reason for you to go back there . . . *ever!*"

I leaned back in the seat. "I should've been there for Grandma when she . . ."

"You can't change that. I'm sure she only wanted you to be happy. You used to write her letters. She knew you loved her."

"Yeah, letters with no return address. That was so immature of me."

"It was the only thing that made sense at the time. Stop beating yourself up. It's not easy living a triple life."

I let her words sink in: *a triple life.* That was exactly what I was doing. I was three women living inside one body.

There was Caprice Tatum — a scared, scarred young girl suffering from intermittent explosive disorder.

There was Ladonna Sterling — the world-traveled, seemingly confident daughter of billionaire Richard Sterling.

And then there was Wicket — the veiled, sensual singer taking the music industry by storm with her first hit album in constant rotation at radio stations around the globe.

No wonder I was so fucked-up in the head!

Sunday, October 25, 1987
2:36 a.m.
Atlanta, Georgia

As I approached the doorway, three college-aged guys were lingering around, smoking cigarettes and carrying backpacks. They had probably come from other HBCUs for the Morehouse homecoming game and were headed back after the parties ended so they could attend class on Monday. One of them had a large boom box. Prince's "Sign o' the Times" was blasting through its eight speakers. That was the thing back then; the bigger the sound system, the better. Nowadays, the smaller the MP3 player, the better. That boom box truly was a sign of the times.

Another guy glanced down at his Swatch impatiently as I brushed past them without a word. I could sense them staring at me and heard one of them whispering something, undoubtedly something ignorant about the scar running down the left side of my face, but I could not have cared less. I was more concerned with the excruciating pain between my thighs, the lacerations on my breasts, and the fact that, hours earlier, I had endured the greatest humiliation of my entire life.

There were fewer than two dozen people scattered around the downtown Greyhound depot; half of them were asleep on benches. All of their worldly possessions were crammed in trash bags, grocery bags, or in stolen carts from local stores. Through my blurred vision, I could make out the ticket counter directly ahead of me. It took all the deliberation within me not to pass out.

Halfway across the lobby, my knees felt like they were about to collapse. It was akin to being on stilts. Pulling my brown bomber jacket tighter around me, I didn't want anyone to see my mutilated body. I tried to persuade myself that if I could make it to the counter, purchase a ticket to anywhere with the $56.78 that I had in my purse, and get the hell away from Atlanta, everything would be okay. I had no clue how far $56.78 would get me or how I would get additional money once I arrived or even afford to eat, but none of that mattered. I had to leave . . . either leave or kill myself. Those were the only two practicable options.

A kaleidoscope of thoughts, accompanied by vivid and horrific images, cascaded through my memory bank as I stood there, weakening by the second. Killing myself would have made the most sense, but I was too cowardly. I had made several attempts; always chickening out when it came down to it. Maybe I would die there on the spot from what they did to me. I would have welcomed such a blessing. I was not meant for this world. They should have made me the poster child for the term "fucked at birth."

People were staring. One woman with big hair, fluffed up so much that it looked like a second head, was clutching on to her purse on the bench like she anticipated me flying across the room like a vampire and snatching it. She shouldn't have been traveling so late if she was petrified of strangers. Crazy people frequented bus stations at night. I was fifteen years old and even I understood that.

Someone else entered the automatic doors behind me. I could tell it was a woman by the sound of her voice. Her perfume was impenetrable and intoxicating and flooded the entire area with her scent. She was speaking with someone, a man.

"I can't believe we have to take the bus back to New York! Why can't we rent a car?" Her voice was indulgent, almost lyrical.

"I don't feel like driving in the middle of the night, Hannah," the man replied. "If we leave on the three-fifteen, we'll be there by dinnertime."

"Shawn, I am *so* not feeling you right now. So not feeling you." She paused and sucked on her teeth. "You're being a cheap-skate, as usual. Let's call a spade a spade."

Shawn sighed. "You just want to hear yourself yack. I'm paying for the bus tickets. It would probably be cheaper to rent a damn car."

"So now you're going to start cursing at me?"

" 'Damn' is not a curse word, Hannah. Could you please chill out so I can check and see if there are any seats? All of this back-and-forth might be a moot point."

I attempted to move again but I remained stuck in place halfway to the window. I wondered if I could get to New York City with less than sixty dollars. His comment about it being cheaper to rent a car than to purchase two tickets had me concerned. Then he had mentioned something about all the seats possibly being taken. I wanted to beat them to the counter and purchase a ticket; I didn't want them to take up the last spaces. New York was the kind of city that I needed to get lost in. From what I had seen on TV, with millions of degener-ates and glamorous people mixed together on an infinitesimal island, I could undoubt-edly drop off the radar. Not that anyone in particular would be searching for me. That was for sure. No one cared whether I was even breathing. Only my grandmother, and she was better off without me. I was a curse in her life, and truth be told, she was also a curse in mine. There was a generational curse in my family that needed to stop someplace, and that *someplace* would be with me. Bringing a child into the world was out of the question. There was no way that I would ever subject another innocent person to the insanity of our family. No damn way.

I would eat out of trash cans if I had to. Sleep in subway stations or on bus benches. I would do all of that until I inevitably starved to death, froze to death, or got up enough audacity to dive directly in front of a train one day. It did not even need to be that melodramatic. I would simply stride off the platform like I was taking the next step on a sidewalk and get it over with. Or maybe I would get a running start off the roof of a skyscraper. Maybe some lunatic would drag me into an alley, slash my throat from ear to ear, and save me the trouble. I would be a mention on the local evening news, might even be a featured scroll on the bottom of the screen on CNN, and would be in a small story on the police blotter and listed on the murder-victim list for the year — and that would be the end of it. "An unidentified black female was discovered in an alley in Manhattan with her throat slashed. She had a preexisting scar on her face, which leads officials to believe she had been disfigured for some time. If you have any information, please call the NYPD at blah, blah, blah, blah . . ."

Somehow I managed to walk to the counter. The couple was behind me, right on my tail. Shawn and Hannah. Hannah and Cheapskate Shawn.

"Can I help you?" the man with the salt-and-pepper beard asked from the other side of the bulletproof glass. I always wondered what they thought could prevent a true maniac from putting the tip of his gun through the transaction slot and pulling the trigger.

"Um, yes," I muttered. "How much is a ticket to NYC on the three-fifteen bus?"

He started typing and suddenly I started shivering like I was in the middle of a snowstorm.

"That will be . . ." The man took one look at me and acted like he had seen a ghost. "Young lady, are you all right?"

"I'm . . . I'm . . ."

I felt someone touch me on my shoulder and then materialize next to me. It was the woman: Hannah. She was striking. She had

27

skin the color of buttermilk, blond hair, blue eyes, and high cheekbones. She reminded me of a model who I had seen one time in a commercial for shampoo. Her hair was fluffed out and big, too.

"Are you okay, sweetie?" she asked, but I could not respond. I was shaking like a leaf and my vision was going in and out. The throbbing between my legs was indescribable. She looked at the man at the counter. "What's wrong with her?"

He shrugged. "Beats me. She asked for a ticket to NYC, and when I looked up, she was looking all sick and crazy."

"Hannah, maybe you shouldn't touch her," Shawn suggested.

I did not even turn around to see what he looked like. I couldn't move.

"Fuck you, Shawn!" Hannah stated with aloofness. "This baby's hurt."

"All I'm saying is —"

Before Shawn could finish his statement, Hannah was gasping at the sight of blood gushing down my legs and onto the floor.

"Oh my Jesus!" Hannah exclaimed. "Call an ambulance!" she instructed the counter man. She looked into my eyes. "Baby, baby, we're going to get you some help!"

"This is insane!" Shawn said. "We're going to miss our bus. Now we won't get back

28

until Monday."

I could not see Hannah, but I heard her curse Shawn the hell out. "Shawn, what part of *fuck you* did you not understand? I'm not leaving this baby here like this. Help me get her to a bench."

"I'm not touching her," Shawn said.

"And you're not touching me, either, never, ever again, you bastard!"

Hannah tried her best to guide me to a bench across the lobby. My eyes were like slits and I could see the three young guys from outside rushing in, toward us, and could hear the man on the phone calling 911. Then everything faded to black.

11:12 a.m.

My eyes flickered at first and then I managed to keep them open for a few seconds. All I saw was a bright light and wondered if all the rumors were true about death. Was I seeing "the light"? Was God going to allow me to go to heaven even though I was tainted, scarred, and worthless? I shut my eyes and prayed for Him to take me instead of sending me to hell. I had lived there for fifteen years already and I desperately needed a break. As I got to the part about walking through the valley of death, I heard Hannah's voice.

"You okay, baby girl?"

I opened my eyes and saw her getting up from the chair beside my hospital bed. Ah, an overhead light? Now I could make things out more clearly.

"Let me go get the nurse." She started toward the door. "I'll be right back."

"Wait!" I exclaimed in a panic.

Hannah turned to look at me. "They need to check you out, ask you some questions." She dropped her eyes to the floor. "They did a rape kit on you. It was kind of obvious; a lot of tearing."

"I don't want to answer any questions. I want to leave this place."

"The hospital? They're not going to let you out of here until you've improved. Not a chance."

I stared at her and fought back tears. "I don't want to be here, in Atlanta. That's why I was at the bus station. I'm not answering any questions and I'm not pressing any charges."

"So you *were* raped?"

I fell silent and then attempted to sit up, searching the room for my clothes. "Where are my clothes?"

"They were ruined, covered with blood. They disposed of them." She walked back over to the bed. "Look, we've yet to even be formally introduced. I'm Hannah."

"Yes, I know. I heard Shawn say your name."

She grinned. "Did you hear me call him a cheapskate?"

I smiled. "Yes."

"We've established that I'm Hannah — and you are?"

"Nobody."

"Seriously, you didn't have any ID on you. They gave me your money, though. I put it in the side pocket of my purse."

"Thank you." I lay back down. It was too painful to sit up. "Thanks for everything."

"Can I go get the nurse now? I don't want anything to happen to you."

It felt strange to have someone care about my welfare. Until the night before, I thought that two of my so-called friends had my back. Instead, they had set me up to be brutalized. I couldn't understand why they would do such a thing. I had never done anything to them.

"Before you go out there, can I ask you a favor?"

Hannah looked uncertain. "And what might that be?"

"If I let them check me out *one time,* will you help me sneak out of here?"

She frowned. "Are you crazy? I already

31

gave them my name and information. I lied and said that I was your aunt . . . by marriage. I started to say that I was your mother but being that I'm white, not to mention my *other issue,* I knew they wouldn't buy it."

I was curious. "What did you tell them my name was?"

What other issue?

She smirked. "Rose Cleveland. First name that popped into my head."

"Rose is an old-fashioned name."

"You don't know who Rose Cleveland was?" She chuckled. "Apparently the person at the registration desk didn't pick up on it, either."

"Pick up on what?"

Hannah sighed. "Rose Cleveland was the first lady of the United States for two years during her brother, Grover's, first term."

"Oh." I felt like such a dummy. Studying was not my strong point, due to all the stress, and I definitely was lacking in my knowledge of history. "Okay."

"Grover Cleveland was the twenty-second president. He served two terms and got married halfway through the first one. So Rose resigned and started a lesbian relationship with a chick named Evangeline who was married to a bishop."

Even though I felt horrible, I had to giggle a little. "Wow, they were getting it on back then."

"And then some. Freakiness was not invented in the twenty-first century." She paused and picked at one of her manicured nails, dislodging something from it. "After he died, Rose and Evangeline moved to Italy to shack up and she ended up dying during the 1918 flu pandemic."

I wanted to ask what a "pandemic" was but opted out of that. "This is fascinating and all, but can we get back to you sneaking me out of here? If you let me go with you, you can teach me anything you want."

Watching a lot of crime shows on TV kicked in. I was a *Miami Vice* addict. Pain or not, I started getting up out of the bed.

"What are you doing?" Hannah's reflexes had her assisting me instead of letting me struggle. "Let me go get the nurse."

"No, that's not happening. I just realized that once they realize that I'm awake, the next thing will be a sex crimes detective in my face asking a bunch of questions."

"They called the police when we arrived in the ambulance, but I told them the truth. That I didn't know anything. I said that we were here on vacation and that you were a mess when you met me at the Greyhound station to head back."

"You're good at mixing fiction with fact." I managed to get up but I only had on the hospital gown. I noticed Hannah's coat strewn across a chair in the corner and confiscated it. "We have to get out of here."

Hannah helped me put the coat on, again so I wouldn't hurt myself, but I could tell she was conflicted about it. "Where are we going?"

"Auntie Hannah, where we both were going in the first place. New York. I promise you that once we get there, I'll get out of your way. I won't even sit beside you on the bus if you don't want me to, but please help me." I fought back tears again. "I'm begging you. I'll do anything you want."

"How old are you?" she inquired. "And don't lie."

I glanced down at the floor and back up into her blues eyes. "I'm fifteen, but I've lived three of your lifetimes."

She stared at me. "Somehow, I believe you. But what about your parents? You're a minor. I can't just —"

"My mother's locked up in an asylum — she's fucking nuts — and my father is dead."

She appeared stunned. "And you're sure you don't want to tell the police what happened?"

"No, I can't deal with that right now. Please. I'll do anything."

"Stop saying you'll do anything. Some of these predators out here will only take you up on that. I speak from vast experience."

I walked over to the door and peeked out. The nurses' station was on the other end of the hallway. Good! "The coast is clear. Let's go."

Hannah seemed frozen in place at first but then jumped into action. "This is *not* a good idea, but I guess that I'm in. Goodness knows that I've done worse." She paused. "I hope you're being honest about your parents. I don't want to end up facing a kidnapping charge. *That* would be a new one for me."

"You're not kidnapping me. And they're not going to come to New York looking for me anyway. They don't even know my name."

"Neither do I."

I hated telling people my name because of the meaning behind it. I blurted it out. "Caprice. My name is Caprice."

Hannah grinned. "What a pretty name. Much better than Rose."

I didn't respond. My name was all part of the generational curse.

We snuck out the room, out the exit door

at the stairwell, and then caught a cab to the bus station. New York City, I was on my way.

Thursday, November 26, 1987
Thanksgiving Day
The Bronx

"Every day, I want you to look into this mirror and say to yourself, 'I'm that chick.' "

I frowned as Hannah stood behind me, holding my shoulders as we made eye contact in the floor-length mirror on the back of her bedroom door.

"But how can I say that when I have this hideous scar on my face?" I asked, not convinced at all by the constant empowerment speeches she had been laying on me since we had arrived in New York a month earlier.

"Baby girl, fuck anyone who thinks they're better than you." She turned me around to face her. "Do you know what I see when I look at you?"

I shrugged. "An unattractive, anorexic-looking teenager?"

Hannah guided me to her whitewashed, wooden, king-size bed and we sat down. "Listen, Caprice, we've talked about your life and all the things people did to you, but the past is the past." She ran her fingers

36

through my hair. "I mean, look at me. All the shit I've endured within thirty-six years. And all I have to show for it is this dump that we live in and a hundred and eighty-two dollars hidden under this old-ass mattress."

"I like this place. It has character."

That it did. Not that I had been anywhere outside Atlanta in my life, and I rarely was in anyone else's residence, but Hannah's one-bedroom apartment in The Bronx had the most interesting decor that I had ever seen. She was a collector of novelty items and was seemingly addicted to loud, vibrant colors. She had her lamps covered with red, green, and purple lace throughout the cramped place and had these huge, flowery floor pillows in various colors in the living room, for guests. She often had company and she was expecting a few friends over for Thanksgiving that day.

We had spent the morning stuffing a turkey, snapping the ends off string beans, and *attempting* to make an apple pie from scratch. It was currently in the oven for another half hour or so and we were keeping our fingers crossed on that one. Neither one of us counted cooking as one of our best traits; we had that in common.

Hannah had a closet overflowing with

fancy outfits, but most were stolen. Hannah was a "booster," a fancy term for an organized shoplifter. She left several times a week and came back with items crammed into her big purses and hidden all over her body as well. She had a tool that she used to remove alarm sensors off items and told me that she had been doing it for over a decade. She would keep what she liked and then sell the rest to other people in the neighborhood.

The Bronx was an interesting place, but it was also scary — especially at night. They were still rebuilding the area after all the fires from times past. Hannah was born and raised there, a fourth-generation member of a Jewish family that had migrated to New York in the 1930s, when the majority of The Bronx was composed of Jews. She said that after rent control was established, landlords stopped taking care of their properties because there was no incentive for them to do otherwise. What resulted was a lot of poor minorities moving in, gangs being created, landlords burning down their own buildings to get the insurance money. Rumor had it that there were so many fires daily that the trucks rarely got a chance to return to the fire stations. Rumor also had it that a lot of tenants were committing the arsons because they could get some money from HUD, no questions asked, for their belongings.

Even though the area was like something out of a World War II movie in some spots, I still enjoyed a lot of the people. The Bronx, specifically 1520 Sedgwick Avenue, an apartment building in Morris Heights, was credited with being the birthplace of hip-hop. DJ Kool Herc referred to the building as "the Bethlehem of hip-hop culture." All throughout the project building where we lived, you could hear "Paid in Full" by Eric B. and Rakim, "The Bridge Is Over" by BDP from their *Criminal Minded* album, and "Rock the House" by DJ Jazzy Jeff and the Fresh Prince. I had always loved music, but listening to it all day and night blasting out of windows and in the courtyard gave me a new appreciation of it.

When Hannah's friends came over, we used to have dance competitions and she would dress me older and sneak me into some of the clubs she frequented. No one really cared about my being underage when we were together. She was so popular and cool. The blond, confident, transgender male-to-female booster with the hot clothing items and shoes on deck that everyone craved but couldn't afford to get from a store.

As it turned out, Hannah's "other issue" in the hospital that day was that everyone was clued in to the fact that she had been born a man except for naïve, sedated, and too-traumatized-to-realize-it me. That was why she had told them that she was my aunt and not my mother, even though the race was another dilemma. She had been completely transparent with me on the bus ride to NYC. I was fascinated with the entire story.

Hannah had been born Amram, after the father of Moses, the leader of the Jewish people in the generation preceding the exodus from Egypt. She knew early on that she did not identify with her assigned sex. Inside, she was a girl, and therefore loved little girl things. Her father, Chanan, was wrought with guilt that he had done something wrong, and up until his death, in a car accident when Hannah was twelve, he could never accept the fact that she wanted to wear dresses and heels and play with makeup.

Upon Chanan's death, her mother, Nava, allowed Hannah to do as she wished. The rest of their extended family shamed and ridiculed her until she left home at eighteen to make it on her own. Nava still lived in The Bronx, but they did not speak. I asked Hannah often why she was shunning her mother when she had been supportive of her desires. Hannah would express that she didn't want to bring her mother any more pain by being around and allowing other family members to badger her with nasty comments. She hoped that being out of their sight would also mean being out of their minds. I could relate to that, because I was hoping the same for my own grand-mother. I had burdened her enough, and my mother's mental instability had de-stroyed any chance of a normal existence.

"This place doesn't have character," Han-nah replied, snapping me back from my thoughts. "I need to get rid of some of this junk around here."

"Just don't get rid of your Cabbage Patch dolls, the Snoopy Sno-Cones machine, or those Moxi roller skates."

She laughed. "Sometimes I forget how young you are." She sighed. "Speaking of which, I'm still trying to figure out a way to get you registered for school in the spring."

"Who needs school? I can get a job and help out around here."

"A job doing what? I can't even get a

decent-ass job and I have my high school diploma. I started boosting to make ends meet, and now I'm all caught up."

"You get a rush from it, don't you?" I asked, recalling the enthusiasm she always seemed to have when she unloaded her "take" for the day on the worn sofa.

"It's partly that, but it is also mostly because I don't have to deal with the bullshit that would come about from a regular job. Sure, I could get some fast-food work or maybe even get into a call center, but people are so judgmental about my choices. I don't have the tolerance to have to defend myself from ridicule day after day. Being a booster allows me to stay off the radar." She smirked. "But I am good. I haven't been arrested in going on three years, and that's a record."

"What happens when they arrest you?"

"A bunch of nonsense, purely for show, then I post a little bail, and walk. They have serious crimes to worry about here. Up until about five years ago, The Bronx was the murder, rape, robbery, aggravated assault, and arson capital of America."

I was stunned. "Really? I mean, I can see that it's rough here, but everyone I've met seems so nice."

"Most people around here are nice, but

that has nothing to do with the crazies who had a total disregard for human life. That's why you need to get your ass back in school. So you can make something of yourself."

I looked down at the floor. "I can't go back to school. Not yet. Are you forgetting what my classmates in Georgia did to me the night we met?"

Hannah grabbed my shoulders and forced me to make eye contact. "Listen to me, nature has a way of weeding out the thorns. Let karma take care of them, and I understand how you feel, but they are more than a thousand miles away and can't hurt you now."

"That doesn't mean kids here won't make fun of my scar." I was on the brink of tears. "It's not like I can cover up my face. My mother should've just killed me that day and gotten it over with."

Hannah pulled me close to her and hugged me tightly. "You're special. Believe me when I say that. You are going to turn your test into your testimony and your mess into your message one day. Don't give up on life, and fuck anyone who thinks they're better than you. They're not. There are not any Big I's and Little U's in this world. We are all unique in our own way."

I continued to fight back the tears. "I want

to believe you, I do. It's just that . . ."

"Just that nothing." Hannah let me go and got up off the bed. "Now go get ready for dinner. All those clothes I've jacked for you and you're sporting sweat pants and my old Beatles T-shirt. Go put on a nice dress."

"Who all is coming?" I asked.

"Sebastian, Crispin, Nigel, and Shayne."

"Oh boy," I said, thinking of the individuals she had just named. "It's going to be a long night."

Hannah chuckled. "Yeah, but a fun one. Bet you've never had a Thanksgiving like the one you're about to have."

"That's for damn sure."

Less than four hours later, we were all sprawled across the living room with stuffed stomachs and chilling to "Don't Dream It's Over" by Crowded House. Sebastian started belting out the words, and the next thing you know, everyone else had joined in, including me.

I was a bit tipsy because Hannah had allowed me a little bit of wine at dinner. I ended up getting up off the sofa and started doing an impromptu dance to the slow song before breaking out into the second verse. It took a few seconds before I realized that everyone else had stopped singing. They were all staring at me.

"Get it, girl!" Crispin yelled out.

"Work it now!" Nigel added.

Everyone in the house was transgender except for me. Nigel and Sebastian were female to male and Hannah, Shayne, and Crispin were all male to female. I loved, loved, loved their confidence and wished that I had it myself.

I started singing louder and dancing even more. Being around them made me feel comfortable. They all got up on their feet and started dancing with me until the song ended. Crispin gave me her white satin scarf from around her neck and I waved it around in the air as I landed in a split on the psychedelic carpet on the last note.

"Damn, Caprice, I didn't know you could sing!" Hannah yelled out.

"That's because I can't sing," I replied. "At least not better than the next person."

"The Devil is a liar," Nigel added. "You can blow."

"Amazing chops!" Shayne chimed in. "You need to go to some Broadway auditions."

"Yessir-ree! It's worth a shot!" Crispin confirmed Shayne's thought.

"Stop kidding with me!" I lashed out, hurt from them teasing me. "I'm not talented!"

"Says who? You?" Hannah walked over and rubbed me across the cheek. "Baby girl, a lot of people don't recognize their own gifts. You can sing *great* and . . ." She paused and looked around the room. "My buddies and I might be a lot of things, but liars we are not. We don't sugarcoat shit."

"Never have, never will," Shayne cosigned. "Now me, I sound like a sick frog when I sing, but I own it. You need to own up to the fact that you have a natural talent. Embrace that bitch."

"Have you ever had any voice lessons?" Nigel asked. "You sound like a pro."

I smirked. "I was barely allowed to go out the house. Besides, Grandma couldn't afford anything like that for me."

Sebastian had been fairly quiet up to that point, but that brought him back into the fold. "Grandma? Is that who raised you? Is she still alive?"

I looked at him in horror, and didn't say a word. I had no idea what Hannah had told her friends about me, but I knew that she was a master of mixing fact with fiction and making it sound plausible.

He looked at Hannah. "I thought you said this child didn't have any living relatives. Are you sure you need to be *involved* in all of this, Hannah?"

Crispin started in then. "What's really going on here?" She looked at me. "How *exactly* did you and Hannah meet, Caprice? And how old are you again?"

I still didn't say a word.

"It's Thanksgiving," Hannah finally said. "My name's not Babe or Dustin Hoffman, none of you are dentists, and this is not going to turn into the interrogation scene from *Marathon Man.*"

I cringed when Hannah said that. We had watched that 1976 flick on VHS a few nights earlier and that scene where a dentist tortured the main character by digging into his cavity had unnerved me to my core.

"Let's just chill and listen to some more music," Hannah continued.

All the rest of them looked at one another. I could tell it would not be the end of it but hoped it would end for that night.

Sebastian couldn't drop the subject. "All I'm saying is you don't need no more felony charges and if, for some reason, Caprice isn't *legally* in your care, anything can happen."

"Why are you all up in my business?" Hannah asked, getting angry. "Have I asked you for shit, to do shit, or for any shitty-ass advice?" She paused and waited for Sebastian to answer. He seemed offended. "That's

47

what I thought. We're cool and all but that's only because you hang with Nigel. He's my fam. But don't get it twisted. I don't need your validation or cosignature on a damn thing I do with my life."

"Damn, Hannah, chill," Nigel stated with disdain. "Sebastian didn't mean any harm."

Hannah glared at Nigel. "I don't know if you two are fucking or what, but he needs to leave me alone. And he damn sure better leave Caprice alone."

Nigel gathered up his coat and scarf off the armchair. "Maybe we should go."

"Maybe you should," Shayne said. "This is getting out of hand."

Hannah and Sebastian stared at each other as Nigel got Sebastian's things as well. Then Sebastian said one word that set me off: "Bitch!"

Now the word "bitch" was acceptable in some instances, and I had grown to understand that, even at my age. Sometimes it was used as a term of endearment or an acknowledgment of being fierce. But when Sebastian straight up called Hannah a bitch and then followed it up with a sneer on his face, something within me snapped in two.

I had had "outbursts" before but this time was different. I leaped over the coffee table and landed on Sebastian's chest as I knocked him backward onto the floor. I started scratching at his face and was determined to rip one of his eyeballs out if I could.

I heard Hannah scream and Nigel and Crispin pulled me off Sebastian, who was flailing around on the floor like a fish out of water. I tried to kick him in the privates — I was not sure what stage of transition he was in, but I was kicking at whatever was there — and the adrenaline in my body up-ticked a notch as I screamed, "I've got your bitch! Don't you talk to Hannah like that, you fucking wildebeest!"

Sebastian still seemed shocked as he stood with some help from Shayne, and was noticeably shaken. Even though he was now a man, he was scared like the female he used to be. I didn't give a fuck what he was or was not; no one was going to talk to Hannah like that.

"Something is seriously wrong with you," Sebastian said to me as Nigel and Crispin let me go. "I can't believe you attacked me."

"You better be glad they pulled me off you!" I lashed out. "You say some more shit about Hannah and you'll be taking a dirt nap!"

Hannah came over to me and tried to console me. "It's okay. They're leaving. They are *all* leaving," she said, making her point clear.

"I should call the police on you, press charges," Sebastian said, still ashamed about getting his ass kicked. "See how you like that."

"No, find your center," Nigel said to Sebastian as he took him by the elbow. "You know good and damn well you can't call no police up in here."

Sebastian sighed, yanking away from Nigel. "Says who?"

"Says common damn sense." Nigel started toward the front door. "Let's just go."

Everyone said their quick good-byes, except for Sebastian, who stomped out without another word, and Hannah put on the five dead bolts behind them. She turned to me. "What was that all about? You could've ripped his eyes out."

"That's exactly what I was trying to do," I admitted. Then I slumped down onto the floor. "I'm not sure what came over me. I'm sorry. Sometimes I lose control. I hope I didn't inherit my mother's mental issues. I often wonder about it, but no one would ever take me to see a therapist."

Hannah sat down in front of me, Indian-style. "They never got you any therapy after . . ."

I glanced into her eyes and ran my index finger over my scar. "After my mother cut up my face? No, not really. Other than DE-FACS asking a bunch of questions before making Grandma my legal guardian. My mother got locked up in a cuckoo house *obviously,* so they considered it case closed. Gave me some stitches and that was that."

"Don't you want to call her? Let her know you're all right?"

"If I do that, she'll try to convince me to come back. I can't go back. Not after what happened at homecoming."

Hannah took a deep breath. "About that. I've been thinking. You shouldn't let that go. You should go back — I'll go with you — and make them pay for what they did to you. Don't let them just get away with it. Don't let them go on with their lives, like nothing happened. They need to pay."

"I can't," I replied. "It's too much to deal with. But . . ."

"But what?"

"I was thinking about writing my grandmother a letter, letting her know that I'm alive but that I need space. I need to think all this through. As for *them,* it's all their words against mine. No one is going to believe me. No one is going to believe that any of those boys would even want to be

51

with me, rather less take it from me."

Even at fifteen, I was aware that most rapes went unreported for a reason. Growing up, I had seen females who accused men of raping them end up being shunned and ridiculed, mostly by other women. I had seen celebrity men on the news get away with mistreating women like they were nothing. I had seen the most beautiful women destroyed after making such statements. And then there was me: a young, poor, deformed girl who had been fucked over her entire life. What was a gang rape or two added into the mix?

Hannah kissed me on the forehead. "Just think about it, but the letter to your grandmother sounds like a good idea. I have some stamps, so let me know. And please consider going back to school."

"You can't even register me for school, remember?" I stood up. "Not that I want to go back. I'll figure out something."

I wanted to go take a shower and try to calm down. I was still upset about the entire scene with Sebastian. I paused at the doorway to the bathroom. "Why couldn't Sebastian call the police?"

Hannah had stood and was clearing away wineglasses and snack dishes. "Huh?"

"Why did Nigel say that it was common

sense that Sebastian couldn't call the police over here?"

"Oh . . ." She glanced at me. "Sebastian isn't exactly walking on the right side of the law."

"How so?"

"He's a big-time drug addict."

"Sebastian?" I couldn't fathom it.

"Yes, Sebastian. You won't see him offering to suck dick on the corner for a vial of crack or anything, but he is a serious cokehead. He's a functional addict. Works full-time in his dad's construction office and helps himself to extra cash out of the safe to feed his habit. Nigel probably knew Sebastian had some drugs on him tonight. That's why he said calling the police was foolish. Popping one can of worms generally leads to popping several. Know what I mean?"

I nodded. "I guess you never know about people. He seems normal to me."

"There's no such thing as normal today. It's the eighties, not the twenties. There is a sense of normalcy that people have accepted but nothing and no one is actually normal in the true definition of the word."

I didn't respond. I went into the bathroom, turned on the shower so the hot water could start making its slow trek up the pipes from the hot water heater in the basement

53

of our dilapidated building, and stripped down to nothingness.

I gazed into the mirror covering the medicine cabinet and whispered, "I'm that chick," even though I didn't believe that.

After I was in the shower, I thought about what Hannah had said about nothing being normal but there only being each individual's sense of normalcy. That was so true because all I had ever known was madness in my life. I was quite sure that most other children didn't have to endure my pain. Then again, I was also sure that some had likely endured much worse. Some were no longer alive, taken away from here by one sick maniac after another.

Since arriving in New York, I had definitely seen and witnessed my share of "questionable things." I hadn't seen all the murders, rapes, arsons, and assaults that Hannah had referred to, but I had seen the hookers lining the corners beside the drug dealers, selling sex and crack or a combination if it was the order of the day. Some of the girls selling pussy looked even younger than me, and that truly made me sad. I understood them, though. They felt like what they were doing was better than the alternative — at least the ones who were not being forced into doing it. I couldn't do anything to save them. Hell, I couldn't do anything to save myself.

The Bronx had gone through a "white flight" phase where most of the white people in the area moved out once things turned ugly. That happened in a lot of cities. But Hannah was white and still there and her family was still somewhere around. I smirked as the water cascaded down my back and into the crack of my ass. Hannah wanted me to contact my grandmother but she refused to contact her own mother. I planned to challenge her: if she would contact her mother, I would contact my grandmother. Fair was fair.

By the time I got finished bathing, Hannah was knocked out over her bed — likely from a combination of wine, laboring in the kitchen, and being emotionally drained by her friends and me. I was exhausted as well so I made my little pallet on the sofa and entered my dream state of the same nightmares that I had endured since I was very young.

Thursday, December 24,
1987 Christmas Eve
7:13 PM
Manhattan, New York City
So much had changed since Thanksgiving

Day, less than a month earlier. Now I understood what they meant about life moving faster up north, because mine had become a whirlwind of activity. I was working in Manhattan with Shayne. She owned a day spa and was employing me under the table since I was underage and nowhere near my legal guardian. She had come by the week after that violent after-dinner event and I had come clean with her. Hannah was out boosting at the time, but something about Shayne made me feel comfortable enough to sing like a canary. I even told her about what happened after homecoming. She broke down in tears and admitted that she had been molested by her older male cousin from age five to thirteen, when her family moved away to another state. She said that a lot of her family members believed that was what made her want to trans from William to Shayne. She disagreed and said the same that thing that Hannah always said: she had always known that she was a woman born into a man's body.

Shayne dated other women, while Hannah dated men. It was kind of confusing to me at times, but I was clear about one thing: they were entitled to live their lives in any way that made them happy about living at all. They were doing better than me because

I couldn't stand the thought of being touched by a man or a woman. I was also clear on that. Maybe one day that would change, but I somehow doubted it. I found guys attractive but didn't believe that any would find me attractive and, even on the off chance that one did, sex to me was associated with violence.

I was Shayne's shampoo girl at her spa and loved it. A few women had been insensitive enough to ask about my scar, but I wouldn't discuss it. Some found it rude and refused to tip me, but most actually felt sorry for me and gave me bigger tips than normal.

Hannah had agreed to my deal about contacting her mother and my grandmother. We both decided upon letters without a return address on the envelopes. That way we could say what needed to be said and did not have to be stressed out over their responses. It was more like: "Hello, I'm alive, love you, don't worry, and good-bye." There were some fluff words in between, but that was the gist of both three-page letters mailed a week before Christmas inside sentimental holiday cards. Hannah's had a Hanukkah theme on the front and I found one with a black angel decoration.

I felt good about letting Grandma know

that I was still breathing. After truly considering it, I found it immature to let her worry. She was not in the best of health and not knowing my fate was probably weighing heavily on her. Hopefully, she would understand why I had to leave. I did not tell her about being raped. That would have been inconsiderate, not to mention pointless. She couldn't have done anything to prevent it from happening any more than I could have. Nor could she do anything to make things right anymore than I could.

I still wasn't feeling Sebastian, and Nigel had cut off his friendship with Hannah over the "incident." I felt bad about that, but Hannah was cool with it. Her exact words: "I'm not about that druggie life anyway. And I damn sure don't want you around it."

I wanted to point out that as soon as we walked out our front door, we were surrounded by drugs, but I got what she was saying about it being in our home. I was just appreciative of the fact that Hannah had even brought me back with her — she could've left me right in that hospital room to fend for myself, or even in the bus station. She had not said a word about Shawn, so I figured that she was truly done with him. I wasn't quite sure who she was dating but I knew she was dating men exclusively. She would skim over discussing this guy or that guy but did not bring them around me. She had stayed out overnight four or five times since my arrival, cautioning me not to open the door or go outside late at night by myself. She was very protective of me and I could tell she had a sisterly or motherly kind of affection for me; two things I had never had, since I was an only child and my mother, along with being insane, hated the fact that I was ever born.

Hannah was the only reason that I stopped plotting to step off a train track and stopped waiting for someone to attack me and slit my throat in an alley. It was obvious that she would be hurt by that, and I didn't want to hurt her. I had grown to love her as, well, like the mother I had never had. We were two people with similar yet different traits that we allowed to hinder us, and that was what made our bond so strong.

My love and appreciation for Hannah is what landed me out in Times Square on Christmas Eve, doing something I never thought I would do in this life. I was walking to the train from the spa, upset that in spite of working my ass off, Shayne could only afford to pay me minimum wage. Back in 1987, the minimum wage in New York was $3.35. So even working under the table, for forty hours a week, I was barely making $135 each payday. My tips added in another $50 or so a week. I would give Hannah most of my money to go toward bills, or purchase groceries for us to share when I could. I had only been working a few weeks, so I had only about twenty dollars saved up. I wanted to purchase Hannah a nice gift, even though she stole most of what she desired. I wanted something to come from me.

I had seen this necklace in Macy's for about thirty-five dollars, so I was short. I didn't have the nerve to try to steal it. With my luck, I would've gotten caught my first time shoplifting and landed in "baby booking" for Christmas. That could've spiraled into a butterfly effect of the police figuring out who I was and forcing me to go back home or into foster care. I wanted to stay with Hannah. I also wanted that necklace.

I had not ventured to sing anything since Thanksgiving when everyone praised my voice. I still thought they were full of shit, but what if they weren't? Every day, on my way to and from work, I had seen people out in Times Square in costumes, or singing, or playing an instrument — even pans — while people tossed money into their buckets, bags, hats, or cups. I was on the way to the train to head home that evening when I decided to go for it. If I could get fifteen people to give me a dollar each, thirty people to give me fifty cents each, or sixty people to give me a quarter each, and a little extra for tax, I could get her that gift. I did the numbers in my head and, of course, Times Square was crammed with people doing last-minute shopping.

I stood there for a moment, trying to figure out what to sing. I needed to keep in the holiday spirit, but we never celebrated Christmas much in my house growing up. Everyone was in their own various states of depression. However, Hannah had been playing some holiday music around the apartment. I tried to think of one or two that I comfortably felt like I knew the beats and music to in order to pull it off.

So there I was in my brown Members Only jacket, a plaid skirt and leggings singing "Someday at Christmas" by Stevie Wonder. I started to give up less than a minute in; I felt foolish. Then a miracle happened. People started tossing money into my right boot, which I had removed and placed in front of me, since I had nothing else to collect coins in. By the time I finished that song, I had lost count of what people were tossing and quickly came up with a follow-up song. Some people stood there like it was a concert, so I couldn't sing the same song again.

I cleared my throat while I thought of something else and several people praised my voice. Maybe Hannah and her friends were right about my talent?

I started belting out "Santa Baby" by Eartha Kitt and, to my surprise, people actually started dancing with each other in front of me, between tossing more coins and even some dollar bills into my boot.

I started truly getting into it then, and some of the other street performers started throwing daggers in my direction. That kind of motivated me more. Even though I was going to have to ad-lib some of the lyrics, I broke out into "Give Love on Christmas Day" by The Jackson 5. I was singing and dancing my ass off. I was executing moves that I didn't even know I had, and realized something important right that minute. When I was performing, it was the only time that Caprice Tatum actually felt free. All my fears, all my pains, all my shame, and all my insecurities faded away. It was such a natural feeling for me; a natural space. I decided right then that in spite of my flaws, I had found my "calling."

Through the crowd, I could see a

chauffeur-driven Rolls-Royce pull up to the curb and the back window roll down. All I saw were eyes at first; piercing eyes. Then the driver got out, walked around to the rear passenger door, and opened it. A tall white man with dark brown eyes got out in a tailored three-piece suit, and a mountain of a man climbed out the front passenger seat. He was not as tall as the first man, but he outweighed him by at least a hundred pounds. His complexion was redder and he looked mean as a snake and glanced around the crowd with caution. I made him out to be a bodyguard. As the taller man walked toward me, presumably to get a closer look and to hear me better, the crowd parted for him like he was the president of the United States. But I knew he was definitely not Ronald Reagan.

He was, however, creating a stir. People started pointing at him and whispering. Several women straightened up their clothes and struck seductive poses. I was completely confused, but one thing was clear: *he was an important, recognizable man and a lot of women wanted to have sex with him.*

I stopped singing after that last song and retrieved my boot. I pulled the money out and did a quick count. I had more than enough to purchase the necklace but needed to get to Macy's before they closed. They were not opening on Christmas Day!

I shoved the money in my pockets as people rushed up to the tall man, trying to engage him in conversation and introducing themselves. I heard a few people refer to him as "Mr. Sterling," but still did not know who he was. The rest of the crowd had dispersed, and the other performers seemed relieved that I had shut the hell up so they could try to get some attention.

I was about to hustle to the train to get to the store when I felt his hand on my shoulder. "Excuse me, can I talk to you for a second?"

I turned to face him. He was extremely attractive and reeked of money, if there was such a thing as reeking of money.

"Do you have a minute?" he asked.

"Look, I'm just a kid," I told him. "I'm underage."

He looked confused and then laughed. "No, it's not about that. I don't have any problems getting women."

"He damn sure doesn't!" some women yelled out. "He can have me in a heartbeat."

He glanced at her and then back at me. His bodyguard approached the woman to make sure she didn't try to make a mad dash to get to him. "My name's Richard

Sterling. I enjoyed your singing."

I shrugged. "And?"

"I'm having this holiday party and I was looking for something exciting . . . someone different to entertain my guests."

"And?" I asked again.

"And I find you to be fascinating."

"This was my first real performance. I only know a few songs by heart." I was wondering how much money he was talking but knew that I was nowhere near prepared to give an actual concert . . . not at a party.

"Oh . . . I see," he said in disappointment. "Well, you're very talented, so you should pursue it. What's your name?"

I ignored the name question. "Funny you should say that because I came to that conclusion right about the time that you drove up. But most people won't hire me because of" — I pointed to my scar — "this."

"What's this? I don't see anything," he said, clearly lying to me. "All I see is a stunningly beautiful young lady who has an amazing voice and some great dance skills to go with it."

I blushed. "Thank you."

"So do you think that I could speak with your parents about you performing at my party, Miss . . . ?"

"My parents told me never to tell my name to strangers, or even talk to them."

"You're not a toddler and . . ." He surveyed the immediate area. "You appear to be out here in the middle of Times Square, one of the most congested areas in the entire world, by yourself." He paused. "How old are you?"

"Old enough to know that it makes sense that someone who is apparently both famous and rich would be willing to let me sing and dance at a party." I eyed him up and down. "What is it? Some kind of orgy where a bunch of old men take advantage of teenage girls?"

He frowned. "Once again, it's not about that, and I'm not that old, for the record." He gazed into my eyes, like he was analyzing me through them, and then sighed. "Never mind. You have a nice night. Merry Christmas."

"Merry Christmas," I said back to him.

He was about to walk away when he added, "Just make sure you don't waste your talent out here on the street corner. I was going to offer you ten thousand dollars to sing at my party. I'll just find someone else to give it to, but you truly are gifted."

I almost fainted. "Did you say ten thousand dollars?"

"I did." He grinned. "I assume you thought it was going to be much less."

"I was thinking more like a hundred dollars. Ten thousand?" I asked again. "Are you for real?"

"I'm for real."

I bit my lip. "But I was being honest before when I said that I don't know a lot of songs. When is your party, where is it, and how would I get there? I mean, if I manage to come up with some songs."

"My party is not until New Year's Eve, it is at my home in Alpine, New Jersey, and I would send a car to get you and your mother or father. That way you won't have to be concerned about anything happening, or having to talk to strangers without one of them."

I was frozen in place, not quite sure what to do, or how to pull the entire thing off. Ten thousand dollars would be one hell of a gift for Hannah. I could pay her back in a lump sum for all of her help and compassion toward me. I forgot all about Macy's and the necklace.

"Well, what do you think?" Mr. Sterling asked. "Do we have a deal?"

"Um, I live with my aunt," I lied. "Her name is Hannah. She'd have to come with me. Is that cool?"

"Cool," he said, and then grinned. He reached into his pocket and pulled out a black business card, then handed it to me. All it had on it was his name and number. "You can call me personally to set it all up."

His bodyguard chimed in. "Are you sure about all of this, sir? That's a private number."

"I'm quite aware of that, Virgil." He looked at his bodyguard and chuckled. "It's *my* private number, after all."

Virgil looked embarrassed and stood back.

Mr. Sterling then gazed back at me. "So I'll look to hear from you, or Aunt Hannah."

With that, he left, and I rushed home to tell Hannah about what happened. I ended up using the money collected in my boot to purchase all the fixings for Christmas dinner, along with a cheap tree that I dragged home myself and decorated with Hannah's lace from around the apartment.

When I told her that I had met a man named Richard Sterling who wanted me to come to Alpine, New Jersey, to sing for his New Year's Eve party, Hannah started screaming. "*The* Richard Sterling? Are you fucking kidding me?"

"Who is Richard Sterling?" I was sitting on the sofa trying to figure out how to solve

68

her squeaky Rubik's Cube but stopped when she had such a fit over it.

"Richard Sterling, the billionaire?"

I shrugged. "I guess. He was in Rolls-Royce with a chauffeur and a bodyguard. I'm assuming that's the one." I paused after what she said sunk in. "Did you say billionaire? Not millionaire but *billionaire*?"

"That's exactly what the fuck I said." Hannah sat down beside me and started waving her index finger in my face. "I told you that you could sing your ass off, baby girl. This is the beginning of something major."

When Hannah made that statement that night, I had no idea how factual it would become. Long story short, I did more than meet a bona-fide billionaire in Times Square. I ended up meeting my protector, provider, teacher, savior, biggest fan, talent developer, and often even my priest. I ended up meeting the *father* that I had never had!

■ ■ ■ ■

PART TWO:
THE REFRAIN

■ ■ ■ ■

It has been nearly twenty-five years since I left Atlanta. While I am grateful for all the success, wealth, and fame I have been able to obtain throughout this journey called life, I have never forgotten what they did to me. The four of them tried to break me and, for a time, they accomplished their goal. As my fortieth birthday approaches, before I celebrate that milestone, before I embrace that significant benchmark, vengeance will be mine.

— Wicket, circa 2012

CHAPTER ONE

Saturday, June 9, 2012
1:42 p.m.
Atlanta, Georgia

The Ritz-Carlton suite was over thirteen hundred square feet with a panoramic skyline view of Atlanta, a music area with a grand piano for me to practice on, an executive study, a butler's pantry attached to the formal dining room, and a bedroom with the kind of high-thread-count bedding that I was accustomed to.

I was soaking in the massive tub with "Rolling in the Deep" by Adele seeping through the surround-sound system and singing along with the words. Her vibe was so relevant. Our musical styles varied somewhat but we were both getting paid to do what we were passionate about, so it was all good. The video for "Rolling in the Deep" had over 400 million views on YouTube, but my video for "The Other Side of the Pillow" had nearly 900 million views. Glad my body was looking tight that week we filmed it in Punta Cana. Otherwise, I would have been worried about people seeing my flaws forever and would have cringed when I heard the numbers. Even though my song was dope, the visual effects of the Dominican Republic made the video truly pop. Most people in the United States would only ever dream of traveling the world. I was blessed to actually do it on the regular. Sounds crazy but I had more than a million frequent flier miles.

Then again, I was actually flawless, keeping it real. I really didn't have any choice other than to remain unblemished and impeccable with both my looks and tastes. Rivalry was thick in the music industry and it was no longer completely about selling records, even though I had sold more than 150 million albums and over a billion singles at that point in my career, shattering all kinds of records. It was about being a *performer.* Selling out arenas for hundreds — sometimes thousands, if bootlegged — of dollars per ticket and making the world believe you were the shit. That you could walk on water, that you were superhuman and unparalleled and untouchable.

Untouchable? I was definitely that for an

overabundance of reasons. I tried to quickly distance myself from the long-ago memories that were persistently clambering back and focus on my upcoming show that evening. As always, I was going to turn it out, but first I had to get dressed and go do a sound check. I hated sound checks. They were nothing but an intrusion on a perfect day. I had been doing the shit long enough that they should have known exactly what settings to have on the soundboards, but each venue space was different, so I dealt with it.

Pure irony that I had never performed in Atlanta before. Then again, I had my reasons. Damn good reasons. Okay, the memories were coming back again. It was time to do something extreme . . . like playing in Thumper, aka my *cooter,* but what with?

I scanned the room as "Rack City" by Tyga came on. *Aw, yeah, some freaky shit for me to get off on!* I stood up, grabbed my back scrubber with the wooden handle, and then sat back down in the tub. I moved the end of the handle in and out of Thumper and closed my eyes. I started gyrating my hips to the music, like I was a stripper named Nutcracker working the pole, except the pole was literally between my legs and inside of me. I slid it in deeper and deeper until I was thrashing around in the tub by the time the song ended. I was an expert at getting myself off quickly.

"Damn!" I yelled out as I reached a toe-curling climax. Then I sighed.

It was what it was and I needed to finish bathing and get dressed. It was only a matter of time before Diederik, Antonio, and Kagiso — my three bodyguards — who occupied the suites surrounding mine, would come to get me for the sound check. One of them was *always* stationed outside my door. Too many damn nuts in the world obsessed with celebrities. One usually stayed in the lobby at all times, by the elevator as well. I felt like that only drew unnecessary attention, but they insisted. There is a very high cost for fame that no one could ever comprehend until they find themselves in that position.

Kagiso was straight from the African bush. At least, I would tease him about that. In all actuality, he was six feet five inches of intelligence, brawn, and fineness. Dark as midnight, with skin softer than butter, these clear brown eyes, and a cleft in his chin that women found to be an instant panty wetter. He had a master's in early childhood education that he had obtained after moving to the United States on a visa to go to school. Don't ask! Imagine a man that size sitting in a circle with five-year-olds. He had done it, though, for an entire decade, before he decided to pursue something else.

Antonio was from East L.A., born and raised, jumped into a gang at twelve, arrested for the first time at thirteen, and tired of living in chaos by sixteen. He ran away to San Diego, hung tight for a couple of years, joined the navy, served his country, and went into private security. At six two, he was the shortest of my bodyguards but was thicker than a Snickers, with muscles rippling everywhere. He had sepia eyes, dimples, cinnamon skin, *and* he was bow-legged — an added bonus.

Diederik was Nordic and get this, *six foot ten.* Looked like a tree walking toward you. Spiked blond hair, ice-green eyes, and a gorgeous bone structure. He looked like "Suck my dick" spelled out.

Yeah, I had some sexy-ass motherfuckers protecting my life, but I had never *technically* messed around with any of them, nor would I ever do such a thing. I happened to know for a fact that they all needed lap bands on their dicks, though. Men like them needed to come with both a warning label and a disclaimer:

FUCK OR SUCK AT YOUR OWN RISK! This dick could possibly tilt your cervix, cause your clit to swell up like a balloon, and you may have to toss cups of soapy water at your pussy for several days afterward because it will be too sensitive to the touch.

Antonio actually tilted a broad's cervix once when we were touring in France. She had the nerve to try to slap me with a $12 million lawsuit. I did not have a damn thing to do with her making the decision to tackle that python in his pants. That shit was on her. People will sue over any damn thing when you have money, even if you've never met them, or even laid eyes on them before. When I saw photos of the chick, my first inclination was to ask Antonio what the hell he was thinking in the first place. But the women in France can be aggressive, and it's not like I expected them all to be celibate year-round before they had to guard me. It was certainly not a prerequisite. They were grown-ass men who did grown-ass things. They were all single and free to mingle, but I was damned if I would pay some floozy for giving it up willingly and getting hurt. The most I would offer someone is a bottle of Advil and my condolences on having a big-ass pussy for the remainder of her natural life.

I had thrown on a sexy little number of a

78

dress and some pumps about fifteen minutes later and put on some makeup. I was not the type to use a stylist, hairdresser, and makeup artist around the clock; only when I was about to go onstage, do a photo shoot, interview, or whatnot. A lot of my counterparts went through all of that shit to walk out on the veranda to do Pilates. It was not that serious. However, I was not going to get caught looking like I just emerged from a cave, either, so I kept it simple and classy. I looked good as shit without makeup but did not feel like dealing with the drama from tabloids and ratchet websites looking for an opportunity to do a caption of me slipping.

The knock came at my door. I grabbed my purse and went to answer it before someone panicked and knocked it down. I was not riding in the bulletproof SUV with my guards, though. I had other plans, and they were about to find that out.

CHAPTER TWO

"Piece of Shit, you better start eating pussy better or I'm going to beat the crap out of you with my shoe!"

We were in the back of a limousine on the way to Philips Arena for my sound check. KAD — what I called my three bodyguards when I was referencing all three of them — was in the SUV following us.

This was not working. "Um, Piece of Shit, did you hear me? Eat your late lunch like a good little boy, eat it all up, or I'm going to take the heel of my shoe and ram it up your chunky, over-fucked ass!"

He stopped for a moment and looked up at me. That fucking did it!

"Did you just look at me? Did you just have the nerve to fucking look at me?"

He quickly looked back down and started eating again, but not before I slipped my right pump off and started beating and scratching up his bare back with the heel.

"Don't you ever fucking look at me!" *Whap!* "I will fuck your ass up, literally!" *Whap!* "I'll find some three-hundred-pound, elephantine-dick motherfucker and present your ass to him like it's a chocolate-covered doughnut, you little bitch!"

Piece of Shit started going hard on the pussy then, slopping and slurping at it like it was his last meal on earth. If he kept fucking with me, it was about to be his most degrading day ever.

"That's a good little pet. Much better," I said, calming down some and feeling Thumper growing more excited. "Um, I'm about to come," I announced. "Just keep eating. Lap it like an ice-cream cone on a hot summer day in the park."

I could feel myself about to explode and let my eyes roll up in the back of my head when Piece of Shit started moaning. That snapped me back to reality.

"Did you just fucking moan?" I started hitting him again with my shoe. "You're not allowed to get any pleasure from this, Piece of Shit!" *Whap!* "I better not find any se-men in those tight little pink panties I have on you, either. I'll cut your damn dick off!" *Whap!* "Stupid-ass prick!"

Even though the partition was up in the limo, and I had a throwback Eminem album blasting through the sound system, I was sure the driver could hear something. He had better keep his trap shut or I would crack his damn nuts open, too.

"You know what," I hissed. "You make my ass sick. Stop eating pussy and suck on some titty for a while. You're acting like a baby anyway, so get to suckling." *Whap!*

Piece of Shit starting sucking like an infant within seconds — hungry ass.

I could see that we were turning into the back entrance at the arena and I was mad as shit. I hadn't busted one yet. Fuck it! I used my other shoe — the one still connected to my foot — and kicked Piece of Shit in the ass, causing him to topple onto the floor of the limo and away from Glaze.

She looked at me in shock, like she had done something wrong. She was my *decent* pet. The one that I actually kind of liked, but I wasn't taking any shit off her ass, either.

"It's okay, Glaze," I told her. "You did all right. Piece of Shit doesn't know how to eat pussy right. I should've come by now."

"Permission to put my clothes on, Mistress?" Glaze asked.

Her pussy juice had soaked down into the seat across from me after having being eaten the entire time, and her nipples appeared

red from Piece of Shit sucking on them so hard, even though it was quick.

"Permission granted," I replied.

I glanced down at Piece of Shit, who knew better than to ask me a damn thing. "Don't you get dressed in my presence, you little fuck. I'll deal with you later."

I could feel Thumper getting angrier by the second. I was going to have to deal with people fawning all over me in a couple of minutes and the thought made me wince. I was habituated to it, but I needed a release. I would have to sneak a few moments in my dressing room to finish the job. I planned to use the heel of my shoe. Sleek, slightly thick, slightly painful. I would have to use some hand sanitizer on it first. Imagine trying to explain a cooter infection to a doctor that came from a nasty-ass heel.

The car came to a halt and Piece of Shit knew to crawl up in the corner so I could get out without anyone seeing him. KAD never asked me questions that they were not about to get answers to. They only knew that, from time to time, I had Stacy (Glaze) and Billy (Piece of Shit) join me somewhere on tour and that they stayed in a room together. In this case, they were staying seven floors below us at the Ritz. Most people assumed they were a couple, good friends of mine, instead of my pets that I humiliated whenever I felt like it.

"Will we see you later, Mistress?" Glaze asked.

I had named her that because she came like a geyser and her pussy was always glimmering with remnants. I had met her on a trip to Oahu. She was a stunning, petite Samoan in her early thirties and a stone-cold, submissive freak.

"No, you *won't* see me . . ." I glared at her. "And don't get too fucking comfortable and start acting like we're homegirls or some shit like that, either." She lowered her eyes before I opened up a can of kick-ass on her. "You and Piece of Shit go back to the hotel and lay low, order room service — but only one meal for the two of you — *and take your asses to sleep.*"

"Yes, Mistress."

"Consider yourself lucky that I'm going to allow you to eat at all. Both of you let me down."

"We're sorry, Mistress," they said in unison, although Piece of Shit's came out as a whisper.

I met Billy when I was in Alabama doing a show. He was working backstage at the concert and our eyes met. The poor bastard actually believed that I would let him fuck me. Stupid ass! He learned fast, quick, and in a hurry when I took him back to my hotel suite that night. At first, he seemed scared to oblige my demands, but we worked the shit out. He was allowed to eat, fuck, and suck pussy — but not mine. Never that!

Billy was average height, average build, and there was nothing special about him. He looked like the average black male that you would find in Anywhere, USA, but he was obedient. I rarely had to actually wear his ass out with a whip, but I would if the occasion called for it.

Diederik opened the door and saw Glaze sitting there in a cute dress and heels, much like myself. He grinned at her as Piece of Shit cowered in the corner in his pink panties. He would look normal again when they returned to the hotel. They would look like a happy couple strolling into the Ritz-Carlton, about to have a romantic evening in their room. They knew better than to fuck each other, or even touch each other, outside of my presence. One of them would be a tattletale and I would fuck both of them up and they recognized that.

I climbed out the back of the limo and looked at Diederik, wondering if he smelled the odor of sex emitting from the back. My other two guards were poised and ready to escort me into the artist entrance.

"You ready?" he asked.

"You ask me that every time and what do I always say?" I snickered. "The answer won't ever change."

He grinned. "You were born ready."

I strolled toward the door. "Damn sure was."

CHAPTER THREE

The *Atlanta Journal-Constitution* article was a lengthy one about how I had decided to relocate to Atlanta as my new home, purchasing a $19 million mansion on Paces Ferry Road. It had nine bedrooms, fifteen bathrooms, was built in 2008, and was a little shy of twenty-five thousand square feet. It was an easy selection for me. I simply told my executive assistant to go out and purchase the most expensive house on the entire market in the area. It was all for show. I could afford it and I would still be traveling a lot . . . after I finished what I had come to the city to do. I wanted the publicity to reflect that I had outdone everyone else so that the people I was there to retaliate against would see it and start circling like a kettle of vultures to obtain a meeting or some type of connection to me.

People in Atlanta really put that entire "six degrees of separation" theory to the ultimate test. They always wanted to mix and mingle with those they felt could contribute to their "brands." Atlanta had become known as "the Black Hollywood," with at least seventeen network shows filming there on the regular. More than half were those ratchet reality shows that showed sisters being willingly exploited as they bullied, badgered, and belittled each other . . . and themselves. They even had to agree in their contracts that they would not sue a fellow cast member for some ridiculous behavior, or they would be fired themselves. Most were portrayed as thirsty, desperate whores fighting over the same pieces of dick, on national TV. But I was not one to knock the hustle. If millions of people wanted to watch human train wrecks on television weekly, and the networks had willing participants, an even swap ain't no swindle. Many had tried to connect with me off the bat, but I was not having it. I planned to entertain attention from only a few people, and none of them were on reality shows, but I was about to give them all serious reality checks. I had been invited to several events and parties those broads were hosting. As if? I was not stepping up their game by allowing them to ride the coattails of my legitimate brand based purely on bona fide talent instead of spreading my legs and bragging about it.

The home had ten-foot ceilings throughout, with a two-story foyer and cathedral ceiling, a pool house, outdoor fireplace, computer room, media room, library, exercise room, and the list went on and on. Excessive for one person, even one with a small entourage of employees, but again, it was all for show and it was a drop in the bucket to me. If money truly bought happiness, I should have been the happiest sister on the planet, but I was depressed, pissed, and ready to seek the vengeance that I had gone there to get. I donated tens of millions of dollars a year, so that was a good thing. I purged my closets every season and donated the clothes to women who needed them, mostly domestic abuse shelters or women reentering society after serving prison terms. Outside of drugs, domestic abuse was the main reason women ended up in such a predicament. If they did not flee and go to a shelter, they ended up snapping on men who had been beating their asses for years and they had to serve time behind it. At the very least, I was able to provide others with some happiness or basic human needs.

The only two things that actually mattered to me in the entire house were my bed — I loved comfort — and my piano that I had had shipped down from my penthouse in NYC. The place needed to be decorated and that was the beginning of the end of my misery. I called it Operation Renovate, Then Destroy.

"Nikki, what time is Mrs. Hudson supposed to be here?" I asked my assistant as I sat at the breakfast counter eating a bowl of fresh strawberries and blueberries with vanilla-flavored granola. "She's still coming, right?"

Nikki was typing away on her MacBook Air, responding to e-mails and requests for interviews and appearances. I had several publicists, but Nikki had a direct line, nearly around-the-clock access to me, so all of them had to go through her to see if I was even interested. Plus, Nikki kept my calendar, so she was the only one who truly knew my availability, even more so than myself.

"Earth to Nikki!"

She finally paused and said, "Huh? I'm sorry."

"Is the interior designer still coming today?"

"Oh, yeah. She'll be here about eleven. That's a good time, right?"

I giggled. "You tell me. All I know is that alerts pop up on my cell phone two hours

before and then ten minutes before I'm supposed to be someplace or do something.
You do a good job at making me look
timely."

"Well, it's a quarter to nine, so you'll be
seeing one in about fifteen minutes telling
you that she's coming at eleven."

We both chuckled.

Nikki was a fantastic assistant. She'd been
with me for four years and I wouldn't trade
her for anything in the world. She always
switched her hairstyles out to express
herself. She was shorter than me, which I
liked, light-skinned, thick, and always
smiled. She had graduated from Spelman in
2004 with a degree in music, so she was
excited that I had moved to Atlanta. In the
entire time of her employment, we had
never traveled there once because I had
never been back since 1987.

That was a year that I wanted to forget
forever. Well, most of it, up until that night
in October where I almost died and was
actually resurrected in the downtown Greyhound station. Hannah had saved me from
other people, and from myself. I was determined to die, one way or another, but she
breathed oxygen back into my lungs.

I clamped my eyes shut when I thought
about what had happened at my high school

homecoming. Those bitches and bastards had actually tried to kill me. It may not have been their exact intention, but it was the most probable outcome. If Hannah hadn't cared enough to save me from bleeding to death, it would have been over. What I had craved and yearned for all the years prior, death, was right there in front of my face. I could almost reach out and touch it, smell it, embrace it.

"Wicket?" Nikki snapped me out of my thoughts. "Did you need anything else from me right now?"

"No, I'm about to work out for an hour." I climbed down off the barstool at the breakfast bar. "I have to keep these tits and this ass tight for the stage."

Nikki grinned. "And you keep them tight, too."

I walked off to throw on a sports bra and pair of sweat pants so I could get in a good sweat before Bianca Hudson, formerly Bianca Lee, showed up at eleven. She thought she was coming to acquire the decorating contract of her lifetime and I was going to give it to her . . . right before I took out the knife that she had embedded in my back decades earlier and fucked the conniving, heartless bitch up with it.

■ ■ ■ ■

"It is such an honor to meet you, Miss Wicket. Should I call you Miss Wicket or do you prefer just Wicket, or do you prefer your real name, Miss —"

"Wicket is fine." I reached out and shook the hand fake-ass Bianca had extended to me. "Please, come in and make yourself comfortable. Nikki, get us a couple of glasses of fresh lemonade. You like lemonade, Mrs. Hudson?"

"Oh, for heaven's sake, please call me Bianca. I want you to think of me as a long-lost, dear friend."

It took everything within me not to spit in her damn face when she spoke those words. Little did she know that we had been friends at one point — *best friends.*

She was putting on airs and was dressed in the latest designer fashion, likely designed by that other bitch: Cherie. Later on in the day, before she left, I planned to fall into the laid trap and have a fit over the dress and ask where I could get one. That was what they wanted; for me to ask about the dress. Bianca would have a chance to introduce Cherie into the mix so she could try to get a lot of my money in her bank account as well. Still the same old slick trifling hoes from high school.

"Why don't we start in the great room?" I suggested. "It's a big space, but I have some thoughts about it."

"That would be lovely. I'd love to hear what you envision."

As we walked into the great room, I started my description. She was feeling it. I really didn't need her ass to design *shit* for me. I was an excellent interior designer myself and owned houses and penthouses around the world that I had decorated alone.

"I *envision* this as my little-black-dress room. I want to put a black, large square rug in the middle of the floor, about twenty feet square and a huge, circular sofa that seats at least twelve that's also completely black. I was thinking a nice, round crystal table in the middle with a light that has decorated edges that shine a pattern on the ceiling when the main lights are off. Something real sexy and intriguing."

"So how does the little-black-dress concept come in?"

"It's simple. You know how we can take a black dress and change the accessories and make it look completely new? Well, I want to be able to change out the objects on the coffee table and the pillows whenever the mood hits me. I might use yellow in the spring, or sea-foam green. Turquoise or peach in the summer. Red or purple in the fall. You get my drift?"

"That's hot." Bianca looked like I had shown her up. That's because I had. "You're about to make me feel useless already."

"It's merely a concept." I shrugged. "I'm open to your thoughts. Everyone sees different things in different spaces. You're the expert, so I'll defer to you."

That made her feel like the shit. She started strutting around like a peacock after that, from room to room as she sipped her lemonade and Nikki took notes to transcribe and share with us both later. I decided not to show her up anymore and pretended like all of her ideas were awesome. Some of them were actually pretty damn good. I could see why she was regarded as one of the top interior designers in Atlanta. Several had put in bids, but I did not even look at the others. She was the one that I wanted to trap in my web, and her greedy ass was about to breakdance right into my slaughterhouse.

Bianca and I were sitting on the veranda drinking two glasses of Moscato when Nikki

95

appeared, as I was about to ask about her dress.

"I'm so excited about working with you," Bianca said with a huge grin. "You're such a sweetheart."

I faked a smile and looked at Nikki, who was waiting patiently to say something. "Yes, Nikki."

"You don't have your cell phone with you so I wanted to remind you that you have a Skype call scheduled with your father at three."

"Thanks." Now, that actually made me happy and my smile became real. "I'm always on time for Daddy."

Bianca looked like she had seen the rapture when Nikki mentioned my father. "It must've been great, growing up with Richard Sterling as your father."

"He's a man like every other man," I replied, upset that she would even regard him like she knew him like that.

"Yes, but one of the richest men in the world. It had to be an amazing childhood."

"He adopted me when I was six," I lied, deducting an entire decade from the truth. "But yes, it was an amazing childhood. Not because of his wealth; because of his heart. He's a very loving man, especially toward me."

I decided not to ask her about the dress. I wanted her grubby ass to grovel for business for her friend. I was sick of staring into her hazel eyes that were clearly fake. Her eyes were brown, the color of walnuts, like her skin. She was wearing colored contacts to make herself more appealing. There was nothing wrong with her natural eye color. I had stared into them enough as a child.

I had a quick flashback of Bianca and me walking down the street to school in the tenth grade, laughing about what had happened on a sitcom the night before. We were both smiling at each other and lightly tapping each other on the arms during conversation. Then I realized she was there, in real time, in my presence, smiling again, but I remembered what evil she was capable of: BITCH!

"You should get going. Please be in touch with Nikki when you have a formal presentation together and she'll fit you into my schedule." I went from being overly gracious to strictly professional in the blink of an eye. "She'll see you to your car, and thanks again for coming by."

Bianca shook my hand and started to hesitantly walk away. She paused and turned around. "Um, by the way, I have a friend who is an excellent designer and stylist. You may have heard of her. Cherie Thompson?"

"No, can't say that I have." I sighed and started acting irritated.

"She's great. Top-notch. In fact" — Bianca spun around like she was ripping up a runway, so I could peep the same dress that I had been looking at all damn day — "she designed this little number exclusively for me. She does practically all my clothes."

"It's simplistic but rather nice," I said, trying to downplay it. "Leave her card with Nikki and I'll consider giving her line a look-see."

Bianca cleared her throat. "Maybe we can have lunch one day later this week, at your convenience."

I rolled my eyes, making sure she would see the gesture. She had a lot of fucking nerve to think that she could commandeer my time like that. I was the celebrity, not her. Stupid whore!

"Or maybe not." She paused. "You take care."

"You as well."

Bianca walked off, trailing Nikki.

"This is going to be like shooting fish in a barrel," I whispered to myself. "Look at you," I said to Bianca's back, "with your fake hair, your fake nails, your fake smile, your fake eyes, and your fake attitude.

Biotch!"

I plopped back down in the chair and drank some wine, trying to calm myself down. Daddy may have been across the globe in Australia on business, but he was far from stupid. Someone had clearly made sure he had seen the reports on CNN or had read the online articles about how Wicket, real name Ladonna Sterling, had decided to relocate to Georgia after giving a spectacular performance at Philips Arena in front of a sold-out crowd of fans. How she had instantly become enamored with Atlanta and had dropped $19 million on a crib. How she was planning to spend the majority of time between tours there, working on her next album.

At three o'clock on the dot, I would have to look happy as a pig in shit on Skype and try to convince him that I understood and totally embraced what I was doing, that I had gotten over the past, and that I was legitimately interested in residing in the same city where I had actually grown up as Caprice Tatum, daughter of a drug-induced, schizophrenic maniac of a mother who had cut the left side of my face with a paring knife when I was seven because she couldn't stand to look at her own image.

Daddy would legitimately be worried

about my welfare, and I could not fault him for that. He had done so much for me; he had paid to fix a broken doll and had rebirthed her as one of the greatest entertainers the world had ever known . . . ever would know. It was hard, but I wouldn't let him down.

Who was I fooling? I wanted to fuck them all up for what they had done to me. For the pain, for robbing me of any chance of a normal, healthy, loving relationship with a man, and for merely being pure evil.

"Calm down, Caprice," I tried to convince myself. "You can pull this off. Daddy can't make you leave. You're damn near forty years old. Just tell him that much."

I finished off my glass of wine and went into my office to launch Skype.

The forty-minute conversation with Daddy did not go off well. He went on and on about how I needed therapy and should leave right away, even if I joined him overseas. He was concerned that I might have some kind of mental break if I ran across any of the people from my past, even though they would never recognize me. I started to say that one had just finished doing a walk-through of my new house to do a mock-up design proposal and that I had played it off without a hitch. But being braggadocious would have only backfired, with Daddy personally flying his private jet to Atlanta by the break of the next dawn.

Nikki had gone out to run errands. She was *loving* Atlanta. I needed some kind of release, so I called Kagiso into my bedroom for a little afternoon playtime. I was not lying when I said that I had never fucked any of my bodyguards. But the reason that I knew they all needed lap bands on their dicks is because I had definitely seen them.

I was standing by a picture window, gazing out onto the courtyard out back, butt naked sans a pair of black Louboutins, when Kagiso knocked lightly on my door.

"Enter," I directed as I turned around.

Kagiso stood there for a few seconds, admiring my sepia skin, flawless after years of treating it both internally and externally with Vitamin E, my shoulder-length onyx-black hair, and eyes the color of a papaya. The papaya eyes were Daddy's idea. They made me distinctive and hid any resemblance to the eyes of Caprice Tatum, whose eyes were naturally a darker brown. Bianca had chosen to wear fake lenses to make herself feel special; my lenses were to mask my past.

"Are you going to stand there in the

doorway and stare at me, or are you going to come in?" I asked Kagiso.

He came in the room and shut the door behind him. Then he started in on me with his alluring, seductive accent. "You plan to tease me again? Dangling a carrot in front of my face that I can never have?"

I walked over to the bed, climbed on, propped my back up on some pillows, and spread my legs so he could get a perfect view of my hairless pussy. It was already wet, but I planned to get it much wetter.

"Answer me," he demanded.

I rolled my eyes and then faked a smile. I needed him to cooperate, and you get more with sugar than you do with shit.

"I want to play Jack and Jill."

"And I want to play digging your back out with my dick."

Same story, different day.

"That's not happening." I bit my bottom lip and stared down at his crotch. "Take off your clothes so I can see that elephantine dick of yours."

"And if I refuse?"

I smirked. "Then I'll call Diederik in here so he can show me his. You and I both know that he'll be down with it."

"Why not call Diederik in here in the first place, then?" Kagiso asked sarcastically.

"Easy answer." I started tapping my clit with the manicured index finger of my right hand. "I love the way you jack off. It's . . . fascinating."

I could tell that he was getting excited. Kagiso loved to be complimented and flattered, especially when it had anything to do with his dick. He was vain and entitled to it. The motherfucker was spectacularly fine.

He started removing his shirt and walking closer to the bed. *That's it. Come here, little doggie.*

"What's so fascinating about the way I beat my meat?"

"Beating meat is such a vile term for it. I prefer jacking off or . . . pleasuring oneself."

"I wanna fuck you, Wicket. These little *excursions* with you are driving me insane. No man can continue to do this without wanting more."

"So leave and send Diederik in on your way out. Tell him to bring a jar of honey. I like the way the honey looks on his pale dick when he uses it to spurt his jism halfway across the room."

I was being cold but not nearly as bad as I was with Glaze and Piece of Shit. My two pets relieved and released an anger in me that could never truly be explained. I equated my sexuality with disdain when I was in their presence and humiliating them was all that mattered. It was my way of making someone else feel how I felt on October 25, 1987, a date forever embedded in my mind. In many ways, it was the date of my death and my rebirth as someone who simply didn't give a fuck about most people in the world. Somehow that made it easier for me to take chances that led to an extreme amount of success in life. Strange shit but the harsh truth.

Kagiso still stood there, pondering over whether he should continue to try to press me for some pussy or cave like always and expose his dick.

"I don't have all damn day, Kagiso," I said. "It only takes five seconds for you to drop your drawers. Let me see Striker." I eyed Kagiso seductively as I went ahead and inserted my index finger into my pussy. "I've missed my baby so much."

Kagiso couldn't hold back any longer, unzipped his pants, kicked off his shoes, and was butt naked within thirty seconds flat. "Ain't nothing babyish about my dick."

I licked my lips. "Damn sure isn't."

Kagiso climbed on the bed and lay down with his head resting on the mattress between my thighs so he could inhale the scent of my pussy. Also, he liked to be close so he could hear the sounds of me playing in it.

His dick, lovingly known to me as Striker, was on full alert and it looked divine. There were times such as these when I yearned desperately to impale myself on his dick, but it was useless. Allowing a man to touch me was out of the question. There was too much pain and agony involved.

"Stroke him gently at first," I instructed in a whisper. "I want to see you pamper him like he deserves to be treated."

Kagiso looked upward at me and our eyes met as he started moving his hand up and down his shaft slowly.

I moaned and slipped two more fingers into my pussy and started moving them in and out to the same rhythm.

"You like this dick?" he asked.

"Um, yeah, I love your dick." I stared at his hand as he started moving slightly faster. I did the same. "I love the blackness of it, the length, the girth; every motherfucking thing about it."

"Sit on it," Kagiso urged, damn near in a begging way.

"You have other women for that. Imagine that I'm sitting on it. Move like I'm sitting on it and I'm going to move like you're inside me."

What ensued was amazing. Kagiso and I both were thrashing around on the bed, him jerking off and moving his hips up and down like I was on top of him, and me gyrating my hips as I bombarded my pussy with my fingers. When Kagiso came, his sperm shot straight up to the ceiling like a geyser and I squirted far enough that some of my juices landed on his cleft chin and in his mouth.

We both moaned and gasped as our bodies convulsed and our breathing patterns returned to normal. Kagiso turned over and licked some of my pussy juice off the sheets and tried to move his tongue up onto my left thigh, where there was a mound of it, but I quickly pushed him away, lifted my leg over his head, and got off the bed. His lips brushed across my ass cheek and that was as close as he was going to get to skin-on-skin action.

I went into the bathroom to wash up with a warm towel, then returned to the bedroom with one for him: our routine. As he stood up and wiped himself off, he glared at me like I had molested him or something.

"What?" I asked. "Didn't you like it?"

"I'm simply trying to figure you out."

"In what regard?" Of course, I knew what he meant, but I wanted to hear it.

"Why you constantly have me doing this and giving me nothing in return. What's up with that?"

"Listen, Kagiso, you and I both know that all of you can get pussy at the drop of a hat. You can smell mine, you can hear mine, and you can even grab a little taste if one comes your way, but I am not giving it up to you or anyone else."

"That's my point. Why is that?" He started getting dressed and then paused, staring into my eyes. "It's certainly not for religious reasons. You're too damn freaky to be shy. Fuck it! Truth be told, you're the best sex partner that I've ever had and I've never even fucked you. So what is it?"

"It's none of your damn business."

I walked back into the bathroom and shut the door. A moment later, I heard Kagiso approaching it. "Wicket, I can only assume that something happened to you. Something that has turned you off like a faucet. For some reason, you don't want to be touched and that's a damn shame."

"Go away!" I yelled through the door.

"If you ever want to talk about it, I'm here for you. You're too beautiful, intelligent, and talented to live your life this way. If I'm not the man for you, that's cool. We started out like this, but you deserve someone to love you."

"I said, go the fuck away!" I yelled louder.

I could hear Kagiso backing away from the door and then leave the room. As he was shutting the bedroom door behind him, I emerged from the bathroom and collapsed on my bed in tears.

"Damn you and your master's in early childhood education," I whispered. Kagiso had read me like an open book and I was not happy about that. Not happy about that at all.

CHAPTER FOUR

The Gracious Swan Spa was a magnificent place. Whoever designed it was on top of their game. It reminded me of a day spa in Milan, Italy. I didn't go to spas everywhere that I visited, even though they were so relaxing. Being Wicket meant paparazzi no matter where I went. In order to go to a spa, it had to be exclusive, so it meant renting the entire space out — not an issue — and having security surrounding the entire building. That meant that KAD had to find at least five to six other big-ass men to back them up. All of that for a facial, pedicure, and steam bath was excessive.

Of course, I had all of that at my home in Atlanta, but I had rented out Gracious Swan for another purpose. It was the only place that made sense for the meeting that I was about to have. Everyone else was across town at the Jeju Spa, which specialized in Korean hip baths, their variation of a sitz bath, that helped to detox the pussy and tighten it up. It was a loud place and they even allowed kids in that joint. A lot of people went to the twenty-four-hour place to sleep in the T-shirt and shorts provided. It was all good. I was not knocking it, but I preferred a more traditional, quieter spa. Besides, if I ever showed up there, I would have been bombarded with people to the point that I wouldn't have enjoyed it for five seconds.

I was sitting on a lounge chair in the aromatherapy room when she entered, wearing a plush, white robe matching the one that I had on, and a pair of snug slippers. She was a stunning woman who looked exactly like her photo on her website. She had her hair wrapped up in a towel, like me, but I remembered that her hair was shoulder-length and dark brown to match her eyes. She appeared younger than she probably was, but black actually doesn't crack until well into one's eighties.

I stood to shake her hand as she approached me. There was not a single other person in sight, including the employees. I had paid eighteen grand to rent the place for three hours.

"Dr. Spencer, nice to meet you."

She shook my hand and stared at me for a

moment. Then she smiled and I felt more at ease.

"Please, call me Marcella." We both took seats on two lounge chairs, facing each other. "And what would you prefer for me to call you? Wicket or Ladonna?"

I hesitated, only because I was trying to figure out if I should cut the bullshit and tell her to call me Caprice. After all, the entire purpose of this was for me to "come clean."

Instead of answering her question, I said, "I'm sorry for the inconvenience of meeting me here. If I had come to your office for an appointment, reporters would have hounded you forever and scared off your other clientele. If I had requested that you come to the house, damn near the same effect. Here at the spa, it makes it appear like we're merely two people enjoying the same place at the same time."

Marcella looked around. "I understand, but if they're extremely clever, they'll realize that no one else is here."

"There are enough cars in the lot to play it off, but you're right. I would never go to a crowded spa, unless I was there to do an appearance." I shrugged. "Well, it's the best that I could think of."

She grinned. "I imagine that it's not easy

being you."

"Millions of people around the world crave fame and fortune, but if they only understood the true price of fame, they'd quickly develop another outlook." I kicked off the slippers and put my feet on the lounger, tucking them underneath me. "I want you to know that this wasn't totally my idea."

"No?" Marcella took a sip of the infused water that was prepared for her arrival. "Then whose idea was it?"

"My father's."

Daddy had practically had a heart attack all the way from Australia that day on Skype. He could read my intentions, despite my efforts to fool him over a computer screen. He insisted that I speak with Dr. Marcella Spencer, who had come highly recommended to him by a business associate. Unlike me, Daddy often had business in Atlanta.

"He's in Australia for the next couple of weeks, then he has to head to Hong Kong for a month. He was quite upset when he found out that I was here in Atlanta."

Marcella looked confused. "And why is that?"

I sighed. "He *assumed* that I'm here for a single purpose. You see, I haven't been in

Atlanta since 1987."

"Oh? So why are you here, in Atlanta? The news outlets made it seem like you wanted a slower change of pace from New York and that you viewed the city as progressive and eclectic."

"I see that you're up on things." I chuckled. "All of that was bullshit, hyperbole, and embellishment."

"I *assumed* as much, but when your assistant called me to request a session, I caught up on recent press. As you know, this is a big deal for Atlanta. A lot of celebrities have homes here, but you're arguably the biggest entertainer in the world at this point."

"Yes, arguably, I am." I stared into her eyes and pondered about ending the entire thing right then and there. "The irony is that I should have been dead a long time ago. In fact, I should've never been born. My mother should've aborted me the second she realized that she would hate me and treat me like a monster under her bed. It would've saved everyone a lot of drama."

Marcella's expression quickly changed as she set the water down. "I don't know much about you, yet, Wicket, but I want you to recognize that I want to assist you. Anything you say to me will be held in complete confidence."

I struggled to find any words, but the tears started to flow.

"If you want to sit here today and just breathe, we can do that," she continued. "Maybe next time you'll feel like talking."

I still couldn't speak.

"Would you like me to leave you alone for a few moments?"

Nothing came out, so she stood up.

"I can wait out in —"

"Please, sit back down," I finally managed. When she had done that, I said, "Dr. Spencer, I mean, Marcella, I'm sure that you're very suitable with what you do but, like you said, I'm not your average client and it's not only because of the fame and money."

"What does your father think you're here in Atlanta for?"

Now she was cutting straight to it. I could appreciate her candor.

I didn't hesitate again. "Vengeance. He thinks that I'm here for vengeance . . . and he's right."

"Vengeance against whom?"

"Are you aware that Richard Sterling adopted me?"

"Yes, I believe *Wikipedia* said around age six."

I smiled. "Good old *Wikipedia* with only

half-accurate information that anyone can put up. He did lie and tell everyone that, but Daddy never laid eyes on me in his life until I was fifteen. He adopted me legally on my sixteenth birthday but had them doctor the paperwork."

Marcella was stunned. "And why did he do that?"

"To protect me from my past. So that no one would ever know who I really am."

"And who are you?"

"I haven't told anyone my real name in decades, but it's Caprice. Caprice Tatum, and I was born right here in Atlanta." I paused. "You're in for a long afternoon, Marcella."

CHAPTER FIVE

Saturday, May 5, 1979
Atlanta, Georgia

It was a Saturday. I remember that well. No school, no plans, only space and opportunity. My best friend, Bianca Lee, had come over early that morning, banging on the back door by eight. I had rushed to the door, hoping that she had not woken my mother. Momma was a drug addict, pure and simple. She had me when she was only seventeen and hated the fact that I was born.

Back then, I did not know what drugs my mother was using, but she was definitely smoking something stronger than weed. We lived with my grandmother, Alice, who did the best that she could . . . *considering.* My mother, Denise, had named me Caprice seven years earlier after the model of car she was raped in by her uncle Donald. Her pregnancy with me was a result of that horrific act. He was convicted and sent to

116

prison, where he was found beaten to death in his cell less than a year after sentencing with an asshole wider than a baseball bat, but that did not negate the fact that an abomination had been created . . . me.

My mother never let me forget that. She would constantly curse me and call me a little bitch. She would beat on me and my grandmother, who was weakened by pleuropulmonary blastoma — a rare form of lung cancer — and would always have to pull her off me. Being so young and having known nothing but Mother's schizophrenic outbursts since my memory allowed, I actually thought it was normal back then. That all children had to suffer at the hands of their parents and then, once they became adults, it would be their turn to chastise and cause pain to their own kids.

Since I was only in the second grade, I was rarely allowed to visit other kids. Mother never took me to the birthday parties that the entire class was invited to, and that was just as well. I was withdrawn in school and barely spoke two words to anyone other than teachers. Bianca was my one exception. She was a vibrant, outgoing little girl who lived two doors down. One of her parents would stand guard and watch her as she skipped down the sidewalk over to my house to see if I could come outside and play.

Mother only let me go out with her because she did not want to be bothered with me. But I would see her constantly peeking through the sheer curtains in the living room, not in a protective way, but almost in a menacing way, like she hoped someone would drive by and snatch me up into a nondescript white van, never to be seen or heard from again. To make an extremely long story short, Denise Tatum hated the one person she should have loved the most — her daughter.

Despite her hatred of me, I was a stunningly pretty little girl. I was Mother's spitting image. While most women would take pride in having a miniature clone of themselves, it was obvious that she could barely stand to look at me. Little did I know when I woke up that Saturday morning in May that my life would change forever.

Bianca and I were standing in the driveway, trying to decide what to do next. We had already gone through Mother May I, Red Light Green Light, Simon Says, and had done three rounds of Miss Mary Mack by slapping hands and chanting the rhyme. Kids back in the day had to actually play outside and come up with ideas instead of becoming zombies to the Internet and video games. We were debating about playing jacks, doing hopscotch, or Bianca going to get her Etch A Sketch while I went to retrieve my Slinky. Playing Lite-Brite was out of the question because there were no plugs outdoors close enough to play and neither one of us could enter the other's house. Her parents would have allowed me to come into theirs, but Mother had made it clear that I could never do that.

I often wondered what Bianca's room looked like. Mine was four plain white walls, dirtied over the years from no fresh paint, a twin-size mattress on the floor that rarely had sheets on it, rather less clean ones, and four dolls with broken parts strewn about. I had only about five complete outfits that my grandmother would wash on the weekends for me to wear to school and two pairs of shoes, with holes in them. Grandma had had to quit her job as a waitress when she fell ill and had no savings to speak of. Mother refused to work and, at twenty-four, was getting food stamps from the state. Otherwise, none of us would have eaten.

"So, do you want to play hopscotch or not?" Bianca asked, smacking on a large piece of bubble gum. "It's getting kind of hot out here."

"It's up to you." I kicked my size-three shoe around in the grass, like I was scaring a colony of ants away. "I'm not hot, but it's probably going to be too hot this afternoon to be outside."

"Do you know your math facts? I always get stuck on the twelves."

"I kinda do," I replied. "You just have to —"

"Bianca! It's time to go!"

We both turned to find Bianca's mother, Mrs. Lee, standing by their Mazda Cosmo with white gloves on and a summery dress.

Bianca sighed. "Shoot! I forgot that I have to go shopping with Momma for vacation clothes. We're going to Disney next month once school lets out."

"That's cool," I said, trying to hide my jealousy. I started walking toward my door. "Have a good time shopping."

"You want to go?" Bianca yelled behind me. "I'm sure Momma will say it's okay."

I wanted to go with them more than I wanted to take my next breath. I glanced up at Mother's window and noticed that she was staring down at me, as if to say, "Don't even think about it."

I turned to Bianca. "Thanks for asking, but I have to go do my chores."

"But you were ready to play hopscotch a minute ago."

"I forgot that I have to do chores," I said harshly, fighting back tears at the same time.

Bianca giggled. "We're in second grade. How many chores could you have? I can ask Momma to wait until you're done."

"No!" I took her off guard with my tone, so I lowered it. "You go ahead. I don't have any money to shop anyway, and it's not like I'm going on any vacation."

Bianca forced a smile and walked away from my house slowly as her mother grew more impatient by their car. I fought back tears, rushed into the house, and slammed the door behind me. Big mistake!

"You little bitch!" I heard my mother scream from upstairs. "You slammed that fucking door again!"

"I didn't mean it," I said in a loud whisper as she practically catapulted downstairs from the upper level. "I didn't mean it."

I ran into the kitchen, hoping Grandma would be able to protect me from the beating that I saw coming a mile away.

Grandma was standing over the sink, using a paring knife to peel potatoes that she had a pot of water on the stove to boil them in. "What's wrong, Caprice?"

Before I could reply, Mother came rushing in and started slapping me in the face and all upside my head. She was screaming something, but I was too busy trying to shield my body to understand any of it.

Grandma walked over from the sink and tried to pull Mother off me, but Mother knocked her backward into the table. She slipped on something and fell onto the floor, with the paring knife still in her hand.

Mother turned to Grandma and this time, I could make out her words since the slaps ceased for a moment. "Momma, she's the Devil! She's the Devil! She never should have been born!"

"Stop talking crazy, Denise," Grandma said, struggling to get up. "We need to get you some help. You can't keep beating on that baby like that. I won't allow it."

"What the fuck you going to do about it?"

The two of them stood there staring each other down for a moment. Looking back on it, I understand that Grandma could not have possibly begun to comprehend the mental issues my mother had, exacerbated by the heavy drug use. Mother's eyes were bloodshot and she was trembling like she was coming down from something.

Grandma spanned out of her shock. "Don't you dare talk to me like that, after everything I went through to raise you.

You're an ungrateful —"

"Ungrateful? Ungrateful? Your brother raped me." Mother pointed at me. "And this is the result. Having to raise his little demon."

"I'm not a demon," I said, not really quite sure of the definition of the word, but I knew it was akin to being a devil. "I'm a girl."

"Donald's paid for what he did to you," Grandma said. "He's dead and gone. I've done the best that I can by you. I had no idea your uncle was capable of such a thing."

"You're a damn liar!" Mother moved toward Grandma, who inched back. Fear was apparent on her face, and I could see her tightening her grip on the paring knife in her right hand, just in case. "You're a liar! You knew he was sick. All of you knew he was a sick pedophile and that I wasn't the first; probably not the last. You wouldn't have even pressed charges if I had come to you first. You didn't press charges when he did the same thing to you when you were younger."

"You have no idea what you're talking about," Grandma said. "Donald never did anything to me."

"Liar! He told me all about it. How he

used to make you suck his filthy dick and lie there in your bed while he fucked you into oblivion."

Grandma stared down at me. "The baby's in the room. Stop talking nonsense."

"Caprice is *not* a damn baby. She better learn quick what kind of world we live in. A world where men use us as interchangeable pieces of meat and where any pussy is for their taking, whether the woman wants to give it willingly or not. I'm not sugarcoating shit for her."

"Denise, stop it. That's enough."

"No, it's not enough." She glared at Grandma. "Look at you. You laid down with some man and made me and he left you before I was born. I wouldn't be surprised if Uncle Donald is my daddy, too."

"That's blasphemy! Shut the hell up, Denise!"

"You shut the hell up, Momma!" Mother pointed at me. "If it weren't for you, none of this would've happened. If you had put a stop to him, this little bitch on the floor would've never been born. I asked you, begged you, to let me have an abortion. You cursed me for life. For life."

"I'm not sure what kind of drugs you're taking, but I will not have you talk to me like this." Grandma raised the paring knife.

"Not now. Not ever."

Mother laughed. "Oh, so what are you planning to do with that? Kill me? Slice me up?"

"Denise, I'm your mother and I love you, but I will not sit by and watch you descend into hell and take Caprice with you. If I have to take you out of this world, I will."

Everything became blurry after that for a moment. I could see Grandma and Mother struggling and hitting each other. I tried to blank it all out and pretend like it was not happening.

A minute seemed like a hundred and I realized that Grandma was passed out on the floor, presumably knocked unconscious by her own daughter. I could see her chest rising and falling, so I was positive she was still breathing. I remember being appreciative for that: her chest rising.

Mother turned to me with the paring knife in her hand and, even at seven years old, I understood that I was in imminent danger. I tried to get up and run from the kitchen, but I was not fast enough. Mother grabbed me from behind and I felt the blade of the knife slicing down my left cheek in a jagged line. She let me go and I toppled to the floor, holding my face. I was speechless, and even if I could have found words, I would have been too afraid to actually speak them.

"Now, no man will ever want you," Mother said. "The curse in the Tatum family ends with you."

CHAPTER SIX

"Turns out that my grandmother was fine. Mother didn't use the knife on her, only me, the demon. She was beaten-up pretty bad, though. We were both hospitalized for about a week."

Marcella gulped down some saliva. "I'm sorry that your mother did that to you. Where are your mother and grandmother now?"

"Grandma died when I was young, right before my twenty-first birthday. I didn't get a chance to say good-bye to her. I was already in New York, but I wrote her letters; no return address." I paused and took a deep breath. "Mother's in an institution not that far from here. Based on your profession, one that I'm sure you're familiar with."

"I don't really do a lot of institutional work any longer."

I drank some water to regain some composure after going back to a place that I never thought I would revisit again.

"Have you seen her?" Marcella asked.

"No. Like I said, I haven't been back here in decades. Even after she first got locked up, I never wanted to see her. Regardless, Grandma wouldn't have allowed it. Not after what happened. I heard that the doctors determined that the cancer finally took her, but it was really the emotional pain created by being raped by her own brother, who raped her daughter in return, and fathered her granddaughter. I've often wondered if Mother was right and Uncle Donald is really her father. It would make a lot of sense."

"Do you want to find out?"

"Hell no," I replied quickly. "My life is fucked-up enough as it is. Why would I want to confirm some sick shit like that?"

"Well, Wicket, I'm glad that you felt comfortable enough to share what happened with me." She stared at my face. "When did you have the scar removed?"

"Several months after I arrived in New York. Daddy paid to have my face reconstructed. It was Hannah's idea. She realized he could afford it and thought it would make me feel better."

"Who's Hannah?"

That one question made me realize that

our session needed to end for the day. I was not prepared to discuss Hannah, or what had happened to her.

"Can we reconvene this later?" I asked Marcella as I stood. "Even though we're in a spa, I feel anything but relaxed." I paused and looked down at her. "Are you willing to see me on a regular basis? Money is no object. I can pay you well for your time."

Marcella stood up. "I would never charge you extra because of your wealth. And yes, I am willing to see you." She glanced around the spa. "But I do have a suggestion. It would be inconvenient to make such elaborate preparations to meet here all the time. I have a hideaway cottage in Pike County, a little ways from here. Population less than twenty thousand and my closest neighbor is literally a mile away."

I was stunned. "And you go out there by yourself." I chuckled. "Oh, mea culpa. You probably have a nice, loving relationship with a man who adores you and goes out there with you."

She looked uneasy. "I've always made it a point to keep my private life isolated from my clients, but I will say that I'm not troubled to go there alone. That's the point of it being a hideaway. Sometimes I need to unwind and diminish the rest of the world."

"I can dig it, but I'd have to bring KAD with me. I would be scared to death to go to sleep out there. I don't see how you do it. I can visit but I need to get out of there before dark."

"KAD?"

"Oh, that's my nickname for my three bodyguards."

She laughed. "First initials?"

"Exactly." We smiled at each other for a moment. "Your cottage sounds lovely and I would like to meet there. What about this same time next week? I prefer to continue to arrange all of these sessions myself. Even though all of my staff have confidentiality and nondisclosure agreements, in this economy, you never know what people are capable of."

"Same time next week. I'll e-mail you the address."

"Thanks, Marcella." I reached out my hand. "Even though it was hard for me to discuss what my mother did to me, I do feel some type of liberation for having said it."

"I do have one last question, if you don't mind."

"Yes?"

"Did you come here to get revenge on your mother? You're not planning to harm her or have her harmed, are you?"

"Relax, Marcella. I don't plan to chop off anyone's head or have them thrown into a pool of acid or lye. And no, this has nothing to do with my mother. She's an extremely sick and revolting woman, and she's right where she belongs."

"Then who is it about?"

"Might we discuss that next week?"

She seemed doubtful, but, being a professional, she recognized when to let it go. "Sure, we can wait until then."

"Feel free to stay and experience the spa. It's paid up for until three. You can have it all to yourself, since you don't mind that sort of thing."

She chuckled. "It's tempting, but I'm going to go change and head back to the office."

"So where is your office?" I asked, making general conversation as we headed off into the dressing rooms.

CHAPTER SEVEN

I really should have been an actress in addition to being a singer. Overall, entertainment is entertainment. But one thing was for sure. The day that I met Bianca Hudson and Cherie Thompson for lunch at Acoustix Jazz on Marietta Street, I delivered an Oscar-winning performance. I had Nikki make arrangements with Frank Ski, the owner, to have a private lunch, since they actually did not open until six for dinner service on Saturdays. The worst thing about being famous is the inability to go someplace and enjoy a meal in peace, so unless you want paparazzi all over the place disturbing your meal and everyone else's meal in the joint, you have to get creative.

After we exchanged pleasantries and I pretended like I had never laid eyes on Cherie in my life, we settled down at a corner table and ordered. I ordered the John Coltrane, Bianca ordered the Charlie Parker, and Cherie ordered the Ella Fitzgerald, which came down to steak for me, blackened tilapia for Bianca, and roasted herb chicken for Cherie. We also did the Frank Taylor crab cakes, Cab Calloway fried calamari, and Chick Corea spinach dip for appetizers. Women tend to order a ton of food when we go out to eat, but rarely ever finish it. Americans, as a whole, order in excess when it means being able to afford to do so. But I went with the flow and even ordered two bottles of wine — one white and one red — to accompany the meals. Since they had invited me to lunch, even though I arranged the place, it was on them anyway to pay, and they wanted to prove they were affluent enough to be in my presence. *Straight bullshit!*

Kagiso and Antonio were out front standing guard, and Diederik was chilling over by the bar, watching a special on ESPN but still completely alert to our surroundings. I stared at his side profile for a few seconds and wondered what it would actually be like to sit on his face one day. He had always asked, but that was a no-go like everything else. I was convinced that all three of my bodyguards traded war stories about how each had attempted to get inside me to no avail. By now, it had to damn near be a game. I wondered what they called it and if any monetary bets had been made. It was all shameful, but it was my life and everything served its purpose for the moment.

Cherie was really trying too damn hard to alter her appearance. Again, at least I had an excuse. The Cherie that I remembered from high school was dark-skinned with a smooth complexion, with dark brown hair and even darker brown eyes. The Cherie sitting before me now, about to hit forty like me, had attempted to bleach her skin and it looked a hot mess, she had dyed her hair blond and had in green contact lenses. She looked completely ratchet, but I had to hand it to her — the outfit was banging. Surely audition-wear to convince me to let her design clothes for me. She had on a strapless burnt-orange dress with shoes to match while Bianca was donning a hunter-green pantsuit with matching shoes. I have never been a huge fan of trying to match shoes and purses exactly with an outfit, but it was working for them. Of course, I was not about to admit that to either one of them.

"Thanks for taking the time out for this lunch, Wicket," Bianca said with her pretentious grin. "We truly appreciate it."

"It's no problem," I lied. "I don't have a

lot of time for this little *soiree,* but Nikki said that you've been blowing her phone up trying to set this up."

Both of them looked embarrassed.

"I wouldn't say all of that," Bianca stated defensively. "I certainly haven't called more than a few times."

"Are you accusing my assistant of lying about you calling seventeen times?" I took a sip of red wine and waited until the two bitches digested that. Bianca did not respond. "I thought not." I sighed, cut my eyes at Cherie, who lowered her head in shame, and then glared back at Bianca. "That's a moot point, so let's get down to business. What do you two broads want?"

Cherie squinted so hard that one of her green contacts almost fell onto her plate. "Broads? How rude!?"

"If you feel like my personality does not mesh well with yours, don't let the doorknob hit you on the ass on the way out." I engaged in a staring contest with her until she gave up and looked away. "Let's not get this shit twisted. I am American royalty and you are trying to jump into my playpen. Both of you want me to expend my hard-earned cash on the shit you're peddling. Whether it's a ten-dollar ceramic mug that I purchase in a Mexican street tent or a ten-thousand-dollar

135

dress or some painting you think will look good over my stove, the shit is still peddling. So that makes you both peddlers."

Bianca and Cherie gazed into each other's eyes. Both of them were itching to curse me out, but neither one of the whores had the nerve. I was intentionally being an ass. If they were two women who I did not know from my childhood, two women who I was not aware were capable of trying to kill me, I would have been pleasant and noncombative. However, the two of them were lucky that I had not taken my steak knife and shoved it into both of the carotid arteries in their necks.

I lightened my mood and let out a laugh. "Don't take it so seriously. It is what it is. We wouldn't be here if you didn't want something from me. Surely, you know I do not want, nor *need,* a damn thing from either one of you."

Cherie cleared her throat. "Actually, I only wanted to meet you today. I admire and respect your business acumen and consider it an honor to even hold a conversation with you, however brief."

It is a damn shame how greed will make someone give up their self-respect so easily, I thought to myself as I watched Cherie resolve herself to basically kissing my entire ass. I was only just beginning.

"That's better," I replied, cutting into my steak. "I always keep it real, and I don't like playing games. We're not here to eat. There is food everywhere. We're here because you want to talk me into giving you money for clothes and design work." I looked at Bianca. "So, I looked over the suggestions you sent over *five times.*"

Bianca started to say something but bit her tongue.

"Or was it six times? I can't recall," I said, adding insult to injury.

Cherie decided to ask what Bianca should have. "What did you think? Bianca's amazing, isn't she?"

"I wouldn't go so far as to call her amazing, but I was feeling a few of the suggestions. Overall, she needs to go back to the drawing board and bring me something more exceptional and unique before I'd be willing to sign a contract. I can't have the most valuable residential property in Atlanta sporting a mediocre interior."

"Mediocre?" Bianca exclaimed.

"Did I stutter?" I replied. "I believe I know the issue with all of this. You don't imagine on my level because you're not on my level. Nowhere near it." I paused so they could let that sink in. "I may have to hire an interior designer from Europe who's done some palaces, citadels, fortresses, or some regal shit like that. I want my home to be a castle and I don't mean like a White Castle burger joint."

"Who in the hell do you think you are?" Bianca yelled, lashing out at me.

Diederik immediately got off the barstool and headed in our direction to toss her ass out. I held up my right palm to stop him. He gave me a confused look and went to sit back down but stopped watching ESPN and glued his eyes on the action at our table.

"If you have to question who I am, you don't need to be here," I replied sarcastically. "You're getting all caught up in your feelings. You're exhibiting a true lack of professionalism. It's obvious that you cannot handle criticism well. This is not a good fit."

Bianca swallowed her pride. "I apologize. I'm just not used to —"

"Being slapped back into reality with the truth?" I asked. Then I turned to Cherie. "Look, Cherise, right?" I pretended like I could not recall her name, even though I had known her forever.

"No, Cherie."

"Cherie, that's a cute dress you have on. Not sure it's my style, but if you want to put together a sample portfolio for me to peruse over, I'll check it out."

"Thank . . . thank you." Cherie seemed relieved. She was willing to take even a slight opportunity to get some of my cash. "I'll have it to you by next week."

"No problem. Take your time." I looked over at Bianca. "I'll come back to you with some specific requests, particularly for the front rooms that my guests will see upon entry. I don't want the wow factor. I want the 'oh my goodness, this shit is off the chain' look."

"I can make that happen for you." Bianca finished off her glass of white wine and pushed her plate away.

"You don't like the food?" I asked, knowing that I was the one who had robbed her of her appetite like a thief in the night. "My steak was incredible."

"No, everything was great." She waved the waitress over to ask for the check. "Thanks again for meeting with us."

I decided to flip the script and act polite for a moment. "It was my pleasure. I don't have a lot of female friends and I realize that I can be somewhat harsh, but you two seem lovely." I was lying my ass off. "Maybe we can become good friends, hangout *buddettes,* over time."

Cherie perked up. In her mind, being able to actually claim me as a friend stepped up her game a million percent. "That would be cool. Bianca and I are both upwardly mobile here in Atlanta and —"

"Upwardly mobile?" I had to suppress a hiss. "I hear that term quite often. Define it."

Bianca and Cherie both looked foolish, using terminology that they clearly had no clue about.

"Does it mean steadily climbing in social and financial status, perhaps?"

"Something like that," Cherie said. "We're constantly striving to obtain more success in life."

"Are either of you married?" I already knew everything about the two fake broads but wanted to feign interest. "Are your husbands successful as well? What do they do?"

Bianca could not wait to brag. "My husband, Herman, is an orthopedic surgeon. He has a private practice in Buckhead with state-of-the-art surgery facilities."

"Oh, that's nice. He gets to play with crusty feet and toes all day." I watched as Bianca pulled out a black American Express to pick up the tab, holding back on a snide comment that was dying to leave her lips to counteract mine. I paused long enough to give her time to swallow it. "How long have you been married?"

She sighed — weak broad. She should've called me on the fact that an orthopedic surgeon was not the same as a podiatrist, but she was too busy kissing my ass. "We were high school sweethearts, actually. We've been together for twenty-five years and married for nineteen."

"Do you have kids?"

"Two; a boy and a girl. Twins. They're juniors in high school this year."

I looked over at Cherie. "And you?"

"Well, I've been with Michael about the same amount of time, but we've never married and have no children . . . as of yet."

I whispered, "Hmm," and gave her a sympathetic look.

It was a damn shame for her to stay with trifling-ass Michael Vinson, who was not even halfway attractive no less, for that long without a ring. She must have been hard up. In retrospect, the two of them deserved each other.

"I assume you're at least shacking." I did not wait for a response. I knew they were. "And what does your man, Michael, do?"

"He's an actor." For once, her face lit up. "He's exceptional, too."

"Oh, what's his last name? Maybe I've seen him in something."

"Vinson. Michael Vinson."

I frowned and said more as an insult than a statement: "Never heard of him. Is he a *working* actor? When was the last time he was in something?"

Bianca seemed embarrassed for her friend. She probably wondered if Cherie was going to tell the truth and shame the Devil or go for broke and make some shit up.

"Well, the last major movie he was in was *New Jack City*. He played a drug dealer who was part of Wesley Snipes's posse."

"I've seen that several times. Did he have a speaking role?"

"Not exactly, but —"

"Baby girl . . ." I decided to stop the madness. "*New Jack City* came out in the early nineties, ninety-one if I remember correctly. If your man hasn't done anything since then, that can't be considered his career. That's like me not putting out an album for years, *decades,* and still calling myself a professional singer. I'm not one to get into someone else's business, but you need to stop being dick dumb and tell his ass to get a fucking job or stop fucking him altogether. We get what we settle for. You know what I'm saying?"

I struck a big-ass nerve with that one.

"So where's your man?" Cherie asked with heavy acerbity. "I've never seen you tied to any particular man in the press."

"And you likely never will," I replied. "I don't have to put my business out in the streets to get attention from the media. My talent trumps everything else. But it's interesting to know that you're clocking my comings and goings like that. What color panties do I have on?"

Bianca's mouth flew open, but no words came out, and Cherie had to make a drastic move to hold her tongue.

"Trust and believe," I added. "There are very few straight men on this planet who would not fuck me if given a chance. That includes *both* of your men. Look at me and look at the two of you. Be for real."

The tension was getting thick and I seriously wanted to hurt someone at that table. It was time to end the farcical luncheon meeting.

I stood up abruptly. "Thanks for the meal. Nikki will be in touch once you send whatever it is that you're . . . *peddling.*"

With that, I strutted out the front door like the queen that I was, with Diederik straight on my tail.

"You really went in on them," he said as

we met up with my other two bodyguards outside and headed to the limousine curbside.

"I hate fake bitches!" I replied and climbed into the backseat.

I could make out Bianca and Cherie through the pane-glass window. Cherie was going off and pounding her fists on the table, surely calling me every venomous term she could come up with. But would the hooker ever be bold enough to say it to my face? Time would tell, and I planned to enjoy every second of it. They had an option to walk away and never contact me again. Greed and a desire for a bigger social status would never allow them to do that, though. I was the closest that they had ever been, or would ever come, to actually being significant in society, and neither one of them would risk fucking it up. I was banking on that, and I was never wrong.

CHAPTER EIGHT

After spouting all of that shit about not claiming something as a career if you have not done it in years, that was my cue to get back to working on my next album. Operation Vengeance in full effect or not, the rest of the world still highly anticipated the release of *Impulse,* my ninth album. I had at least three or four more tracks to lay out but had already recorded an EP in case I did not complete the rest of the songs by my deadline. An extended-play album contained more than one song but not as many songs as a traditional, full-price album. It was the latest craze for newer acts who could not afford to go all-out with at least eight tracks. Even if they landed a deal, record labels were reluctant to fund longer albums for fear that they may do a major belly flop upon release. With the digital age of music taking over, the true money was in touring and being the ultimate entertainer.

145

That was why I was who I was. Outside of talent, it was like playing a game in someone else's body. No one knew that I was Caprice Tatum. Caprice Tatum disappeared off the face of the planet and, just like I had assumed, no one ever even gave a damn.

As I waited for my recording engineer to get everything together to do a take of "Shame on It All," I could not help but chuckle at the irony. Here I was enticing the world with love ballads about sex and being in great relationships, or club tracks about how to get your freak on, and I was doing none of the above. I will admit that I went for the jugular when Cherie inquired about my nonexistent man. Granted, even if I did have a man, I would not have wanted him splayed across every magazine cover with me, or being featured weekly on *TMZ* when we walked out of restaurants. It would be difficult enough to simply get to know a man, rather less have the entire world scrutinizing everything about him concurrently. What man would want to deal with such madness? He would have to be someone already used to the limelight and I had yet to meet a celebrity male who I would have fucked with someone else's pussy. Most famous people traded lovers all over the place, mostly to remain newsworthy. Or both parties would actually be gay and putting on pretenses to cover up the truth. No sir, none of that was for me. All of that was besides the fact that I was incapable of feeling those kinds of emotions in the first place.

I had done a very bad thing when I left the restaurant that day. I wanted to hurt someone so much that I hurt myself. I had not resorted to cutting in well over a decade. Yet, I found myself that night in my Jacuzzi making slight slits under my knee, where they would blend in and look like the normal folds on my legs.

"Ready whenever you are," Brian, my engineer, said, breaking me out of the zone of deep thought that I found myself in. "By the way, 'You Can Lick Your Breakfast' is on fire. I predict it hits number one on the Billboards the first week."

"Thanks, Brian. We think alike."

We both laughed. Brian was cute: Irish with red hair and freckles. He had a boyish look and I often wondered if he had freckles on his dick. I started to ask him to masturbate with me one night while we were working late, but he seemed like a blabbermouth or the type that would try to sue the label if I even mentioned it.

Suddenly, a feeling came over me, so I

147

excused myself. "I'll be right back."

"Okay." Brian started messing with and adjusting buttons on the console while I headed to my private bathroom.

Once inside, I stared in the mirror for a few seconds. "You really have a problem."

I opened up the medicine cabinet and removed my battery-operated toothbrush. I had on a dress — easy access — so I slipped off my sandals and placed my right foot up on the sink counter. I moved my panties aside and put the toothbrush inside of me, inverted, but not before I pushed the on button. The bristles of the brush bounced back and forth over my thick clit while the bottom part shivered inside of me.

I started feeling my own breasts and rubbed my nipples through my dress until they were rock hard. I managed to get myself off in a matter of minutes and then went back out into the studio to get busy. One day, I yearned to feel what actual intercourse felt like, outside of being brutally raped, but it would not be that day. And the question remained: Who could it possibly be with? There was no man who I felt like I could be completely transparent with, no man that I felt would even understand what I had been through. Instead of crying my eyes out, I did the next best thing;

148

what I always did. I went into that studio and left it all there in my music. Everything I ever desired, wanted, or needed.

The next morning, I was scheduled to do an interview with *G-Clef* magazine. I would have preferred to run with the bulls than do it. Sometimes interviews became so redundant that I struggled to find innovative responses to the same damn questions the last five reporters had asked me. At least there was no photo shoot involved. I had done one recently and the label was going to give them exclusive use of some of the images. I had to start promoting the new album, even though it was not scheduled to drop until the end of the year. They were apparently a smaller magazine, but it was recommended that I do the interview.

Nikki came into the theater room to tell me that the reporter was waiting outside on the veranda. She also added, "He's some serious eye candy. Just a heads-up."

I smirked. "I'm surrounded by eye candy, Nikki. Speaking of which, where are KAD?"

"Diederik and Kagiso are off today since you have no plans to go out, and Antonio is in the garden posted up where he can see you without being intrusive."

"Thanks." I sighed. "Might as well get this

over with. What's the writer's name?"

Nikki looked down at the legal pad she had in her hand. "Jonovan Davis."

I froze in place, like I had seen a ghost.

"Are you okay, Wicket?"

"Wha . . . what did you say his name is again?"

"Jonovan Davis. J-O-N-O-V-A-N. You know him or something?"

I quickly gathered my composure before Nikki saw right through me. "No, never heard of him. I thought you said Jonathan Davis at first. I've run across someone by that name, but it's a common one. I don't know any Jonovan."

"Oh, okay." Nikki stood there, hesitating. "Are you still coming now?"

"Actually, I need a few minutes. I need to shoot a couple of e-mails out before noon. Tell him that I'll be right out."

"Cool beans."

Nikki left the room and I almost collapsed on the floor. I had not heard the name Jonovan Davis in decades. It seemed like several lifetimes ago.

Jonovan Davis saved my life the night that everyone else was seemingly determined to take it. He had always been nice to me at Powers High School, but I was too shy to ever take his kindness for genuine interest.

Besides, he had back-to-back girlfriends all throughout school. A lot of it had to do with his incredibly good looks and charm, and the fact that he had a 4.0 GPA. He was voted the most likely to succeed as well. So he was a reporter now? Interesting! I wondered if he was still as attractive. Nikki had made it obvious that he was fine, but was he still *that fine*?

Suddenly, I was concerned about my appearance. I ran upstairs to my bedroom and threw open the doors to my humongous walk-in closet. I picked out a red skintight pantsuit to slip in and opted out of a blouse so I could show off my cleavage. Then I slipped into a pair of five-inch black pumps and a black jade necklace and bracelet to adorn the outfit.

I hightailed it into my bathroom and took about five to six minutes applying makeup. I was not going to put on any powdered foundation that day at all, but I made myself up to look like I was about to do a photo shoot. Actually, my dermatologist told me that I should always protect my skin with makeup. That way all the germs and elements from the day get washed off at the end of the night instead of seeping into my pores.

When I was headed back down the steps,

I almost fell when I got near the bottom. My nerves were shot.

"Get it together," I whispered to myself. "He doesn't know who you are."

My heart felt like it was about to hop out of my chest, it was beating so loudly. I took in three deep breaths and headed outside.

When I saw him, it was like time had stood still. He was sitting there spreading orange marmalade on a croissant as one of my maids poured him some coffee and orange juice. His dark-chocolate skin glistened in the sunlight and he was now bald. Damn! There was nothing that I was more attracted to than a baldheaded man. Back in high school, he had sported cornrows most of the time.

He spotted me and stood up as I walked toward him. "Good morning, Mr. Davis."

"Good morning, Ms. Wicket."

We shook hands and smiled at each other. I was likely to faint at any second.

I pointed toward the chair from which he had arisen, all six foot four of him. "Please, sit back down and enjoy the meal."

"As long as you join me."

"My pleasure."

After we both got settled at the table and my juice and coffee were both poured, the maid left us to some privacy. Antonio was surely in a spot to see all, but at least we could speak without him overhearing.

"So you're with *G-Clef*?"

"Yes, have you read any of our issues before?"

"Can't say that I have. You're local?"

He shrugged and fiddled with the recorder app on his iPhone. "Actually, regional. We're up-and-coming. Right now, outside of a budding subscriber base of about eight thousand, we're circulated in Georgia, the Carolinas, Alabama, Tennessee, and some parts of Mississippi and Florida."

"That's cool," I said, picking up a mimosa that had been prepared for me before I sat down. "So how long have you been working for them?"

Jonovan chuckled. "Since its inception." He paused. "Oh, I forgot to mention that we have a pretty huge digital following . . . to make up for our smaller circulation. I just don't want you to feel like you're wasting your time granting me an interview."

"It's fine. And I get it; everything worth knowing is primarily in the digital space these days. I'm surprised some of the dinosaur newspapers and magazines are even still around. Some that used to be considered credible, intelligent sources of information have converted into thinly masked tabloids to try to keep readers at all."

Jonovan agreed. "Exactly! That's why I started . . ."

I stared deep into his eyes — those sexy-ass eyes. "Aw, so you're the publisher of *G-Clef*?"

Jonovan put his index finger up to his lips. "Shh, it's a secret." He appeared genuinely concerned. "I can't believe I let that slip."

"What's the big deal?"

"The big deal is that when some people, especially those on your level of the music industry, find out that the owner of the magazine is basically the entire magazine, they tend to feel *G-Clef* is beneath them and their brands."

"That is true, but I beat my own drum at the end of the day. I appreciate all my fans, and especially those in the 'Durty South.' I needed a break from the studio this morning and I don't have to do a photo shoot, so it is a win-win for me."

He actually blushed when I said that. *Good!*

"Wow! You're amazing," Jonovan said. "I was waiting for you to toss me out of here any second." He surveyed the area. "I have to say, this estate is the most glamorous one that I've ever had the pleasure of visiting.

What made you decide to purchase it?"

"Is this the beginning of the interview?" I asked playfully. "I want to know when I am on the record and off the record."

He pressed the record button on his phone and said, "This is Jonovan Davis, *G-Clef* magazine and I am here in the A-T-L with none other than the world-famous singer and performing artist Wicket. Thanks for granting me this interview today, Ms. Wicket."

"Just call me Wicket and you are very welcome, Jo-no-van."

He shifted in his seat after I took my time pronouncing each syllable of his name. "So let's dive right in. You recently made the decision to relocate from New York City to Atlanta, Georgia. Could you explain why you made that decision?"

"Technically, I'm still a legal resident of New York State and, of course, I own properties all over the world. However, for the time being, I will be chilling in Atlanta. I like the vibe here and even though I don't socialize much or do a lot of networking, the people who I have met seem down-to-earth and that is a good thing. Most people tend to be intimidated by me."

Jonovan cleared his throat. He was definitely one of the intimidated ones. "Do you

155

think it is intimidation or reverence? You have tens of millions of devoted fans and I would presume, if they actually have the opportunity to be in your presence, that they would be overwhelmed with admiration and a feeling of worship."

I giggled. " 'Worship' is an interesting term. Don't get me wrong. It's great to be able to do what I am passionate about for a living, but I have no desire to be worshipped." That was a lie, because I made Glaze and Piece of Shit worship me — their mistress — on the regular. "When I was younger, some friends of mine told me that I was talented and I was blessed enough to have a father who believed in developing it into something *unique.* If anything I was blessed with a talent from God, the finances to pay for formal voice coaching and the amount of studio time it took to make my first album, and I came into the music industry at the right time with the right sound."

"Speaking of Mr. Sterling, Richard Sterling, your adoptive father," Jonovan said. "There has never been a lot of information provided about how that entire thing happened. He adopted you when you were how old again?"

"Six, and there is not a lot of information

out there because neither he nor I consider that part of my journey to be anyone's business."

I glared at Jonovan, making it obvious that he needed to move on from that topic. Even though Daddy had managed to fabricate one hell of a story, and all the legal paperwork to back it up, the fact remained that all of it was a lie. I had an exotic enough look for him to tell the world that he had adopted me in Guyana from an orphanage he had visited on a business trip. He picked there because he had actually been to Guyana about a decade prior. He was a single billionaire and all his staff and close associates had nondisclosure agreements in place, and he told the lie that he had sheltered me from the madness of his life until I became sixteen and decided to venture into the limelight in the musical space.

It sounded crazy but also plausible because most celebrities allowed little to no access to their kids, or even photographs of them. They were generally homeschooled, which was the story with me, and the truth after he did actually adopt me. I never returned to a school setting, for a few reasons, including the fact that I was not emotionally capable of dealing with being around other teenagers on a regular basis. I never established any true friendships with those my age, nor did I have the desire. My two best friends, Bianca and Cherie, had betrayed me in the worst way, and there was nothing that would make me take that kind of risk ever again. People were simply pawns in a game to me. They all served a purpose to get me what I wanted. Sure, I liked my bodyguards and my assistant, my band members and engineering team, and even a few people at the label, but trust was a different matter.

"I didn't mean to offend you."

I returned from my thoughts to find Jonovan halfway out of his chair. He must have assumed that I was about to toss him out for real.

"It's okay. No need to slide out your seat. You're not the first person to go down that road with me, and you won't be the last. It's simple. I only discuss what I care to discuss and if people want to take it upon themselves to speculate or make up things about me, they can do them. I won't be forced to feel a need to reply to foolishness."

"Well, it's not my intention to make anything up," he said. "I'll only talk about whatever you want to discuss in the article."

I smirked. "If I had a dime for every time

I've heard that." I paused. "For the record, I wasn't implying that you would. I was referring to some others who believe that writing lies about me, sensationalizing rumors, will somehow catapult their careers. Funny thing is, they write their bullshit, it's tossed around by my other haters for a few weeks or months, I am still talented, my fans are still here, and no one even bothers to read their names on the bylines and they definitely don't give a damn about them."

"Yeah, that's one reason I decided to start *G-Clef*. I wanted to put a positive spin on the industry. There is so much negative circulating about people who don't deserve it."

I smirked. "Some of them orchestrate their own drama. Don't get it twisted. A lot of celebrities are encouraged to engage in fuckery in public, or to get into Twitter battles with each other, in order to stay relevant. A lot of them have to act a fool because their talent is mediocre. I've only seen a few who are exceptional do such things, and I'm convinced it is because of deeply rooted issues."

I was talking mad shit, but I always did. I had my own demons, secrets, and debauchery going on in my private life, but I planned to keep it private. There was always that chance that someone would "blow up my spot." My money was on Piece of Shit, which was why I made sure that he always had thick pockets so that temptation wouldn't be there. Glaze seemed more faithful.

As for what happened to me that night at homecoming, the only living person who knew that I was Caprice Tatum was Daddy and, now, Dr. Marcella Spencer. I had yet to tell her everything, but I had already told her the truth about my identity. There was something about her that made me feel comfortable. Even during therapy as a teen, I never told the psychiatrists everything about my past; just enough about my thoughts and behavior to be diagnosed with intermittent explosive disorder.

I had never discussed the fact with them that I would not allow any man to touch me in a sexual manner. I never revealed that I had sex only with inanimate objects or sex toys. I damn sure never talked about my BDSM life with them and my sex slaves that I enjoyed dehumanizing as I watched. I had tried dating a few men in my lifetime — all fine, successful, and kind — but when it came down to being intimate, I could never go through with it.

As I sat there looking at Jonovan, I

couldn't help but wonder what his story was. Was he married? I didn't see a ring, but that meant nothing. Tons of married men stopped wearing their rings by the end of year one, if their wives tolerated it. They did it so they could troll for pussy and their sidechicks could always say down the road that they never knew the men were married. Game; all game. Was he seriously involved? Shacking? Someone's baby daddy? Gay? Bisexual? Did he like to be blindfolded, whipped, and did he get off if a woman put a finger up his ass? So many questions I wanted to ask the one person who cared enough to save me in October 1987. My childhood crush who I had often thought about over the years. I had even tried to find him on Facebook a few years back, not that I would have said anything if I did come across his page.

"Yeah, that's definitely true," Jonovan said in response to my analysis of some other celebrities. "Those Twitter battles can be something else."

I giggled. "I like the ones where thirsty chicks will post photos of them in bed with a male celebrity to prove that they're manpooling with his other women."

"Manpooling?" Jonovan was lost.

"Yes, that's actually one of the songs on

the new album I'm working on. A lot of women manpool like they carpool. Basically, the song is about sharing dick."

He grinned. "Can't wait to hear that one."

"Oh, it's fire. And nothing but the truth."

"You're a cold piece of work. You know that a lot of women are going to get in their feelings over that?"

"A hit dog will holler. No reason for them to get offended if it doesn't apply to them. Even if it does apply, if they are willingly sharing dick, it should become their national anthem. You'd be surprised at how many chicks are actually proud to be a man's side-ass action."

"You definitely have a way with words."

"You're surprised? Where do you think my song lyrics come from? If I'm not going to go hard, I might as well go home."

"So it's a fact that you write all your own music?"

"I pen all my own lyrics and then, as I'm sure you know, I have a few producers who I collaborate with on the music itself. I bring the thoughts to life and they give me the beats to flow with. It's a lovely thing."

"So when is your next tour?"

"After this new album drops. While some may be able to pull it off, I can't tour and work on new cuts at the same time. Those are two different lives completely. Touring is a twenty-four-seven process. Between traveling, sound checks, rehearsals, and the actual shows — where I cannot afford to disappoint — there is no time to go into a zone and create new music."

"I've always admired those of you who do big tours. It has to be exhausting. I get tired even watching the performances. You must work out."

I stood up and turned around, tapping myself on the behind. "With an ass like this, you know good and well that I have to keep it lovely in the gym." I walked around the table and grabbed his left upper arm. "All this muscle you have on you, you must hit the gym daily."

"I actually have a gym in my home."

"Oh, do you and your wife work out together?" I asked, being nosy.

He looked up over his shoulder at me. "I'm not married. Well, I'm divorced actually."

"That must be hard on your kids." I let his arm go and sat down on the edge of the table, with my hip rubbing against his wrist. "How many do you have?"

"What makes you think I have any?" he asked, looking up into my eyes.

"You have a *daddy* feel about you." He

163

smelled so damn good as I inhaled his cologne. "We seem to be roughly the same age. Most men my age have a gaggle of kids."

"Gaggle?"

"A flock of geese not in flight."

"You're a brilliant woman. I love listening to your choice of words."

"Again, it's the nature of my business. I would think that the other artists you interview are creative spirits. At least, they should be." I sighed. "So how many kids do you have?"

Here is what Jonovan had to be thinking at that very moment:

Is Wicket coming on to me?

Oh my God, is Wicket really trying to pick me up?

This shit is crazy! Wicket's coming on to me.

Truth be told, I had no idea what I was thinking. What I was doing was foolish, reckless, completely irrational, and unwise.

"I have a son, Jonovan Jr. He's thirteen and he lives in Seattle with my ex-wife."

"Why all the way in Seattle?"

"Her job transferred her there. She's in IT." He cleared his throat. "My father actually lives with me. He has Alzheimer's and I didn't want to put him in a home. At least, not yet." He seemed to be visibly upset.

"I'm doing the best I can."

"That must be hard."

"It can be a challenge."

I got down off the edge of the table and walked back around to the other side. "I apologize for getting off track from the interview. Sometimes I enjoy hearing about other people."

"It's no problem. I'm just surprised you would even be interested in my life."

"You have a very kind aura about you. I find it sweet that you would take care of your father. Is your mother still living?"

"No, she succumbed to breast cancer when I was in my early twenties."

I remembered seeing Jonovan's parents at school functions at Powers High School. They seemed so happy, and Jonovan was his father's twin. It looked like he had spit him out and that his mother had been the carrying vessel. Strong genes, so I could only imagine that his junior was his split image as well.

"What about your parents?" he asked. "How did you end up in the orphanage in Guyana? Do you know if you have any existing family there? Were you scared to come to the United States? How long did it take you to learn English, or were you already speaking it? Did you have a thick accent at first?"

I chuckled. "You are really good. Journalism is about trying to get information, and even though I made it clear that I don't discuss such things, you went for it anyway."

He lowered his eyes. "Maybe I should go. I apologize. It's just that —"

"I started getting into your business, so you assumed my guard was down."

Jonovan gazed into my eyes. "Actually, I forgot about the interview and I only asked those questions because I was interested in knowing more about you." He hit the end button on his recorder. "Again, I didn't mean to offend you."

Shit, this was starting to feel like a date!

I spotted Antonio out the corner of my eye. He was probably wondering why I was doing such a long interview, even though we had never gotten to an actual one so far. He knew that if I ran my fingers through my hair two times, he was supposed to break it up. I didn't do it. Instead, I guzzled down the rest of my mimosa.

"Off the record? Just two people shooting the breeze?"

He grinned. "Definitely. You fascinate me, but I'm sure that doesn't surprise you. You're a fascinating person."

166

Then I blushed. "Guyana actually is the only South American country with English as its official language so, yes, I was already speaking it."

"Wow, never knew that."

Richard Sterling had known it, which was why he made up that lie about adopting me there.

"As for an accent, I did have one but I'm not sure when it went away. Daddy provided me with the best teachers that money could buy and one of those was a speech coach. I had a stuttering issue as a child," I lied so easily, and now it was time to go into the truly big lie. There was another reason why Daddy had fabricated the Guyana adoption in 1978 when I was six. "Do you promise never to talk about what I'm about to say next?"

"I promise."

I was not a trusting person, but even if Jonovan did betray in the name of press freedom, it could never be proven one way or another.

"My parents were killed during the Jonestown Massacre!"

"Wha . . . what?" He was stunned.

"When Jim Jones rented that land to build a compound in Guyana, my parents were among the few locals who joined his cult. I can't explain why. I was too young to know what was going on. So when everything happened on November 18, 1972, my father willingly drank the poison, but my mother refused. She tried to save me, but they stuck her in the neck with a syringe."

"Oh my God!" Jonovan exclaimed. "And you saw all of it?"

"Yes, I did," I continued lying. "When this man was poisoning my mother to death, she let my hand go and screamed for me to run. So that's what I did. One man almost caught me, but I slipped out of his grip and ran into the woods."

"This is unbelievable! I heard that there were a few survivors — even saw a documentary about it on CNN — but this is crazy."

"It's past crazy," I added.

"So what happened next?"

"More than nine hundred people died that day, including nearly three hundred kids. Many were never identified. I fell through the cracks. Since I was a local, no one assumed that I was a by-product of Jonestown. They assumed that my parents had been killed by the PNC regime. The seventies and eighties were hard times in Guyana."

"But how did you even end up in the orphanage?"

168

"I kept running and running until I got to a village, and this American doctor found me and took me to the orphanage. I refused to speak, so they made assumptions and I let them. I was too traumatized and in shock to speak the truth. Seeing all those people die. I can still smell the poison to this day and can't stand the smell of almonds, since it's so similar."

Jonovan reached over and took my trembling hand. I had the physical reactions down to a science. I had learned how to connect emotions in acting classes. Even though I was relating a fake story, I was remembering what had really happened to me. I had yet to actually act in a movie, even though I was constantly flooded with scripts. Outside of music-video skits, I had never ventured there. I was waiting on the right opportunity. I no longer feared that someone would recognize me. I was older, looked completely different, and was convinced that the world had long forgotten about Caprice Tatum. *Who the fuck was she anyway?*

"I am so sorry that you went through that. But . . . do you have any idea how many people you could inspire if you told the truth about your past? An escapee from the Jonestown Massacre in another country becoming the biggest musical star in America, possibly the entire world? Wow!"

"You promised," I stated angrily. Maybe he couldn't be trusted after all.

"And I will keep my promise."

I ran my fingers through my hair twice and Antonio appeared within seconds. "Wicket, you need to get ready to head to the studio."

Jonovan seemed disappointed.

"Sorry," I said. "Time's up."

"I guess I blew it," he replied, standing up. "I'll make my story work with what I have."

"Minus what we just talked about?"

"Definitely. You don't have to worry."

I started walking toward the house with Antonio on my tail, leaving Jonovan to be showed out by Nikki, who had also appeared suddenly, after realizing the interview was over.

"What was that all about?" Antonio asked. "What don't you have to worry about?"

"It's all good. Jonovan has always been a good guy."

"Oh, you know him?"

Damn, I fucked up!

"No, just heard that he was a good guy from some other peeps in the industry."

I was about to walk upstairs, and Antonio

would have headed off to watch his tele-
novelas, but I paused and turned around.

"What are you about to get into?" I gazed
into his eyes seductively.

"Hopefully you one of these damn days."

"You know that's not happening, but you
could help me relieve some stress." I
dropped my eyes to his groin. "With that
lap band-needing dick of yours."

He chuckled. "You and your jokes. My
dick's not that big."

"Shit, in whose world? Your dick is an
urban legend. You have fucked up many a
pussy and you know it. That's why you're
never going to disfigure Thumper."

Antonio moved close enough for me to
taste his breath as I stood on the third step
and he was at the base of the steps.
"Thumper might enjoy being with someone
so legendary."

"I didn't call you a legend. I said your dick
was a legend." I giggled. "So you want to
play with me this afternoon or what?"

"Depends on what playing entails. But
you know that I can never refuse you."

"If you can never refuse me, then it
doesn't depend, does it?" I turned and
started up the steps. "Give me twenty
minutes to prepare and then make it
happen."

When Antonio entered my bedroom exactly twenty minutes later, I was showered and ready with the blackout curtains closed, candles lit, and I was wearing a sports bra and biker shorts with no panties.

"What's this all about?" he asked as "Workout" by J. Cole played through the speakers in the walls.

"I thought we could do some Tantra Yoga. It makes me come."

Antonio laughed. "That again?"

"Didn't you enjoy doing all those poses and stretches with me before? Gazing into my eyes?"

"I want to fuck you, not do *poses.*"

"But you know we're not fucking, so let's cut the bullshit." I walked over to him and ran my fingers over his chest and then pulled his T-shirt out of his pants and pulled it over his head. "Damn, what have you been eating?" I teased. "You buffed up some . . . since last time."

"You need to start calling me up here more often. K and D don't know what to do with all of this." He grabbed my hips and pulled me closer to him so his dick was poking me in my ribs. It was rock hard.

172

"Can't you imagine all this dick up in you?"

"I do imagine it — all the time."

"Then let me hit it."

"Hit it?" I pushed him away. "Um, no. But I'll tell you what. Since you're topless, I can rock with that." I pulled off my sports bra, revealing my tatas.

"You're so lovely. You could at least let me suck them."

I contemplated actually letting Antonio suck my tits as "Adorn" came on and Miguel started singing about how his lips couldn't wait to taste some chick's skin. So apropos for the moment.

"You hear that?" Antonio picked up on the song lyrics fitting the moment as well. He moved closer to me and licked his lips as he started rubbing my right nipple with two fingers. "Let my love adorn you, baby."

I took a deep breath and threw my head back as the magic in his fingertips got to me.

You're almost forty, Caprice, I told myself. *You've got to learn to let go.*

Antonio picked me up by the hips with his other muscular arm and carried me to the bed as he started licking my other breast with the tip of his tongue.

"Aw, shit," I heard myself say as he laid me down.

173

He took my breast deep into his mouth and I could feel Thumper start pulsating in my shorts.

"Ummm, you taste so good, baby," he whispered as he came up briefly for air and moved his mouth over to my other breast.

I stared up at the ceiling, taking all the sensations in. I had played with my tits throughout my life, often masturbating with a toy, or even a towel between my legs if I was without a toy on tour, until I climaxed. But one of the major problems was that I never thought about what would be considered "traditional sex" when I masturbated. There were always at least two men involved, even if one of them was watching and waiting for his turn. I wondered if it was because the only time that I had ever actually been penetrated was under such circumstances. The men in my fantasies weren't violent or raping me or anything like that, though. There was just always at least two, or more. It concerned me that I might not have been able to be content with a sexual encounter with one man, if I ever took it that far. I planned to open up to Dr. Spencer about that, if I could.

Antonio did suck the hell out of my tits that day, and suck some damn tits he did. He tried to get my panties off so he could eat my pussy — damn near begged me to feed him — but I couldn't bring myself to allow it. So we ended up jacking off together and never got to the tantric yoga. I had to get back into the studio and work on "Manpooling."

CHAPTER NINE

The ride out to Marcella's cabin was relaxing, the views breathtaking. None of my bodyguards asked me any heavy questions — they knew better — and Nikki was in Miami handling some business for me. I was looking to open a restaurant there and she was doing some location scouting, gathering some lease proposals, and interviewing some chefs. I planned to come up with the names of the menu items myself, all named after my song titles, and I wanted to call it Wicket's Thicket and have it surrounded by dense landscaping. That way people would feel like they were far away from the beach, and the shade of the bushes and trees would mask the intense Miami heat while they were dining.

Daddy had called to Skype that morning and I assured him that I was fine. He was pleased to discover that I was on my way to a second session with the psychiatrist he suggested. I understood his concern, but it was time for me to deal with my past. Avoiding Atlanta forever made no sense, and while actually residing there for the time being was a bit drastic, I still had my plans for Bianca and Cherie. There was no way that they were getting away with what they did — them or their men.

Jonovan had crossed my mind quite often. I had even searched his address on Google Earth and checked out his small, brick rancher and surrounding neighborhood. He had only moved roughly ten miles from where we attended high school together at Powers. I had yet to go past my old school. The memories would have been too painful. Plus, it would have been too hard for me to explain that visit to KAD. Sneaking out to the boonies to visit someone in a cabin was one thing, but driving past a high school that I supposedly had no connection with would have been a red flag.

I had actually told KAD the truth about Dr. Spencer — to a point. I told them that I was seeking therapy for my issues and they certainly knew that I had them. They didn't know the extent of them but, clearly, the way that I toyed with them sexually, coupled with the fact that they never saw me bring any men into my bedroom or hotel rooms, were signs that I was not normal when it came to intimacy.

They also knew about my adoption, and I had made up different variations of the Jonestown story with each of them over the years. It was really more about laying the groundwork for people to back up the story if it ever surfaced. It always helped to have people who could say that they had known blah, blah, blah for years.

"We're almost there," Antonio said. He was still feeling some kind of way about getting to second base with me and getting shut down. "Five minutes."

"Cool," I replied as I played *Little Shop of Treasures 2* on my iPad. "I'm almost on week eight."

It's amazing how people can come up with the stupidest, brain cell–wasting games and apps and millions of people become addicted to them. I had beat the app dozens of times, but I still did it to kill time and to take my mind off things. In this case, I was trying to mentally prepare myself to come clean with Marcella about more details from my life — not the fabricated ones. The *real* ones.

Exactly five minutes later, we pulled up to an oak cabin that was definitely hidden away in the woods. It was "adorable," for lack of a better term. Like something out of a Disney movie. Flower beds out front held various perennials and there was a flagpole with a decorated floral flag to match what lay below. There was a two-seater Mercedes convertible parked out front, black on black, and Marcella was sitting on the wraparound porch drinking lemonade out of a mason jar. She had on jeans and a button-down, pin-striped shirt. Her hair was in a ponytail and she had on sneakers.

I felt completely overdressed in an Alexandre Vauthier gold minidress and a pair of Manolo Blahnik lace-up, high-heeled sandals. I saw her grin as I was guided out of the truck by Kagiso. He had complimented me earlier on my outfit.

"Looks like she thought this was a casual meeting," he remarked in a whisper.

"It is," I replied. "But you know I always like to have my shit on point. Never know when some cameras might be snapping."

He surveyed the area. "Doubt that'll be happening out here."

"And that's the point," I said. "But we still had to get here and we have to go back. Besides, I'm thinking about making a pit stop on the way home. Call Nikki and see if that Bianca broad is still hosting a party this evening at 444 Highland."

179

"That Bianca broad?" Kagiso laughed. "Why do you even hang around her if you can't stand her?"

"It's not that I can't stand her," I fabricated. "I actually like some of her suggestions and want to see what kind of references she might have. She's talented but seems to have a bit of an attitude."

"Maybe that's because you have one with her, Wicket."

I pinched Kagiso on the cheek and walked toward the porch. "You all try to look inconspicuous in case someone else stops by."

"How in the hell are we supposed to do that?" Diederik asked, overhearing my last comment.

"Blend in with the trees or something," I stated jokingly. "Or you all could head back into town and have lunch at that diner."

"Mr. Sterling would have all our heads on platters if we left you alone," Diederik said. "We're not that foolish."

"Besides, that diner had grease packed on the windows," Antonio chimed in. "I could tell that when we drove by."

It was just like Antonio to peep out every single food establishment we passed. Even though he was technically the smallest of the three, he liked to eat the most food. It was rare that he would pass up food for his iron-clad stomach, so the place must have truly looked foul.

"Then back to blending in with the trees!"

Marcella stood as I started up the porch steps. Turns out that she had a pitcher of lemonade waiting and another jar for me packed to the brim with ice to pour it over.

"Good afternoon, Wicket. Did you have any trouble finding me?"

I glanced over my shoulder. "Not with three bodyguards and a driver. Even though men hate following directions, they had enough common sense to use GPS to get out in this forest."

We shook hands and she motioned for me to have a seat. "We can sit out here, if that works, or go inside if that will make you more comfortable."

"Actually, I would prefer indoors, if that's cool. I'm not big on bugs, and I'm allergic to bees."

"Oh dear," Marcella said in a panic. "Let's get you on in then."

I was not allergic to bees, but I didn't want to put myself in the position of pouring out my feelings on her porch with KAD right there. I helped her carry the lemonade and jars inside. The place was nicely decorated. Again, looked like a movie set. It was a Pottery Barn house, with everything in its place like a furniture catalog. Most of the furniture was a dark mahogany and appeared to be expensive. Marcella had a bookshelf lined with books, mostly fictional titles. That surprised me as I walked over and ran my fingertips over the spines. She had all of Allison Hobbs's and Cairo's books.

"Um, let me find out you have a little bit of freak in you," I said to her.

She giggled. "When I come out here, I prefer to relax. No point in bringing my actual work out here with me, so I read a lot of fiction. And yes, I'm human, so I have a little bit of a freak in me."

I turned to face her. "From reading your bio, I realize that you are a general psychiatrist, but do you deal with a lot of patients who have sexual issues?"

"What sort of issues?" She sat in an armchair and waved toward the sofa for me to take a seat. "Do you have intimacy problems?"

I plopped down on the sofa. "That's an understatement."

"To answer your question, yes, I have several patients who are dealing with concerns and disorders surrounding their sexual identities or behavior."

182

"Such as?"

She poured me a jar of lemonade. "Addiction; survivors of rape, incest, and abuse; fetishes; hypersexuality disorder; gender identification issues; erectile dys—"

"Got you," I said, cutting her off. When she said "gender identification issues," I thought of Hannah. "Well, I most certainly have issues with intimacy, and I'll open up about that at some point. Right now, I'd like to tell you about Hannah."

"Yes, I remember you mentioning her before. It's obviously painful for you to discuss."

"Not all of it. Not the beginning of it, at least. Hannah was my everything. She rescued me and —"

"Rescued you from what?"

"Hell!"

I told Marcella about how Hannah had sought help for me in the bus depot but did not go into the details of the earlier part of that evening. I described how she had taken me to The Bronx, protected me from harm, shared her personal space and belongings with me, and was my ride-or-die after I met Daddy that Christmas Eve in Times Square. I talked about how she had been my nanny, my confidante, and my surrogate mother and sister that I had never had.

"Where's Hannah now?" Marcella asked about an hour into the discussion.

A single tear began to cascade down my cheek when I replied, "Hannah's dead."

CHAPTER TEN

Saturday, June 11, 2005
10:47 a.m.
Paris, France

I'll never forget the day Hannah died. It all started out so perfectly. There was no way in the world that I could have suspected that June 11, 2005, would be the day I lost my only friend. She was fifty-four and I realize that a lot of people do not even make it that far. But she still died far too young. I needed her for another twenty or thirty years. I needed her to be here for me and since her death, and up until I met you, Marcella, I'd only had Daddy.

We were in Paris. I had a concert later that evening at La Flèche d'Or. The first show had sold out in less than ten minutes after the tickets went on sale, so a second show had been added the following evening. I was excited. I had never performed in Paris before.

185

"I'm kind of nervous but extremely excited at the same time."

We were seated on the balcony at Hôtel Fouquet's Barrière on Avenue George V. We had arrived a few days earlier on my private plane and had been chilling in the presidential suite most of the time. That's the thing about being recognizable — another ugly price of fame — unless I wear some kind of disguise, it is damn near impossible to do a lot of touring. At least not in the traditional sense. People are not as overbearing overseas, but I still was not in the mood to be bombarded with a lot of the public.

We did sneak out one day to go see the Eiffel Tower and the Louvre. The night before, we had taken a gondola ride down Canal Saint-Martin. It was breathtaking. This was before KAD was hired, so part of my father's security detail were with us. Big difference, because they were all older, with beards and big bellies, but any one of them could shoot a penny off a rooftop. Most were former military and weren't scared of shit.

"Why are you so nervous?" Hannah asked as she took a bite into a croissant. "You know you've got this."

"It's different when you're in another country. People are not the same. My show

186

might bore them."

"Yeah, right. Your fan base is thick here, or there wouldn't be a second show. Judy said you could probably have sold out a third."

Judy was my tour manager, and she was bat-shit crazy if she thought I wouldn't pass out from exhaustion doing shows three nights in a row. As always, I vocalized my thoughts. "Judy must be bat-shit crazy. I'm not hurting myself like that. I'm getting old."

"Thirty-three is far from old, Ladonna."

"For regular people with regular careers, maybe. But there isn't a damn thing normal about my life. One week is like one year for most people."

Hannah nodded. "You have a point. But imagine how I feel then. I'm in my fifties and time is moving like a TGV train." She was referring to the high-speed train system in France that went up to more than two hundred miles per hour. "Life is passing me by."

I started giggling.

"What's so funny?" Hannah asked.

"I was just remembering the old days. How your place looked when you first brought me there. Hanging out with you and your squad."

Hannah laughed as well. "I was pretty eccentric. Richard wasn't having any of that loud lace and flowery shit once we moved in with him."

"Hell to the no, he wasn't."

Shayne still owned her spa and Crispin had moved away to the West Coast but still kept in touch with us.

"What ever happened to Nigel and that fool Sebastian?"

Hannah sucked her teeth. "Nigel's still around and in love with some dude he met online, some dating site. He said Sebastian's taking a dirt nap."

"For real?" I am stunned. "Drugs?"

"No. Actually, he was in one of the Twin Towers when they came down. He was working for some marketing firm."

"I'm so sorry to hear that."

Hannah shrugged. "We all have to go sometime." She sighed. "You never know when life is going to throw you for a loop. Like they say, you don't beat the grim reaper by living longer. You beat the grim reaper by living better."

I chuckled. "Who the hell says that? I've never heard that before in my entire life."

"Well, someone said it or my ass wouldn't be able to recite it, baby girl. You know my ass isn't creative enough to make it up."

188

We both laughed.

"How are things going with that guy you met?" I asked, referring to a man who Hannah had connected with on the banks of the canal two nights prior. They had been burning up phone lines; I knew that much.

"They're going. We're planning to hook up tonight. I put him and his brother on the list for all-access passes for your show."

"Look at you, giving that man perks and things."

"Hey, I have to pimp your ass out some way. Backstage passes to your shows are a big fucking deal."

"It's cool. I wanted to meet him anyway. You were all bummed up in the dark the other night. I couldn't even see what he looked like, on the real."

"Paul is definitely a cutie pie. I just hope he doesn't trip when —"

"You haven't told him?" I asked in astonishment.

"It hasn't come up."

"Hannah, you and I both know that being transgender is not just going to come up. Do you think he could tell when he met you?"

She shrugged again. "Who knows, but he'll find out tonight if things go the way I've imagined. Time is of the essence. We're leaving on Tuesday, and he's leaving on Thursday. If things go well, I might have to stay a couple of extra days and meet you back in New York."

"I'm not leaving you behind," I stated without hesitation. "You left the States with me and you're going back with me."

"I'm grown, Ladonna. Even though you have me spoiled with riding the friendly skies on private jets, my ass is not above riding commercial."

I was glad that Hannah had met a man she liked, but I was also very concerned. At fifty-four, she had had her share of both good and bad relationships, like most people. Most men had been accepting of the fact that she had undergone hormone therapy to grow breasts, reshape her hips and waist, and her face was stunning. Always had been, in fact. Some people would stare at her hard enough to figure it out, and even though she was transgender — meaning that she lived her life as a woman and her outer appearance was that of a woman — Hannah still had a penis. It wasn't that obvious in her clothes, because it was small. I had seen it before. Plus, she tucked it in, according to her. I imagined that to be painful, but it was important to her to live as a female.

I was concerned, however, because a few years earlier, one guy had not taken the "great reveal" that well. In fact, he had beaten on her in his apartment after they were making out and he reached between her legs. I understood that she wanted to get a fair chance to get to know men before admitting the truth, but I didn't consider it a good idea.

"I don't feel right about this," I said with honesty. "You just met the guy and we're over here in another country. Where is he from, anyway?"

"He's from Sweden, here on business."

"And what kind of business is he in?"

"He's an architect. That means he's good with his hands, if you know what I mean." She blushed and giggled. "I can't wait to find out how good."

"Don't get me wrong. I'm excited for you, but please don't go off with him after my show without me."

"What are you going to do, baby girl? Watch the action?"

"No, of course not," I replied. "At least promise me that you won't go anywhere without a bodyguard. People disappear all the time when they're traveling."

Hannah got up and glanced down at the street from the balcony of the 2,700-square-foot suite. "You're overreacting."

"I'm being protective of my best friend."

"More like overprotective, but I love you for it." Hannah came over and kissed me on the forehead. "I love you, Ladonna."

"Love you, too."

As Hannah walked off to get dressed so we could leave for the sound check at the arena, this eerie feeling washed over me. I couldn't describe it, but I know what it was all about now.

The concert went off without a hitch and I was more confident afterward. The Parisians adored me and my music, so by the third song, I was in my element. I put on one hell of a performance and was looking forward to really showing my ass the next night. In fact, I was going to make some wardrobe changes and wear something even more shocking and revealing on Sunday night.

I was in my dressing room when Hannah came knocking, and then walked in arm in arm with Paul. His brother was not with them, and I inquired about him after brief introductions were made. "Did your brother come to the show?"

"Yes," Paul said uneasily. "He met a chick and they went to some club. Sorry about that. It was rude of him not to at least come speak."

"It's not rude at all. I was only wondering. Everyone is star struck by my presence and this is Paris. The place to get romantic with strangers." I grinned at both of them and winked at Hannah. "You and Hannah have sure been getting along well. Every time I've looked around, she's been on the phone with you."

Paul looked at Hannah and grinned. He was roughly about the same age as her. He was kind of on the shorter side but still had her by at least two inches in her heels. He had a pudgy nose and dark brown hair and it was obvious that he had a full set of dentures. But he had a cuteness about him, and his personality seemed pleasant. I started to ease up a little on my concerns.

"So what are you two going to do tonight?" I asked. "Hannah has to take security with her, as a precaution. I hope you don't mind. They'll stay out of the way."

Paul seemed uncomfortable then. "But I thought you were the celebrity? Why do we need security?"

Hannah cleared her throat and glared at me. "We don't. Wicket's just fucking with you. We're rolling solo, Paul."

"Are you sure?"

Hannah let go of Paul's arm. "Baby, why don't you wait for me out in the hallway. I'll be right out."

Paul shook my hand. "It was nice meeting you, Miss Wicket. Great show, by the way."

"Thank you." I waited until he exited and closed the door behind him. Then I pounced on Hannah. "I thought we had an agreement!"

"Ladonna, it's obvious that Paul's not comfortable with that scenario, and I'm not blowing this opportunity."

"Please, let's just think about this. Even if the two of you hit it off, you live in two different parts of the world. How is any kind of relationship going to work?"

"I'm not worried about that at the moment. But I'm sure you would travel with me to see him if that's what I want. Right?"

I rolled my eyes.

"Right?"

"I guess, but I need you with me." I pouted. "You've always been here for me."

"And I always will be. But you're not a baby anymore. There's a huge difference between fifteen and thirty-three. You know how to handle yourself. You're Wicket, international superstar, dammit!"

We both laughed.

"I'll be back at the hotel before sunrise.

194

Don't wait up for me."

"Where are you going?"

"Out for drinks and hopefully back to his hotel room. That's where the magic will probably happen. Did you see those architect hands?"

"I shook one of them, but I didn't stare." I giggled. "It was rather soft, though."

Hannah grinned. "Exactly. I can't wait for him to lay both of those soft hands on me."

Hannah rushed from the room as I started stripping down to take a quick shower. I always shower after a show and before I head back to my hotel. A lot of entertainers wait, but I simply can't take it. I need to rinse all the sweat residue off as soon as possible.

I ended up dragging my security detail to Crazy Horse Paris, also on Avenue George V. A cabaret club where a lot of celebrities hung out, the acts were very sensual and not to mention creative as all get-out. It was there that I first gained an interest in BDSM. When I saw this woman beat a man with a whip onstage, it made me feel some kind of way between my legs. I wanted to bring pain to other people, the way that they had brought pain to me. I wanted to humiliate them and give commands that they had to follow.

I stayed there until about 3:00 a.m., and then headed back to the hotel. Hannah wasn't in her room when I got back to our suite. I drank some wine, took a sleeping pill, stripped nude, and passed out in my bed.

I woke up about ten and dragged myself out of bed and into the shower. When I came out into the living room, I noticed that Hannah's door was now closed. She had gotten back safely. I ordered some room service and it took damn near an hour for it to get there. Once it did, I figured Hannah might be hungry, so I went to wake her.

I knocked lightly at first and she didn't respond. I considered letting her sleep, but something urged me to knocked louder. I tried the knob and it was locked from the inside, making me wonder if she had brought Paul back to our suite with her. That would've been a first, but maybe he was sharing his room with his brother. I continued to knock, and then I started shouting.

"Hannah? Hannah, are you all right?"

Now I was escalating into a panic. I leaned my ear up against the door and heard nothing. I tried to ram my shoulder against it to get it open and then kicked it.

I rushed over to the phone and called the front desk, demanding that they send someone up right away with a key to the door. While I was waiting for them to come, I kept trying to get the door open and by that time, I was in tears. Something wasn't right and I only prayed that she was okay. Just passed out drunk or high, even though she didn't use drugs.

The three minutes or so it took a manager and maintenance man to arrive seemed like thirty. I was the first one in the room once they unlocked it. The bed was empty and still made. I rushed into the bathroom and collapsed.

Hannah was submerged in the bathtub and her wrists were slit. There was a straight razor lying beside the tub on the white marble tile. Blood was everywhere, from the water to the walls where it had splattered, and on the floor. I realized that I was sitting in her blood and screamed. They had to pull me out of there and out into the living room area, where the manager radioed for them to alert the authorities.

By that time, Daddy's security detail was all over the place. They probably had assumed that I was still asleep until all the action started. I heard one of them, Thomas, on the phone with Daddy filling him in.

They had to sedate me to calm me down. I was moved to another suite while the Parisian forensics team and police took over the presidential suite. When I woke up hours later, one of the officers asked me a bunch of questions. Then she handed me Hannah's suicide note, addressed to me. I'll never forget what it said:

Baby Girl,

I'm so sorry about this. I know that we just talked about how much you need me and I do love you. I'm your best friend. Always remember that. But I'm tired. I'm tired of this life and being afraid of what people will think about me. I really believed that Paul was the one. That he could accept me for who I was and would fall in love with me. All my life I've searched for the real thing, and while we both know that I had some hit-or-miss relationships, I don't want to grow old alone.

I hope that you will open yourself up to someone eventually and let go of the past. I realize how much your so-called friends hurt and betrayed you, but please don't let them win. You have fame and fortune, but you deserve someone to share it with.

Please tell my mother that I died still loving her, even though she could never love me back after I decided to live as a woman. Please tell Richard thank you for taking me in along with you, and being tolerant of my lifestyle. He is an amazing man and he loves you dearly. Please remember that I love you.

Don't blame yourself for this. It was a long time coming. I used to lie in bed at night and think about all the things I fucked up in my life. You are the only good thing that I have ever nurtured, and I am so proud of you. I just feel like I would make a better ghost than a human being. So remember that I will always be there for you in spirit. I'm not sure if my soul will still be around. People tell all kinds of stories but who the fuck knows? I just know that I have had enough.

As my last act, I plan to leave the world the way that I wanted to live in it. I want to die happy, as the woman that I was. I am sure some will say that I was crazy, but it was not about that. Once I cut it off, there will be no turning back. My wrists will be the easy part.

Good-bye, Ladonna. May you continue to thrive and walk in your gift.

Mourn me for a few days and then let me go. I know that you'll miss me, and I'll miss you, too. Please don't get too emotional over my death. I'm happy now. Do me one last favor. I cut off my dick for a reason. Don't bury me with it.

Love,
Hannah

CHAPTER ELEVEN

I was sitting on Marcella's sofa with tears streaming down my face as I finished relating the events of that day.

"Maybe we should end this session for the day. I don't want to emotionally drain you. We should take baby steps," Marcella suggested.

I jumped up. "Can I use your bathroom?"

"Sure, it's the second door on the left." She pointed down the hallway.

"Thank you."

I walked to the bathroom on wobbly knees and closed the door behind me. I closed the toilet seat and sat down and really let the pain release. I stifled my cries with a guest towel and then turned the faucet on to cover it up even more. The pain of discussing Hannah was almost unbearable.

After a few moments, I heard Marcella on the other side of the door. "Are you okay?"

"Yes, I'll be right out," I whispered.

It dawned on me that she may have been worried about me doing something crazy in her bathroom. After all, she was a psychiatrist and I had just finished recounting my best friend's suicide.

I ran some water over my face, demolishing what was left of my makeup, took a few deep breaths, and then opened the door. She was standing there waiting for me, concern written all over her face.

"Are you okay, Wicket?"

"I'm fine." I walked past her and went to sit back on the sofa. "This is the first time that I've discussed this with anyone since that day, except for my father."

"Why do you think Hannah killed herself?"

"Like she said in the letter, she was sick of the intolerance of this world. It wasn't about that guy, Paul. It was a culmination of fifty-four years of suffering. I understood why she did it; not sure if that makes me as frustrated with the world as she was. But I've been suicidal before. When she met me, I was prepared to kill myself, but I was too much of a coward." I sighed. "I even understood why she cut off her own penis. All her life she had one desire, to be a woman. She always identified with being female, and she stood up for what she believed."

"Do you feel like you've gotten over her death?"

I stared at Marcella with disbelief. "Does it look like I've gotten over it?"

"What I mean is, does it disturb you all the time, or are you in this current state because we were discussing it?"

"I've always recognized that I can't change what other people think or do. I'm sure that there was nothing I could've done to change the outcome of what happened. If she didn't do it in Paris, it would've only been a matter of time. It was clear that it wasn't something that had popped in her head that day, or even that week. She picked a moment and left me a note explaining why. I'm glad she did that. Otherwise, I would've always wondered."

"Did you carry out her last wish?" Marcella asked.

"Yes. Daddy came to Paris and arranged to bring her body back to New York for burial. We left her . . . we left it at the medical examiner's office in Paris. The unbelievable part is that her mother attended her funeral. First and last time I ever met her. She mourned over Hannah like they had never been apart. I was stunned, and so were her friends who attended."

"I actually recall reading about this in the

news back then. How your traveling companion had committed suicide when you were on tour, but there were not many details."

"And there never will be," I said, staring at her. "I don't want her to be embarrassed posthumously."

"Her self-mutilation goes no further than here. That I promise you."

"Thank you. I appreciate that."

"Your privacy goes without saying. Can I ask what she meant about your friends hurting you?"

"That goes back to why I'm here in Atlanta." I stood up. "In fact, I need to be somewhere."

"I don't want to press the issue, but I hope you're not planning to hurt anyone today."

"Not in the physical sense, no. I admit that I am extremely angry with several people here in Georgia, but I'm not willing to get locked up behind them."

"That's good to know."

"Thank you for your time, and enjoy the rest of your day."

Marcella walked me out. Antonio and Diederik were sitting on the porch drinking spring water out the cooler in the SUV, and Kagiso was sitting by a tree meditating.

"Sorry I took so long, guys," I said. "Told

you to go get something to eat."

Antonio chuckled. "I was about to go find a fast-food joint or something, for real. Anything but that diner."

"Well, now we're headed to that party, if it's still going on."

Kagiso had joined them by then. "Yes, it's confirmed. Also, Nikki said she found a hot-ass spot for Wicket's Thicket in Magic City."

"Can't wait to hear more about it." I turned to Marcella. "Thanks again for everything."

"You're very welcome, Wicket. Have a nice time at the event."

I could tell she was unnerved by the thought of me going some place where people would be present that I couldn't stand. What she didn't realize is that I held all the cards and all the advantages. They all wanted something from me, and they didn't even have a clue about who the fuck I really was!

■ ■ ■ ■

PART THREE:
THE CHORUS

■ ■ ■ ■

In its purest form, an act of retribution
provides symmetry, the rendering of
payment for crimes against the innocent,
but the danger of retaliation lies in
furthering the cycle of violence. Still, it's a
risk that must be met when the greater
offense is to allow the guilty to go
unpunished.

— Emily Thorne

Chapter Twelve

We stopped back by the house so that I could redo my makeup before the party. I didn't believe in having a makeup artist all up in my grill for anything outside of photo shoots or performances. Daddy had paid a ton for me to be naturally beautiful, so it wasn't that serious. However, I realized that people would be taking photos of me all evening at Bianca's event and, quite frankly, I wanted them all to be pressed to even get next to me. It was all a part of the plan for Wicket, *the Wicket,* to attend the event of an opportunist in Atlanta was a big fucking deal.

I also decided to change. All the emotions that broke out of me at Marcella's had me thrown for a loop. I had intended to speak with her about Hannah. She was such an integral part of my life and it had to be addressed if I ever wanted to be helped. I hadn't expected it to practically throw me into a mental break, though. I was being honest when I said that I believed that there was nothing I could've done to save Hannah. Her mind was made up and, if I were being honest, she was entitled to end her life if she saw fit to do so. I had watched several documentaries and news stories about "right to die" laws and controversies. No, Hannah was not battling terminal cancer or excruciating brain tumors but, to her, it was just as painful.

I remembered how I felt when I was disfigured. From the ages of seven to almost eighteen, I believed that I was subpar to others. I felt like no one would ever want me. After all, that was my mother's intention when she slashed my face that day in the kitchen. She wanted to break the Tatum curse, but as I matured, I realized that the curse began and ended with my uncle Donald. He was the sick one, and I would never know why he was so sadistic. Maybe he was touched by someone, raped prior to being attacked in jail, as the rumors had it upon his death. Maybe it did go back for generations, but all that I ever knew about was him raping my mother and, according to her, also raping Grandma. What a crazy notion that he could have been both my father and my grandfather.

I needed a drink before that fucking party. I hit the buzzer on the intercom and instructed one of the housekeepers to bring me a bottle of 1990 Henri Jayer Vosne-Romanée. Nothing like a five-thousand-dollar bottle of wine to calm the nerves.

Once she brought it up in an ice bucket, I had her draw me a bath while she was there. I put on "Make Me Whole" by Amel Larrieux as I ditched the gold minidress and heels. I sunk down in the suds and closed my eyes, thinking about what my next moves would be with Bianca, Cherie, and their bitch-ass men. I really, really wanted to see them all die but knew that wasn't right. Even though they deserved it, no one had made me their executioner. But I would most certainly make them pay, one way or another.

I heard someone stirring in my bedroom. "Who's there?"

"It's me," Diederik responded. "Just came in to check on you, but I see you're in the tub." He could see me through the open doorway. "You still planning on attending that party? Maybe you should just chill. You seemed upset earlier."

"No, I'm good. I still want to attend. You all have time to change if you want."

"All right, if you're sure."

He was about to leave when I called out to him. "Can you wash my back before you go?"

"Sure." He walked into the bathroom, already rolling up the sleeves of his white, button-down shirt. "My pleasure."

Like Kagiso and Antonio, Diederik had seen me naked plenty of times. I didn't feel like doing anything kinky right then, though.

"Thanks," I said as he picked up a loofah and started gently scrubbing my back.

He worked in silence as "Never Make a Promise" by Dru Hill came on. I closed my eyes and listened to the lyrics. Once it ended, Diederik said, "That good?"

"Perfect, thanks."

He got up from the side of the tub and was about to leave when he paused in the doorway. "Can I ask you something?"

"Sure. What?"

"What's going on? Why are we really here in Atlanta?"

"Change of pace. We won't be here forever. What? You and the other guys don't like it?"

"Where you roll, we roll. You know that. It's just that you seem different: like this place is doing something to you."

"That's silly. I've never even been to Atlanta until we came here," I lied. "If

212

you're referring to me seeing Dr. Spencer, that has nothing to do with this city, or the people in it. I'm trying to work through my issues that have been around for a very long time."

"You've been through hell," he admitted. "We all know that."

You don't know the half of it, I thought.

"I want you to know that if you ever need us to do anything . . . *anything,* if you get my drift, all you have to do is ask."

Diederik was talking about killing someone for me!

"No one will ever suspect a thing. We're very good at what we do."

I sat up further in the tub. "We need to end this conversation right here. I get your drift and I don't want to know about whatever any of you did before you started working for me. You dig?"

He gazed at me with his ice-green eyes. "I feel you. But remember that we have your back at all times. Nothing's going to ever happen to you on our watch, especially mine."

"Thank you. I love and appreciate you for that."

"I'll go tell Antonio and Kagiso to be ready to leave in about forty-five minutes. That cool?"

"Perfect."

When he walked out, I realized that I needed to "find my center." I wasn't pulling things off as smoothly as I planned. I needed to calm down and not be so obvious about my animosity toward Bianca and Cherie. Of course, all of that flew out the window the second I laid eyes on them.

Four forty-four Highland was a nice spot. It was a mixed-use space with a theater and entertainment venue downstairs, and some offices and apartments upstairs. The theater held a couple of hundred people tops. There was not any parking, but of course I was driven there, so it didn't matter. As always, when KAD emerged from the SUV first, all the women started drooling. No doubt that I had the hottest security team on Planet Earth. Their days off varied, so I am sure they were collecting phone numbers — and pussy — by the pound. Tonight would be no exception. The chicks were thirsty and not even trying to pretend otherwise.

My entrance caused an uproar, as it should have. Being there was out of my element. Bianca rushed forward to greet me and then escorted me over to the step and repeat so people could snap flashes all up in my face. I was perfect, as always, in a Hermès white floor-length gown with my boobies halfway on display. My hair was up in a bun, and I was wearing a couple of million dollars' worth of diamonds.

"I'm so glad you made it," Bianca exclaimed. "Everyone is dying to meet you."

"I'm sure," I said sarcastically. "I decided to grace you all with my presence, but if too many people get up into my personal space, I'm leaving."

KAD was not about to let that happen, but I was spitting shit anyway. As soon as I saw her face, I wanted to knock all her teeth out — *fake bitch!*

Bianca looked ashamed because a few people had overheard my comment.

"So what exactly is this little shindig all about?" I eyed this one chick who was clearly jealous of me. She may have been an aspiring singer or video vixen who wasn't getting any play. People always want to blame someone else for their failures. I've never kept a single fucking person from achieving their dreams by going after mine. "Are these supposed to be the who's who of Atlanta? I don't recognize a soul."

Bianca had to bite her tongue and then she said, "Yes, at least a dozen or so reality show stars are here. This is just a reception to thank my current clients, and I have a display of some of the interior designs I have created right down those steps." She pointed to a crowded area down a few stairs and I could make out photographs on easels. "In about thirty minutes, Cherie will be putting on a fashion show with some of her designs in the theater."

I glared at her and grinned. "In other words, you and your road dawg are peddling your shit. I ain't mad at you."

That "peddling" implication always got to her. I made a mental note to use it as much as possible.

"As for the reality show stars, I don't watch train wrecks. What's so appealing about watching thirsty-ass broads argue and scrap over community dick?"

"That's not what reality shows are about!" Bianca exclaimed. "If you don't watch them, how would you know?"

"Did you just break bad with me?" I stared her up and down. She wanted to curse me out but knew better. I would be her biggest accomplishment in her entire pathetic life if I hired her. "That's what I thought."

Kagiso was shaking his head, and Diederik looked concerned. They were both probably wondering what my purpose was in even going. I was such a private person. Networking and "being seen" were never on my radar. I was a household name and a household face already.

I smirked at them as I pushed Bianca out of my way, practically knocking her to the floor. "No more pictures. This is beneath me."

"Well, we have a . . . a seat for you on the front row for the fashion show," Bianca said, catching her breath.

"I'm not sitting on no damn front row so you all can pretend like I'm a groupie for her shit." I stopped walking and turned to face her. "Besides, I won't be here for thirty minutes. You need to be appreciative of the fact that I came at all."

I wasn't watching where I was going as I started walking backward. I bumped right into Jonovan. He was standing beside Antonio — *and some chick.*

Antonio pointed at Jonovan. "He's the one who came to interview that day at the house. He saw me outside and asked if you were here."

"Mr. Davis," I said, taking in all his fineness. "Nice to see you again."

He frowned. "I thought we were on a first-name basis, but good evening, Miss Wicket."

Jonovan had on a black tailored suit with a russet tie, and his date had on a dress that

217

matched his tie. She was light-skinned with a weave on fleek and had a pretty smile. She still couldn't hold a candle to me, though.

"Is this your little friend?" I nodded toward the woman. "You two look adorable together."

"I'm Marilyn." She reached out a manicured hand to shake mine. I barely touched hers but made a slight gesture of a handshake. "It's such a pleasure to meet you. I'm a huge fan."

I wanted to say, *Of course you are, bitch,* but instead I replied, "Thank you. I appreciate it."

She eyed Jonovan, who had all eyes on me. "Baby, I'm going to find the ladies' room. I'll be right back."

"Okay," he said, still looking at me.

"Why are you staring at me?" I asked, after Little Miss Marilyn had scattered away to take a piss. "You didn't even look at your woman when she walked away. Just a word of advice: most females are offended by that kind of thing."

"I'm sorry." He broke his stare and looked in the direction where she had headed. "It's just that . . . that . . ."

"That what?"

"There's something about you that seems so familiar."

My knees almost gave out.

"It feels like we've known each other for a lifetime. I felt that when I left your house that day, too."

"Some people say that I've never met a stranger," I lied. "I have that kind of personality but only with certain people."

He started staring at me again, gazing in my eyes. "You remind me of someone I used to go to school with . . . here in Atlanta."

Oh no! He recognizes me! How?

"Well, that would be an amazing feat, since I grew up in New York and was home-schooled my entire life."

"I realize it's silly. It's just that I often wonder what happened to her."

The logical thing would have been for me to ask questions about her, but that was not going to happen. He was talking about Caprice Tatum, and that was not a conversation that I wanted to have — ever.

"It must've been cool to actually have classmates and a lot of friends," I commented.

Then it dawned on me why he was even there. We had all gone to school together and he was still connecting with the rest of them. But why, if he knew what they did to me?

"What brings you to this event?" I asked.

"Covering it for *G-Clef*?"

"Pretty much. There are a couple of local singers here tonight, and one of them invited me. I actually know the hostess. We went to high school together, ironically." He paused. "We don't really speak like that, though."

"You mean Bianca Lee?"

"Yeah, Bianca."

I saw his eyes become dark and realized that he wasn't feeling her after all. It was just business for him.

"She's sweating me about decorating my house, so I stopped by. I'm not sure that I'm vibing well enough with her to utilize her services."

"You may want to look elsewhere," he said. "There are a lot of designers here in town."

Good! He's not trying to get her any business because he knows she's a fucking liar!

"Miss Marilyn's coming back for you." I spotted her headed in our direction. "I'm about to roll, but have a good night."

"She and I are not serious," he made sure to tell me. "She's actually more like a friend."

I giggled. "Does she know that?"

I walked off before she got back to us. KAD followed as I searched for that other whore. I found her with her asshole of a man, Michael, cheesing for photos on the lower level.

She spotted me and rushed up to me. "Wicket! I'm so glad you're here! I have a seat for you in the show!"

"I'm not staying for the little performance," I said with disdain. "I'm on my way out."

Cherie's face almost dropped to the floor. "But I wanted you to see my fashions, and then I have some media that wanted to ask for your opinion afterward."

"Unless you're paying me five hundred grand to peddle your shit for the evening, I'm not giving any opinions. You do realize that people of my stature get paid to show up at events, to tweet or post status updates, and whatnot?"

"I realize that it could work that way, but —"

"And actually, I don't even do any of that. Those are the ones stressing over exposure and who need the money."

Michael walked over to introduce himself. "Hey there, I'm Michael Vinson."

He reached out his hand and I just stared at it until he pulled it back.

"You must be the actor." I smirked. "Cherie said you were in *New Jack City* decades ago, but I don't remember your face."

Kagiso and Antonio chuckled. Diederik didn't get the joke because he had likely never heard of the Wesley Snipes movie about the crack explosion in NYC.

Michael seemed ashamed. "I've done some things since then. I'd love to be in one of your music videos, if you have any about to go into production."

"And what could you possibly do in one of my music videos?"

He shrugged. "Play one of your love interests or something. We're about the same age."

I laughed and pointed at KAD. "Do you see my bodyguards? I mean, do you *see* them? It takes more than good looks to be in one of my videos. They're a walking video."

Michael was getting upset. Poor Little Tink Tink.

"Well, maybe I can have my agent submit my information just in case something comes up."

A lightbulb went off in my head. "Tell you what. Give me your cell number and I'll be in touch personally. Now that I think about it, I may have a role for you. I'm cutting my new album and soon I'll be working on the title-cut video."

The expression on his face went from disappointment to euphoria. In his mind, he was thinking that he might be able to resurrect an acting career that was never breathing in the first place.

"Sure, let me give you my card." He reached into his jacket pocket and handed me a tan card. "My cell's on there, and my e-mail. Whatever works for you."

Cherie was starting to get uncomfortable about her man giving me his personal information. "Michael, she really could contact you through me. We're already friends."

"Friends?" I rolled my eyes at her. "Yeah, whatever."

Diederik was eyeing me suspiciously again. I was doing the most and decided to cut it out.

"I'm ready, guys." I started walking toward the stairs that led up to the entrance. "We need to get to the studio."

As we were leaving, I spotted Jonovan and his *friend.* Once again, he forgot all about her and started staring at me. It was all so confusing. He thought I reminded him of Caprice and it felt good to know that he had never forgotten her. I was still attracted to both his looks and his spirit, after all that time. But what could become of it? There I was, hell-bent on getting revenge on people for being wolves in sheep's clothing, but what the fuck would that make me?

Chapter Thirteen

Brian and I were in my new studio. Instead of continuing to rent one in the Atlanta area, I had one built on my own property. It was finally ready, and I was loving it. I had it completely decorated in white. Something about white calmed me when I was singing. I also slept to white noise most of the time. The blankness of it all helped me zone out everything and everyone else. I spent a lot of time meditating as well. Sometimes it helped; sometimes I had problems relaxing and controlling my breathing and thoughts.

I used to think that meditation was complicated, and while some people do make it that way, the overall idea is to sit still for at least twenty minutes — I tried to do it both in the morning and the evening — and control your thoughts. Obviously you will not be able not to think or worry — especially when you are going through a lot of shit — but you put your thoughts and worries into compartments and analyze them one by one. Tons of meditation music was available right on YouTube if you didn't want to pay for it.

That night, after seeing Jonovan, I decided to work on a new song impromptu. I was going to call it "Surge" because that was how I had felt the two times I had seen him. Just seeing him brought out something powerful in me, in my soul. The sad part was that it was as plain as the nose on my face that I couldn't do a damn thing about it.

One of the things that I had learned in therapy when I was younger was that being delusional was very damaging to me. Over the years, I had fantasized about being in normal relationships with various men. I had detailed, vivid dreams about our lives together. Cooking and eating dinner together via candlelight; curling up and watching movies on the sofa or in the bed; making love all night until the break of dawn; celebrating holidays together, especially Christmas, New Year's, and Valentine's Day.

There was only one thing that I never fantasized about when it came to men. I never dreamed of having children. A few months earlier I had come across an online survey — I spent a lot of time alone, so I read a lot on the Internet — where they had interviewed about three hundred women regarding why they had made the decision to never have kids. I read through each and every one of them. The list included:

Concentrating on their careers
Not having financial stability
Their man already had kids and had a
  vasectomy
They'd rather have pets
Too scared to carry a baby in their bodies
They have an illness
They don't like kids
They haven't met a man they want to have
  kids with
The world is too fucked-up to bring a
  child into it (*I totally agree.*)
They were stuck raising siblings and
  didn't want to raise their own
They didn't believe it was in God's plans
They have never married and don't want
  to have kids outside of it
They are lesbians
They are too selfish to be mothers
All the work falls on the women
Too much responsibility for them to
  handle emotionally

The list went on and on, but what I found fascinating is that none of them said because their own mothers were bat-shit crazy. Surely there were women on that list who had been abused. A few made note that they grew up in a dysfunctional home but did not go into details, even though everyone was kept anonymous. All I saw was denial, denial, denial. I recognized it because I was the same way.

I often wondered what would happen if I ever told the truth. No one had a heaven or a hell to put Caprice Tatum in. What would have been the reaction if I held a press conference, or wrote an open letter to the world, and confessed who I really was? How would my fans have reacted to me? Would they look at me differently if they knew that I was the by-product of incest and rape? If they knew that my sick-ass uncle was my father and possibly my grandfather? If they knew that I was ugly and disfigured as a child? If they knew that several boys had run up in me raw dog after my homecoming during my freshman year in high school? If they knew that instead of facing them, and pressing charges, I ran away in a suicidal state?

I really hated living a lie. Even though I had it all — based on societal views — I was lonely, depressed, and the only thing that made me happy was my music. I didn't and couldn't truly trust anyone. That would have been the case if I wasn't a celebrity, but being a celebrity made it a hundred times worse. It never escaped me that there were strangers who wanted to see me fail, for no other reason than they couldn't stand a black woman being successful. Yes, there were some famous white female singers in the same boat. It was part of the industry, but the hatred was always worse when it came to celebrities of color. If we made mistakes, or nasty rumors started about us, people were ready to rejoice in the streets like they had gained something from it.

I would have loved to see the expressions on the faces of Cherie, Bianca, Herman, and Michael if they ever found out that I was Caprice. They had no reason to do what they did to me. I was always kind to them and I thought we were cool.

CHAPTER FOURTEEN

Monday, May 27, 1985
Memorial Day
4:56 p.m.
Atlanta, Georgia

"I can't believe school's almost out!" Cherie was flipping burgers on the charcoal grill in her backyard. "Two more weeks and summer vacation!"

"You act like your father's actually going to take time off to go on one." Herman was playing DJ on the boom box that he had brought with him to Cherie's customary Memorial Day cookout. "Raspberry Beret" by Prince was going off, so he pulled that cassette tape out and popped in another one. Within seconds, "Cool It Now" by New Edition was pumping through his speakers.

There were about two dozen kids there — most of us twelve or thirteen and heading to the eighth grade — and the boys were sporting high-top fades while the girls all had "big hair." Back then, the bigger the blowout, the better. It was the age of Madonna and her pointed bras that every teenage girl wanted while they felt "Like a Virgin." The Pointer Sisters had everyone doing the "Neutron Dance," the Commodores were working the "Nightshift," Phil Collins wanted "One More Night," and Aretha Franklin was cruising on the "Freeway of Love."

Life was so simple then, even for me. My mother had been safely tucked away in a sanitarium for years and even though the scar on my face was a constant reminder of her hatred toward me, I felt safe because I knew she wouldn't be sneaking into my bedroom to finish killing me. For years after "the event," I wondered why she hadn't simply taken my life. It was clear that she was not prepared to take care of a child, and while I understood that she was forced to have sex with Uncle Donald, that didn't give her just cause to disfigure me.

Most of us had snuck in to see *Rambo: First Blood Part II* over the weekend. It was the big picture for the weekend. Back then, movie theaters weren't tripping so hard on kids seeing R-rated movies. *The Breakfast Club* had come out for Valentine's Day Weekend that year and Cherie, Bianca, and

I had gone to see it.

We pretty much had Cherie's house to ourselves, as usual. Her father was indeed a workaholic. He had his own garage and worked on cars daily, even on the holidays. He only had two workers and neither one spoke good English, so he didn't want to miss out on any possible money by leaving them in charge. They were beasts when it came to fixing cars, but giving estimates and explaining what was wrong to people was a challenge. Cherie told me that he was seeking a bilingual mechanic so he could take some time off.

Cherie's mother was a trip. Best way for me to describe her. She was afraid to embrace her aging. She dressed young, acted young, and was completely irresponsible when it came to parenting. She rarely cooked, but she would go grocery shopping. She wanted to be in control of the finances. Cherie's father would bring home the money, or put it in the bank, and her mother would write the checks and spend it. She was out shopping somewhere that day. She was always shopping and returning home with her Chevrolet Camaro IROC-Z packed to the brim with bags. Half the stuff ended up staying in the bags and shoved into corners and closets throughout the house.

Michael emerged from the back door carrying a twelve-pack of Coca-Cola and a bag of ice. He had made a run to the corner store to replenish our supply.

" 'Bout damn time," Herman said, getting the naps out his fade with a hair pick. "I thought I was going to have to come find you."

"Man, you should have seen these honies at Quick Stop. They were phat as all get-out. They go to Mays."

Herman smirked. "Don't no high school babes want to roll with you, shorty."

Michael was still short back then. Herman was taller than all the girls in school, but Michael hadn't hit his growth spurt yet. He would later shoot up within the next couple of years, but at that moment, he looked more like nine than twelve.

I got up off the lounge chair that I was sitting in, trying to stay in the shade, and decided to help out. "You want me to put ice in the cups?" I asked Michael.

"Yes, do your woman's work," he replied jokingly.

He ended up helping me while Bianca flirted with most of the boys there. This was well before Herman and Bianca hooked up in high school. Michael had confided in me that he liked Cherie, but she wasn't feeling him at all. Not until he was tall and his dick had grown several inches.

"You still want to go to the pool next weekend?" I asked him. "The passes are almost sold out for the summer. I need two more dollars to get mine, but I can ask Grandma."

"I've got you on the two dollars, Caprice." Michael hit the bag of ice on the side of a picnic table to bust it up some more. "I'm doing that paper route, remember?"

"I know, but I hate to take your money."

Michael put down the ice and then sat on the edge of the table. "It's cool. All the rest of us have parents, or at least a mother in my case. Your grandma's sick and all. Two dollars isn't a big deal."

Michael and I were actually kind of friends. Grandma started allowing me to have company sometimes, after Momma was put away. He used to come by and play *Super Mario Brothers, Gauntlet,* and *Xanadu* with me. My video game system was on its last leg — along with my television — but we still had fun. I didn't like him, either, not as a boyfriend. Besides, I didn't want to get my feelings hurt. Even though boys were nice to me, I couldn't wrap my head around

234

one of them actually believing I was pretty; not with that hideous scar.

"Thanks, Michael."

Time slipped by while we had fun listening to music and eating hot dogs, hamburgers, and consuming sugary drinks. Before I realized it, it was dark and Grandma didn't play that.

"Can someone walk me home? I'm afraid of the dark."

Several kids were coupled up and slow dragging to "Smooth Operator" by Sade. Yeah, they were fast as all get-out. People think the newer generation is doing more than previous ones. Such is not the case. People were feeling all over each other, dry humping and some were even fucking in middle school in the eighties; probably the sixties and forties as well.

Michael was dancing with this loose hot tamale named Olive. He didn't even hear me ask. Herman was also all up on some girl, and the only other boy who I ever really spoke to at the party was Jonovan. He had arrived late because he had a lacrosse game earlier that day. While other boys in the neighborhood were playing typical sports like football, baseball, and soccer, Jonovan was the most valuable player on his lacrosse team. Our school didn't belong to a league, but his parents transported him to the better part of town to play. He was so good that the league paid all his fees. His father was of the belief that he should not have to pay to play organized sports. He was that good.

Jonovan was sitting down over by an oak tree on a makeshift bench that was actually a piece of a tree trunk that had been chopped down. People made out however they could back then. If a dead tree had to come down, parts of it were going to be utilized for one damn thing or another.

I walked over to him. "Hey, Jonovan."

"Hey, Caprice. How are you?"

"I'm okay. Just wondering if you wouldn't mind walking me home. My grandma's going to sound the alarm and call the police if I don't get back soon and I'm scared of the dark."

"I've got my bike. You mind riding on the back of it?"

"How am I going to do that when you only have one seat?"

"I stand up and pedal. You've never ridden like that before?"

I was embarrassed to say that I really was not even good at riding bikes. I had never owned one. We couldn't afford them. My experience was limited to taking a turn here or there on Bianca's when we were younger.

"No, I've never done that, but I'm open. Can we leave now?"

"Sure. I need to be home by nine myself."

As we were leaving together, I heard Herman say, "Uh-oh. What's going on with you two?"

We both blushed.

"I'm making sure she gets home," Jonovan replied.

"You coming back?" Bianca asked.

"No, I need to get home. Don't any of the rest of you have curfews?"

Cherie said, "Bianca's spending the night, and some of the other girls. Caprice, you want to stay? Call your grandmother and ask."

"No, I can't."

There was no hesitation in my reply. I wanted to be home every night to keep an eye on my grandmother. She was in poor health, and my biggest fear was that she might fall and hit her head and I wouldn't be around. Crazy because about two and a half years later, I would leave her for good. My biggest fear transformed into something much worse. I felt like staying would only bring her heartache and shame. She had endured enough of that. Everyone was always talking about Mrs. Alice Tatum, whose daughter went crazy and cut up the face of her granddaughter.

I was trembling all the way to my house on the back of Jonovan's bike. "Noooooooooooooooooo!" I screamed out as he hopped a curb, dashed out into the street and then hopped another curb to get onto the opposite sidewalk.

"Calm down, Caprice," he said.

It was clear that he was showing off in front of me. At least, that is what it seemed like. When we finally pulled up in the front yard, I was so ready to get off that Hutch BMX.

Grandma was sitting on the living room sofa staring out the window.

Jonovan waved at her and yelled, "Hey, Mrs. Tatum! Sorry she's late!"

She waved slightly at him, but I could tell she was highly irritated and had been sitting there concerned. I felt bad, but at least I was home. Some of the kids I knew couldn't have cared less about worrying their relatives.

I climbed off the back of the bike and straightened up my jean shorts that had been embedded in my crotch from the seat and my neon T-shirt. I had on pink jelly shoes and my feet were killing me. Some things change and some remain the same. By the time most girls are ten, they are already wearing shoes that cut into their toes, mess up their arches, or give them corns and bunions. They eventually graduate to high heels and stilettos, all in an effort to look cute for men who pay little attention to the shoes. Some men like "fuck-me pumps" but most are more concerned with what kind of tits and ass the chicks are working with.

"Thanks again for bringing me back."

"No problem."

"So this is how the magic happens when you deliver papers, huh?"

"Yeah, sorry if I was going too fast, but I do my entire route in less than thirty minutes. I get my money fast and then get home."

"You like delivering papers?"

Jonovan shrugged. "I guess. It was part of the deal. My dad agreed to get me this bike if I worked off the money, so I'm working off the money."

I giggled. "Makes sense."

Grandma was up off the sofa and suddenly swung the front door open, staring at me through the screen. "It's late, Caprice."

"I'm coming, Grandma."

"You better get in there before she comes out here and beats us both with her cane."

We both chuckled.

"She'd never do that," I replied. "Ground me, yes. Beat me up, no."

Jonovan seemed like he was hesitating to say something.

"What is it?"

He zipped up his Wrangler jean jacket. It was getting cooler outside.

"Seriously, what is it?" I asked again.

"I was just thinking about something."

I glanced at Grandma, who was standing there waiting.

"What were you thinking about?"

"I was thinking that you're a nice girl and you shouldn't feel bad about your scar."

"Jonovan, you know I get bullied a lot. Not by our friends but the other kids." I started kicking through the grass with my jelly shoes. "I've learned to accept it. It's been five years since my mother did this to me."

"Well, I think you're pretty."

We stared into each other's eyes for a brief moment, and I was in shock.

"Caprice, get in here now!" Grandma's patience was gone and, to top it off, we were disrespecting an elder by not obeying.

"I have to go. Thanks again, Jonovan."

I went inside and dashed up to my bedroom so I could look out the window and see him ride off down the street. For a few seconds, I actually thought I could get a boyfriend. Jonovan was so cool.

That fantasy was short-lived. I called Cherie to tell her that I was back home and she burst my bubble quickly after I told her that Jonovan had told me that I was pretty.

"He told me the same thing. He tells every girl that she's pretty. *That's what boys do.*"

The last sentence was dripping with sarcasm.

I wished them a good night with their sleepover. Grandma locked up the house and then came upstairs, peeking her head into my room to make sure I hadn't climbed out the window.

"I'm still here, Grandma."

"Just checking. I know how kids can be once they hit puberty."

"Well, you don't have to worry about me. I'm a good girl. Cherie wanted me to stay over with her and the other girls, but I came home to be here with you."

"I would've let you stay."

"Really?"

"Yes. Maybe next time."

"Thanks, Grandma, but I'd really rather be here with you at night."

"I love you, Caprice."

"Love you, too."

She closed my door. I turned on my General Electric alarm clock on low. I set the dial to 96.7 and fell asleep to "Who's Holding Donna Now" by DeBarge.

CHAPTER FIFTEEN

Wednesday, August 22, 2012
11:38 p.m.
New York City

"So what are you really doing in Atlanta?" Daddy took a sip of his Dalmore 62 whiskey. He owned one of the twelve bottles of the sixty-two-year-old aged whiskey that was released from the distillery from Scotland in 2012.

"How much did you pay for that bottle again?" I asked, attempting to change the subject.

"Two hundred grand."

I shook my head.

"Hey, I can't take billions of dollars with me, you're my only child, and you're filthy rich yourself."

"I'm not a *billionaire*." I stressed the last word.

"Close to it, and besides, you will be once I kick the bucket." He held his glass up like he was doing a toast. "That's a guarantee."

"There's no amount of money that could ever replace you, Daddy."

"And I know you mean that. Ditto."

He glanced around my penthouse apartment on Park Avenue. I had put it on the market for $18 million. It would take a while for anyone to come along who could afford it — likely another celebrity. But they had to be approved by the board of the building as well. It was sometimes shocking when celebrities were denied by a group of stuck-up floozies and pedigreed old-money folks. Like who really gave a fuck about them?

"That's why I'm concerned about you. So what are you doing in Atlanta? Really?"

I sighed. "Daddy, I came back here to celebrate your birthday with you."

"My birthday's the day after tomorrow."

"Doesn't mean we can't celebrate early."

I kicked off my black heels and put my feet up underneath me on the sofa. We had gone to a premiere of *Lawless* with Tom Hardy's fine ass in it. If I'd had it in me to actually let a man blow my back out, he would have been tied with Dwayne "The Rock" Johnson to rip my panties clear off my ass. God bless both of their sets of parents.

"Did you enjoy the movie? It was good to see so many of your old friends at the premiere. That red carpet was bananas."

"Isn't it always?" He took a puff of his Cohiba Behike cigar, something else ridiculously expensive. Only one hundred humidors were ever made, with forty rolls each in them. A single cigar was worth four to five grand. "You keep thinking that you can change the subject, but that's not going to work. You know me better than that."

Daddy owned several properties in New York City, but he'd decided to chill with me at my place so we could spend a lot of quality time together. I hadn't been there in months and wanted to be in my own space.

"Do you think someone will take this place off my hands? Why don't you buy it, Daddy?"

"Not a chance. I told you this was a bad investment when you purchased it. Park Avenue is getting played out. You may end up taking a loss on it. The real estate market has tanked in certain parts of town."

I shrugged it off and took a sip of my distilled water. I was trying to get the liquor out of my system from the after party of the premiere. I had lost count at five cosmopolitans, and heavy drinking was not my thing in the first place.

"Are you really going to make me ask you again? Don't insult me!"

"Daddy, I've already explained to you that I'm posted up in Atlanta because it was time. It was time for me to stop avoiding my past. I'll be forty next month, for goodness' sake. How long am I supposed to let them dictate my moves?"

"It's not about people dictating your moves. It's about you keeping your condition under control."

I glared at him. "I haven't gone off, or snapped in a long time."

"Not to an extreme, that I know of, but we both know what you are capable of. Have you been taking your medication?"

"Prozac, Dilantin, Ativan, and Lithobid, the breakfast of champions!"

"I realize you hate taking all that stuff, but it's better than the alternative."

"Don't worry. I have no plans to shoot anyone or run them over in the street."

"I don't want you to hurt yourself, either. That's happened in the past."

"You say that like I wasn't there." I was getting upset about the entire conversation. "Look, Daddy, I'm sure you already knew that I was still on my meds. Even with patient-doctor confidentiality laws, they're all on your payroll one way or another. They know what side their bread is buttered on."

Daddy took another sip of whiskey and followed it up with a puff on his cigar.

"I'm not privy to what you're doing with Dr. Spencer."

"I'm surprised. Then again, she doesn't seem like the type that could be bought."

"You must admire that trait about her. The two of you have that in common."

Daddy was referring to the fact that some of the richest men in the world had tried to date me. One Arabian prince had even offered me $10 million for one night of sex. Another man offered to sign over the deed to his skyscraper in Milan for an opportunity to date me. Then there was my refusal to perform concerts in countries where women were mistreated and undervalued. That was truly a sensitive issue for me. Women being stoned to death for cheating, even if there was no proof. Women being shot to death on their wedding nights if they weren't virgins; their own fathers providing their grooms with the guns and bullets. Young girls being forced to marry their rapists so that their families won't be shamed by their communities. Female circumcisions and mutilations. The Sworn Virgins of Albania who were forced to live as men if they did not engage in arranged marriages.

The list went on and on.

"I like Marcella a lot. Something about her makes me feel comfortable."

"That's good. You've never really connected with your past therapists."

"I feel like I'm evolving. Unfortunately, I've discovered that there are no shortcuts. I wish that I could jump inside a time warp and suddenly become the new me."

"And who is the new Ladonna?"

"I guess we'll both find out at the same time."

I giggled and got up to look outside the window. Park Avenue was nothing like Times Square late at night. The streets were not crammed with people, and it was rather quiet. All the fancy stores were shut down, and even the restaurants closed their kitchens earlier than those a few blocks over.

"I hope that I can finally beat my depression. Have some kind of normal existence."

"What about a love interest? Met any intriguing men in Atlanta?"

Thoughts of Jonovan immediately popped into my head.

"It's complicated." I turned to look at him. "Why are you always pressuring me to get a man?"

"Ladonna, I'm barely in the country, rather less putting pressure on you to get a

248

man. However, I'll admit that I would love to know that someone will be here to take care of you once I'm gone."

"Why do you keep talking like you're dying? Are you sick, Daddy?"

He chuckled. "I'm as strong as an ox, but I'm also a realist. You're about to turn forty and I'll be seventy-three the day after tomorrow."

"And still a player player," I said jokingly. Daddy had women posted up in several different countries. He never settled down, because he always thought women were all gold diggers. I was the only female he'd ever trusted with his cash, and most likely his heart. "Don't be fucking around with that Viagra, either. It might mess you up."

Daddy shook his head. "This is not an appropriate conversation for a father-daughter evening."

"Oh come on, I'm Wicket. I know all about older men still trying to swim in the ill na-na."

He chuckled. "You and your choice of words."

I went back over to sit down across from him. "I'm writing this song called 'Surge' for my new album."

"Oh yeah. What's it based on?"

I looked him in the eyes. "This guy I went

249

to high school with."

Daddy frowned. "Not one of the ones who —"

"Absolutely not. Jonovan was actually nice to me. He's the one who got me out of there that night when . . ."

"Have you seen him since you've been back there?"

"Yes, but it was by coincidence both times . . . so far."

"You didn't tell him who you really are, did you?"

"I have all kinds of mental issues, but being stupid isn't one of them. That's too risky. I can't ever tell him."

"But you're interested in him?"

"He's still nice." I finished off my water. "He's seeing someone, casually according to him, but it's just as well. Maybe I'm too fucking complicated for someone to love."

"You can't live a positive life with a negative mind."

"I hate getting flashbacks from things I don't want to remember."

"So what's Dr. Spencer doing about that?"

"I haven't even told her about that night yet."

"Because?"

I blinked hard twice and then looked down at the floor. "Those people . . . the ones who did it. I've been spending time with them."

Daddy almost dropped his expensive bottle of whiskey — mid pouring — when I revealed that. "What does *spending time* mean?"

"They're swarming around me like the damn opportunists that they are, trying to connect with the biggest star in the city. Trying to get me to hire them or hook them up."

"Don't do anything ridiculous, Ladonna!"

"I won't."

"Promise?"

"If I ever feel like I'm about to end up on that show *Snapped,* I promise that I'll call you to stage an intervention. I've been doing pretty good, all things considered. Nothing like the extreme rough patches in my past."

I was referring to the cutting I used to engage in, the times that I used to be destructive to items around the house — breaking them or flinging them at servants across the room, and the few times I had actually hauled off and attacked people, like I had with Sebastian that night at Hannah's apartment.

"I did tell Marcella about Hannah."

"I'm sure that was difficult."

"All the pain came rushing back. It was like I was still in that hotel bathroom in Paris, sitting in her blood. And her note was so horrific. Her cutting off her . . ."

"We've been over this. There was nothing you could have done."

"I realize that life goes on, but sometimes that's the hardest part."

Daddy leaned on the arm of the chair and put his right hand over his head. "We should turn in. Don't forget we have reservations at Norma's for brunch tomorrow."

Daddy loved the selections at the restaurant inside the Le Parker Meridien on West Fifty-Sixth Street. They only opened for breakfast and brunch until three in the afternoon daily. My personal favorite was the Foie Gras Brioche French Toast with asparagus and onions. Daddy preferred the Duck n' Eggs with confit hash, peppers, and onions. We always split the Nova Smoked Salmon Ring with eggs so we wouldn't look greedy or have to waddle up out that billy.

"Yeah, I am kind of exhausted. Those cosmos still haven't quite worn off yet."

"You're going to be up and down all night from drinking all that water."

"Plus I need to get up at six and go for a run."

KAD was back in Atlanta because Daddy's detail was with him.

"You're running through the park?"

"Uh-huh. You should join me."

"I've gotten lazy, baby."

"You need to get unlazy and get motivated. After all, motivation is what gets you started; habit is what keeps you going."

"On that note, I'm motivated to go pass out." He put the cap back on his whiskey, closed up his humidor, and stood up to stretch. "Don't be up too much longer."

"I'm right behind you," I said as he walked up the staircase to the second level of the penthouse. "I'm going to shut everything down."

Daddy's security guards were stationed in the lobby and across the hall. I also owned the smaller apartment there so no one else would be on that floor. I planned to keep it, even once the penthouse sold. I didn't need a lot of space in New York, but I wasn't about to not have a spot at all. I enjoyed my independence but was elated that Daddy was staying with me on this quick jaunt back into town. He was leaving for the Dominican after we celebrated his birthday, probably to hook up with some exotic beauties who loved money and were open to trading it for sex.

Whenever I ran across males who claimed

to do a lot of business in the Dominican, I knew what time it was. A lot of wives even sent their husbands there on vacations alone so they could get the fantasy out of their systems. That was another reason I didn't trust men. Being faithful was more than a notion for most and they could have perfect wives who put dinner on the table every evening at six and pussy on their faces every night at ten. It didn't matter. At the end of the day, they felt variety was the spice of life. As far as I was concerned, being single was better than being lied to, cheated on, and disrespected. I had seen too many of my counterparts destroyed by men who humiliated them in public. Not this kid.

I was closing up the blinds when I spotted a couple in the building on the other side of the street fucking the shit out of each other. He had leathery skin and looked like a foreigner. He wasn't white, black, or Hispanic, but he was sexy for damn sure. Plus, he had a big dick. I stood there and watched as the redheaded woman with a cooch to match pounced up and down on his dick like there was no tomorrow. And I wasn't mad at her.

I loved watching other people have sex, and I yearned for my pets. I wished that I could've flown them in, and actually contemplated it for a hot second. I could've put them up in a hotel suite and snuck away from Daddy for some afternoon playtime the next day, but I wanted to spend as much quality time with him as possible. Glaze and Piece of Shit would have to wait. But I was definitely making a pit stop on my way back to Atlanta. I'd have them meet up with me someplace so I could beat some ass and get off at the same time.

I ended up masturbating myself to sleep that night. While it did the trick, it just wasn't the same as digging into Piece of Shit's back with a stiletto heel.

CHAPTER SIXTEEN

Sunday, August 26, 2012
9:32 p.m.
Hilton Head Island, South Carolina
I made a detour on my way back to Atlanta and truly pulled a fast one, but only for one day. KAD thought I was still in NYC with Daddy, and Daddy thought that I was headed straight back to Atlanta. I convinced him that I didn't need security detail on the private jet because Kagiso was picking me up from the hangar in Atlanta. I told the pilot that he better keep his fucking mouth shut about my flight plans. Archie, short for Archibald Witt, had a major crush on me, so the idea that he might actually get to whiff my pussy one day, or fuck me up in the friendly skies, made him want to impress me.

I put on a disguise — light brown wig, silk scarf, and sunglasses — and hopped a ride up to the main airport terminal and then caught a cab to the resort.

I needed to relieve some stress. When I arrived at the four-bedroom villa in Palmetto Dunes, Glaze and Piece of Shit were already there. They had rented the place under Glaze's real name and were both butt-ass naked, as I had instructed when I arrived.

Piece of Shit crawled to the front door to answer it for me. I could see him on his hands and knees through the frosted glass. He did have a spiked collar around his neck, connected to a diamond-studded, four-foot leash.

He sat up on his hind legs after he opened up, and stuck his tongue out, holding his hands in front of him like paws.

I grabbed the leash in the middle. "Good boy! You ready for some fun tonight?"

He nodded and kept letting his tongue hang out of his mouth. Drool was trickling down his chin and onto his chest.

I yanked on the leash, forcing him back down on all fours as I kicked the front door shut behind me and locked it with my free hand. I walked him through the foyer, then the living room, and out onto the balcony. It was dark, but I could make out the waves of the Atlantic in the close distance. We had a private beach at our disposal and I planned to make the most of it.

Glaze was lying on a floral-covered lounge chair, digging into her pussy with three fingers. She was already nice and wet.

"Who told you that you could play in your pussy?" I yelled at her. "I'm going to beat your little ass for that!"

She pulled her fingers out in a panic. "I'm sorry, Mistress. I thought it would please you, if I —"

"What the fuck is so pleasing about walking up in here and catching you playing in that nasty snatch of yours?" I glared at her. "Huh? Answer me, dammit!"

I yanked on Piece of Shit's leash harder, and tightened it up around my wrist by looping it several times. He was all the way up to my hip bone and choking within seconds. I glanced down at him. "Let me find out that the two of you have been up in here fucking and whatnot while I was en route."

"No . . ." Cough. "We didn't . . ." Cough.

I loosened the leash a bit. Didn't need anyone dying on me. Imagine the headlines:

Wicket Discovered with Dead Naked Male and an Unidentified Samoan Female in Hilton Head Mansion

Is Wicket More Wicked Than We Thought? Secret BDSM Lifestyle Uncovered After Man Chokes to Death in Hilton Head

Famous Singer Wicket Caught Up in Sado-masochistic Murder!

The press would have had a field day; especially the bitches trying to make names for themselves by talking shit about talented and famous people. The funny part was that no one ever remembered their names, or even read their bylines, and they were still nobodies with no talent at the end of the day.

"Listen up, I want both of you to get your asses into separate showers right this second and get to scrubbing. I don't know if you've been up in here fucking or not, but I won't tolerate no bitch-ass behavior up in here!"

"Yes, Mistress," they whispered in unison.

"Get to moving. I'm going to check out the rest of the house and make myself a drink. Did you get my fucking liquor?" I eyed Glaze with disdain.

"Yes, Mistress. Your Absolut Crystal is on the bar."

"It fucking better be!" I let the leash go completely. "Now get the hell out of my face! Both of you!"

Glaze got up off the lounger and walked past me. I hit her on the ass with my Hilde Palladino bag that I'd purchased on tour in Norway. She jumped a little. "Bitch, you better not flinch from that little hit. Wait

259

until I rip into that ass out there in the sand. You better get prepared."

"I'm ready, Mistress," Glaze replied. "I love pain. Bring it on."

I fought back a grin. Instead, I frowned. "Oh, I'm going to bring the shit on, all right. Now go get your filthy ass into a shower. You smell like dick."

Piece of Shit and Glaze were not crazy enough to be fucking outside my presence — at least I didn't think they were — and she didn't smell like dick. It was all a part of blowing off steam for me.

As she walked off into the house, Piece of Shit had the audacity to try to get up on two legs and walk. I pushed him so hard that he fell backward and hit his head on the porch ledge. "Motherfucker, are you insane? You better crawl your ass into the house. Matter of fact, once I fix my drink, I'm coming to check on you in that shower and you better be on all fours like the affenpinscher that you are."

He started crawling. "Yes, Mistress."

I kicked him in the left buttock as he entered the house.

I walked into the house to find the bar. While I was pouring my drink, I got a text alert on my cell phone. It was Michael. I'd been messing with his head since the night he gave me his number. I made it seem like I could get him an acting job. Technically, I could, but there was no way in the world that I would actually make it happen.

MICHAEL: HEY, WICKET. JUST CHECKING IN. ANY GOOD NEWS FOR ME?
ME: GIVE ME A FEW MORE DAYS. WAITING TO HEAR BACK ON A POSSIBILITY.
MICHAEL: OKAY, COOL. THANK YOU.
ME: NO WORRIES. IF I CAN HELP YOU, I WILL. YOU HAVE MY WORD.
MICHAEL: YOU'RE THE BEST.

I started conniving a plan in my head right then and there. So far I had merely been stringing him along. Now it was time to actually exact some revenge on his ass. Time kills all deals so I was sure he was starting to panic. He kept texting me to try to seem relevant somehow. Soon he would start lying about having other opportunities that he didn't want to pass up if I wasn't serious. He would try to spin the tables and act like he was doing me a favor by offering up his acting skills, instead of the other way around. It was the oldest game in the book, but what people never realized was that artist development executives, publishers, agents, and the rest invented the game. Sure, there were some truly significant people who did have deals coming at them right and left — I was one of them — but most were peddling a crock of shit.

Michael was a peddler just like Bianca and Cherie. I was still stringing them along as well but planned to save the best for last. I wanted to ruin all of them — even if it was by reputation only — and make them pay for the rest of their natural lives.

As Glaze came out of one of the bedrooms, freshly bathed and wearing a towel, it all became clear.

"After this trip, I want you to meet me back in Atlanta. I'll get you a room at the W, and fill you in. I need you to do something for me."

"Will it be fun?" she asked with a wink.

"Yes, it'll be a lot of fun, but don't you dare wink at me."

She lowered her eyes. "I'm sorry, Mistress."

"I'll be right back. Put some music on up in this bitch!"

"Whatever you say, Mistress."

I walked down the hallway to find Piece of Shit. I heard a shower running in the last room at the end on the left as "Sexy and I Know It" by LMFAO starting emitting from the built-in speakers throughout the home.

I walked into the bedroom. It had twin beds decorated in pink and yellow. The room for the kids — little girls — and Piece of Shit knew that was exactly where he belonged — *biotch!*

The bathroom was adorned with pastel wallpaper and pink and yellow soap dishes and towels. Piece of Shit was on all fours, looking pitiful as he tried to scrub as water got all into his eyes.

"Look at you," I started in. "A sick-looking runt of the litter, with a wet ass, soggy ass."

He didn't respond. He just kept scrubbing himself.

"Scrub harder! Get all that stank bitch's pussy off you. I know you two were doing disgusting things before I got here."

He wanted to say something but knew better.

"Scrub that dick raw! I want it to be red when you crawl out that motherfucking shower!"

I kicked the toilet seat down with my foot and then sat down on the lid. I spotted Piece of Shit's toiletry bag on the counter and started rummaging through it. He was an attractive man, but too average to be seen with me. He also kept himself well-groomed. I pulled out a half-empty bottle of aftershave and grimaced.

"Did you scrub that dick raw?" I asked.

"Yes, Mistress."

"Stand up and let me see."

He didn't look up at me but hesitated.

"You have my permission to stand up, Piece of Shit."

As he stood, I could see that his dick was hard — my meanness turned him on — pulsating, and clearly irritated from scrubbing it so hard. He had rubbed a layer of dead skin away and exposed a fresh layer of epidermal cells . . . and some new nerves.

Before he could stick and move, I splashed all the remaining aftershave on his dick. He stifled a scream and then took all the pain. I halfway admired Piece of Shit at that moment.

"Yeah, claim that pain!" I yelled out.

He took a series of heavy breaths and then grinned. And there it was: the reason why Piece of Shit and Glaze engaged in such debauchery with me. It satisfied their individual needs to be dominated. I personally was not down for the pain, but I was more than willing to inflict it. Some people in the

BDSM community liked to be both a giver and taker of pain. Not the kid. I had endured enough pain by the time I was sixteen. Besides, I was not about to trust anyone to put me in bondage and not take a ton of photos and make them go viral. Hell to the no!

When I was younger, I had run across this chick who got paid to fuck married men in their asses with strap-on dicks. Their wives would hire her and then watch her while she did it. It was then that I realized that people never really knew what the fuck other people did in the privacy of their own homes. Some believed that everything was acceptable in a marital bed. And some simply wanted to fuck the masses, have one-night stands, and live their lives. Whatever worked for them! What worked for me was having an outlet for my pain and that meant controlling other people in the process of hurting them physically!

We ended up out on the beach that night. It was a crazy time. Glaze had purchased and brought everything that I asked for. I put a bridle on Piece of Shit and had him give me a ride up and down the edge of the water. Glaze had a ball gag in her mouth and a zip strip — a row of clothing pins along a line of twine — connected to her nipples, underarms, and clit. When she least expected it, I walked up behind her, pulled the twine, and ripped them all off her at the same time. She was a trooper and didn't scream. She did almost lose it when I made Piece of Shit scrape her ass with sandpaper and I pushed her out into the salty ocean with all of those small, open cuts.

I started to go hard and bring some electricity into the mix but, again, I was worried about going too far and ending up on *New Day* on CNN with Chris Cuomo or *CNN Tonight* with Don Lemon.

All three of us had a good time, in our own ways. I left the next morning via cab, in disguise again, and met Archie back at the plane. He had grabbed a room at a hotel right by the airport. He had no idea where I had gone off to, and he never would. He probably assumed that I was secretly seeing some man who I didn't want the world to know about — another celebrity, someone married, a young bull, or a combination of the three: a married celebrity nearly half my age.

I had a big grin on my face as we took off. I was totally relaxed and ready to put Plan A into action!

Chapter Seventeen

Friday, August 31, 2012
2:30 p.m.
Atlanta, Georgia

Cameras, lights, action. The scene was set. I had to pat myself on the back. It was one hell of a plan. I was going to set Michael up for the okey doke and distance myself from the fallout at the same time.

Glaze had met me in Atlanta and I had her go rent a temporary office space in midtown with cash. She put up a placard on the wall beside the door that read PROVISIONAL ENTERTAINMENT. Even the name was pure brilliance, since "provisional" meant "arranged or existing for the present." In this case, "the present" was less than a week and no company by that name actually existed. I made sure by googling it.

I had Glaze call up Michael, express that she was a Hollywood producer currently casting for a new film scheduled to shoot in

Atlanta in the spring. I told her to toss out a few heavy-hitter A-list actors and actresses as confirmed leads and send Michael bogus sides that I had fabricated out of my vivid imagination. I didn't write an entire script but just enough to make it seem realistic. I had turned down enough roles to know what a script layout looked like. I purchased some cheap script-writing software offline and made it happen within the span of an afternoon.

He was going to be auditioning for the role of Choad, the older brother of the main character, Domino, a hit man from Compton, who had come to Atlanta to exact revenge for the murder of his wife by an adversary. The name of the film was called *Vindication.* Every name was well planned out. I was there in Atlanta to get them all back, the name Domino stood for the domino/butterfly effect that my life had turned into that night in October 1987, and Michael was too stupid to put two and two together in regards to Choad. Most people had never heard of the term. However, being the freak that I was, I knew that a "choad" was the area between the penis and the anus and also a common nickname for a dick that was actually wider than it was longer. In other words, Choad was a moniker for "little dick motherfucker."

We had cameras and microphones set up throughout the office that could not be seen and a DSLR — digital single-lens reflex camera — on a tripod on the opposite side of her desk. She was dressed in a black blazer without a bra, so her tits were titillating — no pun intended — and a short beige skirt with no panties and black fuck-me pumps. She had on glasses to make her seem studious and professional, but I was banking on Michael getting horny the second he walked through the door.

To give the temptation some additional momentum, Glaze had an "actress" there to read with Michael for the role of Choad. She was an up-and-coming porn star named Mrs. Teasedale. She was about five foot four, petite, with couveture skin, meaning that she was like chocolate rich in cocoa butter. Her skin was flawless all over. She drove men crazy. I only hoped that he had not seen any of her work yet. It could've ruined my plans. I needed him to believe that she was a real actress. It was customary for someone to read the other part in auditions so that those casting could see how it would all play out on-screen.

Michael knocked on the door promptly at two o'clock. I was across town watching it all on web cam in my studio. That was the only way that I could assure I would be alone, by lying and saying that I wanted to work on my music alone. Diederik and Antonio were off for the day since I had no concrete plans and Kagiso was out by the pool perfecting his moves. He had tried to teach the art form to me, both for self-defense and to relieve stress. Little did he realize that doing those slow, graceful moves were the exact opposite of what relieved my stress. I liked beating asses.

Since my studio was soundproof and I had barricaded myself in there by not only locking the door but by also placing a security bar under the knob, I had my laptop on as loud as it would go so I could hear everything.

"Come on in, Mr. Vinson," Glaze said as she greeted him at the door and led him into the central office space. "This is Duchess."

Mrs. Teasedale was going by the name of Duchess for the afternoon. It sounded like a great actress name to me. Being that I used a fake name myself, I was always fascinated with the fact that so many celebrities utilized them. Mine was obvious because of Wicket, and most people knew that I was also Ladonna Sterling. They just had no idea that I had started out as Caprice Tatum.

Some simply wanted more exotic names, some had long-ass names, and some had names that were too hard to pronounce. Some of my favorites were Nicki Minaj "Onika Tanya Maraj," Akon "Aliaune Damala Akon Thiam," Jane Seymour "Joyce Penelope Wilhelmina Frankenberg," Stevie Wonder "Stevland Hardaway Morris," Ralph Lauren "Ralph Lifschitz," Cher "Cherilyn Sarksian," and Woody Allen "Allen Stewart Konigsberg." It always amused me how some papers insisted on using my real name whenever they did an article on me, stating that it was their policy — a damn lie — when they would write articles about tons of other people and *never* use their real names.

"It's nice to meet you ladies," Michael said, grinning from ear to ear as he shook their hands. I had the screen split into four so I could see it all from various angles . . . and record it. "I'm so excited for this opportunity."

"How old are you?" Glaze asked, looking at his headshot and information on the back. "You look older in person. When was this headshot taken?"

Glaze was playing her role and going for

271

the jugular from the onslaught like I had commanded her to do.

"Um, it was taken a year or two ago." Michael watched as Glaze looked back and forth between him and the photograph. "It might be this goatee," he added, rubbing his chin.

"So how old are you?"

Duchess looked on, trying to suppress a giggle.

"I can play midtwenties to early thirties."

Glaze sat down in the leather chair behind the desk, leaving Michael standing in the middle of the floor.

"Have a seat on the sofa with Duchess. Did you memorize your lines?"

"Indeed." Michael grinned as he sat down. "I'm your Choad."

"So have you done any love scenes before?" Glaze asked, eyeing him over the top of her glasses. "Are you in shape?"

"I'm in great shape. I work out five to six times a week. As to your other question, no, but I'm not opposed to it, either."

"Marital status?" Glaze looked over his paperwork. "It doesn't say on here."

"Single."

"Good. That means no one should be tripping if I give you this role."

He cleared his throat. "I don't recall any

mention of simulated sex scenes in the sides you sent me."

"Look . . ." Glaze slammed his information down on the table. "I don't have time for games. I have to get this film casted and into preproduction by the end of the year. If you're too shy to work that tongue and ass on camera, you should leave now. This is a major motion picture with A-list stars and it is also gritty, violent, and sensual. Moviegoers love sex and violence within the confines of a loud-ass theater. There's nothing better."

"I agree," Michael said anxiously. "Sex and violence are hot together. Like I said, you won't get any opposition from me. I was merely asking a question."

Duchess sprung into action then, perfecting her role. She reached over and rubbed him on the thigh. "Don't worry, baby. I don't bite . . . unless you're into that sort of thing."

Michael pushed her hand off.

"I knew you were a punk ass," I said aloud to myself. "Let me find out you're scared of pussy unless you're controlling it."

Michael had always seemed like that type to me in high school. He seemed to shy away from the aggressive girls and lean toward naïve and gullible chicks like Cherie. Bianca was probably too self-secure for him, so he left her to Herman. He needed a weak-minded broad like Cherie. Because her father worked all the time at his garage, and her mother was too busy trying to recapture her youth on a daily basis, Cherie was always starving for attention. She wanted to be the party person with the party house and while it seemed cool back then, the fact that her parents were rarely around spoke volumes. Yes, I had a lot of nerve, but both my parents were fucktards and her parents were at least normal. They just didn't care to be bothered with her.

"What? Are you gay or something?" Duchess asked as Glaze continued to look on over her glasses.

"No, hell no, I'm not gay." Michael shifted on the couch to face her better. "It's just that I don't know you and this is a professional audition. It's not appropriate for you to start touching me like that out of the blue."

"What kind of cockamamie bullshit is this?" Glaze said loudly. "How the hell do you call yourself an actor when you get all up in your feelings as soon as another thespian lays a finger on you?"

Michael opened his mouth to say something, but Glaze cut him off.

"When people act together, it's a group effort. They have to hug, shake hands, kiss, pretend to fuck, and even give mouth-to-fucking-mouth resuscitation if it's in the script."

"I understand that, but the sides you sent me didn't —"

"So if the longer script calls for you to suck Duchess's toes, what are you going to do? Break down in tears and cost a hefty part of our production budget to be wasted while we replace you?"

"No, I assure you, I'll do whatever the script calls for."

Glaze got up and walked in front of the desk, then positioned herself on the edge with her right thigh elevated, so Michael could see her freshly shaven, glistening pussy.

He stared at it like she was taking pictures of his face and then swallowed his own saliva in a big gulp.

"You seem kind of suspect to me. You were recommended to me by a friend of a friend of a friend for this role, but I'm not so sure about this."

"But I thought you know —"

Before he could say my name, Glaze cut him off again. *Good little pet!*

I had been extremely careful not to actually say that I knew the people at Provisional Entertainment. Michael was so excited to get an audition, based on my recommendation, that he had asked very few questions. Glaze had contacted him from casting@provisionalentertainment.com and had given him the number for a burner phone.

Cherie had called to thank me personally for getting him the chance to read and I played kind of dumb. "Oh, I don't really know anything about the project. One of my agent's friends has something to do with it. She said it's legit, though. I wish him luck."

"Okay, okay, this is how we're going to get through this." I could see Glaze's eyes rolling on three out of the four cameras. "We need to get this moving because we have other people coming in today."

Michael was in a panic. "Are they trying out for Choad?"

Glaze smirked. "A couple of them are, but some are trying out for other supporting roles. I need to get back to Los Angeles tomorrow, so time is of the essence." She sighed. "I'll be up-front and tell you that everyone else is way more experienced than you. I decided to give you a shot, but you're going to really have to bring it with this audition."

"I'll do whatever it takes!"

Duchess and Glaze made eye contact and grinned mischievously.

"Before we go any further, I need to do a quick body check. Strip down to your underwear."

Michael was quick to get out of his clothes. I chuckled there in my studio. "You have no idea what's coming! Go Glaze! It's your birthday!" I got up and shimmied my hips a little in pure delight. The fool was falling for it.

"Nice," Glaze said as she ran her fingertips down Michael's chest once he was down to a pair of plaid boxers. "I'm feeling these tight abs. Is that an eight-pack?" She turned him around to face Duchess. "Duchess, check this out!"

Glaze was totally exaggerating about his abs. He was not that cut, but he was toned. Duchess decided to take it further.

"Who gives a fuck about the abs? My eyes are glued to he who walks behind the rows." She licked her lips and then bit her bottom lip as she kept her eyes glued to his groin. "That's what I want to see."

"Your wish is my command."

Glaze yanked Michael's boxers down, where they landed at his ankles. He looked shocked as Glaze took his dick in her hand and started bouncing it up and down in her palm. "Umm, blessed are the flexible for they will not be bent out of shape."

Michael was clearly nervous but, as suspected, wanted that damn role. His dick was average, but it didn't feel that way when he robbed me of my virginity in such a brutal fashion.

"Wha . . . what do you mean by that?" he asked, nervous.

"It just means that you have a nice dick, Choad. I like the way it moves so fluidly in my hand. Makes me wonder what it would feel like in my mouth, my pussy . . . and my ass."

"Listen, maybe I should go." Michael backed away from Glaze and pulled up his boxers.

"You were right," Glaze directed toward Duchess. "This motherfucker is light in the loafers."

Duchess shrugged. "Too bad. I was curious to see what he was working with."

"My girlfriend would kill me if she found out I did something like this for a role," Michael said.

"I thought you said you were single?" Glaze pouted. "Wipe your mouth on the way out. There's still a tiny bit of bullshit around your lips."

"I am single, technically. I'm not married, but I do have a woman. So I'm *not* gay."

"Well, one lie is enough to question all truths. It's not the lie that bothers me. It's the insult to my intelligence that I find offensive."

"I'm not saying that you ladies aren't attractive," Michael said, as he gathered his pants to step into.

Damn right, I thought. *They're fucking gorgeous. Go ahead and cave already.*

I wish that I could've been there to tell Glaze not to let that motherfucker leave before she got what I needed. I grabbed my phone and sent her a quick text message on the burner phone.

ME: DO SOMETHING DRASTIC. START MAKING OUT WITH THE OTHER BROAD OR SOMETHING.

I heard a text chime go off on her phone and she walked over to read the message. Since I was the only other person with that number except for Michael, she realized it had to be from me.

GLAZE: OH, HIS ASS ISN'T GOING ANYWHERE.

"That's my girl!" I exclaimed.

Right then, Kagiso started rapping on the studio door.

"What?" I yelled out. Then I realized it was soundproof and got up to go to the door. I cracked it open and glared into his eyes. "What is it?"

"Just checking on you."

"I'm all good."

"You need anything?"

"Nope. Just some privacy so I can be alone with my muse."

Kagiso looked concerned and then walked off. I locked the door and put the security bar underneath the knob.

By the time I got back to the split screen on my laptop, things were on and popping. *Mission accomplished!*

Glaze was in her most comfortable state — naked. Duchess was topless and the two of them were tonguing each other down on the sofa. Michael had dropped his pants back on the floor and was taking it all in.

Duchess started sucking on Glaze's tits as Glaze threw her head back in ecstasy and started moaning and saying, "Oh yes! Umm-mmm, that's what I'm talking about!"

"You two are some serious sluts," Michael said. Poor thing was getting angry about the entire situation, but his ass wasn't leaving, either. "I can't believe you all are doing this shit in auditions."

Duchess stopped slobbering all over Glaze's tits long enough to say, "We're only sluts because our sexuality scares you."

Glaze pushed Duchess back on the sofa and started pulling her panties off with her teeth.

"I'm not scared of shit!" Michael lashed out.

"Prove it!" Duchess challenged. "Are you over forty? They say most men over forty can't keep their dick hard anyway. You probably can't even handle all this pussy."

That did it!

"I don't give a fuck about the role anymore. I'm about to teach you two bitches a lesson."

"There's that wildebeest!" I exclaimed out loud in my studio. "Bat-shit-crazy motherfucker!"

The three of them fucked and sucked for the next two hours and I got all of it on camera. Both Glaze and Duchess sucked that rat bastard dry, then got him hard again and one rode his face while the other rode his dick. Then Glaze lay on top of Duchess's stomach and he ate them out in stockpile fashion with their thighs held open in V's

281

with their hands, greedy fool. I had to admit, it was an amazing spectacle to view. I could've made a ton selling it on the Internet!

After that, he fucked them on top of each other, putting his dick in Glaze's pussy, pounding her, and then pulling out, lowering a few inches, and pounding out Duchess while Glaze bit on his nipples and stuck her finger up his ass. They really had his ass going. He thought he was doing something, but it was just another day at work for the two of them, especially Mrs. Teasedale. She was a Mrs. because she was actually married, had been for a few years. Her husband was a — get this — epidemiologist, meaning that he was responsible for investigating public health concerns and preventing them from spreading. Hmm, okay.

Before they let Michael go — he never asked about the nonexistent other people who never showed up for auditions — they both stood in the middle of the floor with their backs to each other and leaving enough room between them for him. That shit was my idea! They bent over and grabbed their own left ankles and each other's right ankles so that it was a tight squeeze as he fucked them in turn. He was balls-deep in Glaze and then struggled to turn around and go knee-deep in Duchess and so forth and so on.

Then that bastard ran out of semen, energy, and he was barely coherent by the time they got done with him. Glaze and Duchess went and lay on the couch, scissoring their legs together as Michael got dressed in silence. What the fuck could anyone say after all that?

As he was leaving out the door, Glaze whispered, "I'll be in touch."

That wasn't true. She wouldn't be in touch, but those recordings were about to make Michael Vinson the famous actor he'd always wanted to be. All I had to do was edit out the women's faces, lay some freaky background music to it, and make sure that Cherie was the first one to see it.

I was so fucking proud of Glaze. I shot her a quick text.

ME: YOU'RE THAT CHICK! CLEAR EVERYTHING OUT AND HEAD BACK HOME. CALL YOU TOMOR-ROW.

CHAPTER EIGHTEEN

"Thanks for seeing me on such short notice." I was sitting on Marcella's sofa in her cabin on a Saturday afternoon. "I realize that I'm constantly imposing on you outside of your regular business hours."

"Psychiatrists don't really have regular business hours, Wicket. I see some of my patients in the office, but I also have some in psychiatric hospitals. Not many, but some, and I do some pro bono work."

"That's nice of you."

"Sure, but it also gets me an opportunity to stay on top of the trends in my profession."

I crossed my legs. I was casual that day: tan leggings and a button-down white shirt. "There are trends when it comes to being crazy?"

"Of course. A lot of people are affected by illnesses that mess with their brain activities, and those change all the time. A lot of insane asylums first popped up back when tuberculosis was extremely active. The sanitariums were named that because most were near clear, open air, and were constantly cleaned to kill germs. The theory was that if patients were kept in sanitized conditions, it would improve their health."

"Did it . . . improve their health?"

"For some, it did, but others were too far gone."

"I never knew that. You've taught me something."

"Initially, most were started in private family homes. I'm talking a century ago and then some. Wealthy families with relatives who were suffering from mental incapacity would donate their homes, or convert them to facilities to house them and others. Searching for a cure."

"Kind of like a lot of drug and alcohol rehabs are started by former addicts or relatives of those who need recovery?"

"Now you've got it."

"Well, I know one thing for sure. My mother can't be fixed, she can't recover, and there is no cure for her crazy ass."

"Have you even checked on your mother?"

"Why the hell would I do that? Why would I give a flying fuck about someone who never gave a flying fuck about me?"

"Maybe it will give you some kind of closure, if you see her and forgive her."

"I'm not showing up at that place so that someone can run their mouth to the tabloids about my being there. People are too hard up for cash that relatives of celebrities are selling photos of them on their death beds and in their caskets for six figures."

Marcella flicked a piece of lint off her lightweight peach sweater. "It was merely a suggestion. At least consider it. As for someone being a whistleblower, we may be able to work around that."

"I'm not even trying to hear that shit. My mother can kiss my *entire* black ass. I truly don't care if she's alive or dead. Grandma and Hannah are both long gone and she's still breathing."

"And how would you know that?" Marcella raised an eyebrow. "You keep a check on her, don't you?"

I glared at Marcella. I had to hand it to her. She was good at her career.

"It's not that serious and don't get things twisted," I replied. "It's actually not me. Daddy makes sure that she never has a chance of getting out. It's about his concern for my welfare, not that bitch's."

"From what you've told me about your mother, it's apparent to me that a lot of her

286

issues come from being victimized."

"And?"

I had told Marcella about the rape and incest during another session and went into further details about the day Momma slashed up my face, and all the craziness and abuse that led up to it.

"Your issues stem from things that happened to you in your childhood, but you expect people to be tolerant of your issues and your behavior."

I was heated. "Are you comparing me to that maniac? She is a maniac. You do realize that? She's violent and she's dangerous and —"

"Aren't you violent and dangerous? Intermittent explosive disorder can lead to violent outbursts where you harm yourself or others."

"Thanks for the update," I stated vehemently. "I take my meds every damn day. Thank you very much."

"Good, but psychotherapy is also important. I realize that you've had therapists in the past and that Dr. Lamb is still giving you prescriptions, even though she is based in New York. But we need to address the underlying issues."

"That's what the fuck we've been doing, Marcella. You think I've been coming up here because I don't have anything else to do?"

"No, but I also don't think that you're being honest about why you came to Atlanta."

I stood up and started pacing the floor. "What did Daddy tell you?"

She glanced over her shoulder at me. "What makes you think Mr. Sterling told me anything?"

"Marcella, honesty is always better than sugarcoated bullshit. What did Daddy tell you?"

Marcella sighed. "He's worried that you came back here to get some kind of retaliation on people who went to Powers High School with you. And he's also concerned that you may have a violent outburst, or several of them, in the process. He doesn't want to see you get into any trouble."

"I don't plan on it! But they need to pay and . . ."

I didn't mean to let that slip!

"Who needs to pay and what for?"

I walked back over to the sofa, but instead of sitting on it, I lay down on it and covered my eyes with my right arm.

"You can talk to me freely," Marcella said.

Part of me wanted to rush out of there and tell Kagiso and Antonio I was ready to go. Diederik was off that day, dealing with some drama. Some crazy whore had shown up at the house, trying to get into the gate the night before, talking about how she was carrying his child. I knew all of their asses were fucking broads in Atlanta. It didn't bother me, but they needed to keep their floozies out of my presence.

The other part of me said that it was time to be completely transparent. It was all for naught unless I told Marcella where my mind was really going. However, her comments about my disorder leading to violent behavior had upset me. Only because I knew it was the truth. When I was much younger, even prior to the rape, I used to self-mutilate. I would make tiny cuts on my thighs or burn my leg with a lighter or match. Sometimes, I would stick the tips of safety pins into my skin or bang my head against my bedroom wall. It was my way of expressing my emotional pain that I could not put into words. Not that I had anyone to talk to anyway. Grandma was sick and my friends already felt pity on me because of my facial scar.

"Caprice?"

When Marcella used my real *real* name, it was apparent that she was trying to get me to go back there.

"When I was in Germany a few years ago

doing a concert, I saw this beautiful sign in a window. There was a photo of a sunset over the ocean. I asked the escort the label had assigned to me to translate it. It read: 'Leave the bad memories behind and have faith in a greater tomorrow.' It was in front of one of the few homeless shelters in Berlin. They do things totally different over there. Their education, health insurance, and all of that is paid for by the state."

I paused and took a deep breath. "Their constitution, called the Grundgesetz, calls for all Germans to be able to 'live in dignity,' meaning that they are guaranteed to have access to all their basic needs. What I noticed about the homeless people that I did see — they only have about six hundred out of three-point-four million people — was that most of them had mental issues."

I looked at Marcella. "The same goes for a lot of homeless here in the United States, except we tend to discard people who need our help. It's a damn shame that men and women can go and serve in the military, protect us from terrorists — foreign or homegrown — and then end up eating out of trash cans or pushing all of their worldly belongings around in shopping carts."

"You're rambling because you're trying to avoid the issue. Who needs to pay and for what?" She sat up further in her seat. "Caprice, you can avoid reality, but you can't avoid the consequences of avoiding reality."

"I'm just tired of my memories sneaking out of my eyes and rolling down my cheeks. I hate crying, Marcella, and if I go where you expect me to go, I'm going to definitely exhibit my weaknesses."

"You inspire millions of women and young girls. That's not a sign of weakness. That's a sign of strength. My hope for you is to liberate yourself the exact same way you have liberated so many others."

"I'm fucked-up in the head, so I say unto you: bye, Felicia."

I got up from the sofa and headed toward the front door.

"Go ahead and leave if you so wish. But know this. You're only leaving because it's easier to walk out than fight for what you really want."

I turned and gazed into her eyes. "And what is it that you *believe* I really want?"

"Ultimately, love, but right now, you need to prepare yourself emotionally to receive that love."

I put my hands on my hips and smacked my lips. "I don't want or need a man. Men want love. I'm incapable of loving anyone.

Men want sex. I can't give them that. Men want commitment. I can't give them that, either. Men want kids. There's no damn way I'm bringing any kids into this world."

"Why can't you give a man love, sex, or commitment?"

I shrugged. "Partly because I'm a coward and partly because I'm too damn selfish. At least I admit it."

"Please, come sit back down." Marcella motioned toward her sofa. "Your birthday's in a few weeks, isn't it?"

"The big four-O!"

"Good, then let's work through this. Tell me who needs to pay and what they need to pay for."

I stood there in silence for a moment and looked back and forth between the sofa and the door. One meant an escape and not having to deal with all my bitterness and baggage. The other meant taking a huge risk and taking myself into a deep, dark place that I'd never wanted to revisit. But Marcella was right; it was time.

I walked back over to the sofa and lay back down. I concentrated on one of the lightbulbs in her ceiling fan and then closed my eyes. Then I was suddenly fifteen-year-old Caprice Tatum way back in 1987. Not one but two, Ladonna *and* Wicket, lifetimes ago.

CHAPTER NINETEEN

Saturday, October 24, 1987
9:43 p.m.
Atlanta, Georgia

Spirit Week had gone well at Powers High School, leading up to the homecoming game. Our football team was ranked third in the state of Georgia and everyone was excited about winning the state championship in another month or so. It would mark the first time that Powers took the championship since 1968. Our starting lineup was over the top and it was predicted that all the seniors would end up getting full-ride scholarships to the colleges or universities of their choice.

We were all freshmen — Cherie, Bianca, Herman, Michael, Jonovan, and me — and high school had presented both new adventures and challenges. Well, in my case, making new friends was always a challenge. Outside of the ones I just mentioned, the other kids in middle school had either ignored me completely, made it their personal plight to bully me whenever a chance presented itself, or remained neutral and didn't give a damn about me either way.

I often read background stories of other celebrities to see if they were popular in school. From what I'd gathered, most merely blended in, and some were bullied, but all of them ended up being at the top of their game when they became celebrities. The major difference between them and me is that they could go back to their high school and college reunions and show off the fact that they were the shit. I could never do that . . . not ever.

Every day of Spirit Week had been themed and a load of fun. Monday was Crazy Hair Day, Tuesday was Twinsie Tuesday, Wednesday was Pajama Day, Thursday was Beach Day, and Friday was School Colors Day, where everyone wore burgundy and gold. Now it was time for the big game. We were playing against Hiram Rhodes Revels, a school named after the first African-American to ever serve in the United States Congress. Their colors were navy and white.

The bleachers in the stadium were overflowing. It was the one game of the season where everyone showed up, including the parents, grandparents, and other various relatives of the players, the kids from the surrounding schools — including all the girls who were sharing players' hearts and bodies — and even the school outcasts. It was the opportunity to see and be seen, the chance to make hookups with the cuties from other schools in Atlanta, and a way to ensure that you didn't miss out on any drama that might have popped off when you were out doing something less important.

The game was tied 21–21 with less than a minute left in the fourth quarter. The cheerleaders from Powers were damn near going at it as hard with their cheers as the players were going at each other on the field. Bianca and Cherie were both cheerleaders and were prancing around the sidelines in their skorts and sweaters with PHS embroidered on them.

They were chanting:

You may be good at basketball
You may be good at track
But when it comes to football
You may as well step back.

You may be good at baseball
You may be good in school

295

But when it comes to football
We're making you look like fools.

Powers has the knowledge
Powers rules the game
And once we wipe the grass with you
You're headed home in shame.

Go Tigers! Go Tigers! Go Tigers, Go!

The school band was playing the instrumental version of "Victory" by Kool and the Gang as Jonovan, who was actually the school mascot, danced in front of them. It was hilarious, and I wondered if he was hot under that costume. He had actually asked my advice when they first asked him to be the mascot. He was on the fence about it but didn't want to play in the school band during high school. He had played the trumpet in middle school and was tired of all the practice time involved. But he still enjoyed participating. I told him that it seemed like being the mascot would be the best of both worlds. He didn't have to practice with the band — or practice the trumpet at home — and all he had to do was dance and still be able to hang around everyone and get caught up in the excitement at the games. He decided to agree to be the mascot for the football season and then revisit it for basketball in the spring. The good part was that since he was wearing a costume, someone else could take over without missing a beat.

The band kicked into "Lean on Me" by Club Nouveau as the Tigers got ready to try to pull a Hail Mary, a term coined by Roger Staubach but arguably dates back to 1922, when Notre Dame played Georgia Tech and prayed a Hail Mary before each of two fourth-down plays that resulted in touchdowns. Jonovan jokingly snatched the baton from the drum major, whose elaborate uniform was doing the most, and the two of them started doing the cabbage patch. That ignited everyone in the stands on the home team side to start doing the same. Next thing you knew people were moving from side to side and snapping their fingers . . . until the ball was snapped and then the music, the dancing, the talking all stopped.

Malcolm Briggs, better known as "Golden Arm," grabbed the ball in the snap, took four quick steps back, and threw a thirty-nine-yard pass into the end zone that was caught by Cedric Parrish, better known as "the Steel Curtain," due to his size and agility. It took about two seconds for everyone to realize that they had won the game before complete pandemonium started.

Even I was excited and I really didn't have shit to do with the accomplishment. That is what's so amazing about school spirit. Winning takes a lot of work and effort on the parts of various people, but everyone gets to celebrate the triumph. I was on the third row of the bleachers and rushed down to the field, almost getting trampled by the others who didn't have shit to do with winning, either. The key players were being lifted up and tossed around like rag dolls instead of the two-hundred-plus pounds they were actually carrying. Some players had three to four girls — their own rosters — trying to fling their arms around their necks and shower them with kisses. I was trying to find Bianca and Cherie, since we were planning to attend a party together. I didn't want to get lost in the madness, so it was better to hook up with them then.

Jonovan walked past me in his costume and roared at me. I gave him a high five with my hand against his paw but didn't engage in conversation. The idea was for him to really pretend to be a tiger, and tigers don't speak. He had to act out all of his emotions and speak through his movements.

I did ask, "Did you get where the cheer-leaders went?"

He pointed his right paw toward the other side of the mass of people.

"Thanks." I walked off and started push-ing my way through the crowd again.

I eventually found them and, looking back on it, searching for them was the worst mistake of my entire life. If I had gone back home that night instead of trying to hang out with them, my life would have taken a much different turn.

I stared at Marcella and decided that I couldn't go any further.

"What happened next?" she asked. "Take your time, Caprice."

"I can't do this."

"Then maybe that's enough for today."

"Or maybe it's enough forever. I'm sure you get the gist of what happened. My best friends set me up to be raped that night by the boys I had always trusted, and others. It was humiliating, painful, and I thought that they were going to literally fuck me to death."

Marcella stood up and came over to sit beside me where I lay on her sofa. She took my hand. "I'm so sorry, but please under-stand that you're not alone. A rape occurs every —"

"Why do people always go there? How does knowing that tons of other women, and men, have endured the same thing help matters?" I sat up, angry. "So that means that I shouldn't be so upset because Peggy Sue was raped back in 1952 in Peoria, Illinois, walking home from third grade and Tiffany will be raped tonight leaving work at a diner in Milwaukee, Wisconsin?"

"No, I'm not implying that," Marcella said, taken aback by my statement.

While I understood that I was far from the only person who had ever been victimized, I was fighting my own damn demons. There are two different ways to tell someone that they aren't the only ones who have dealt with a traumatic experience, such as rape, death of a loved one, or even an addiction. One way is for it to come across like: *you did nothing to deserve this and there are others who can be a support system for you because they have dealt with similar things.* The other way is for it to come across like: *you need to suck it up, get over it, and deal with it like everyone else because this is life and shit happens.*

I decided to take Marcella at her word, that she didn't mean to come across abrasively like I had taken it.

"I just don't want to go into further details," I said. "It was horrific and inhumane and now I'm back here to make sure they pay for what they did to me."

"Okay . . ." Marcella tightened her grip on my hand. "Let's not talk about that night. I'm sure that it was an atrocious experience. But I do need to know what you are planning to do to Bianca, Cherie, Jonovan, and —"

"Jonovan was the one who saved me that night. He showed up in his tiger costume and started pulling them off me. He wanted to call the police."

"But you refused?"

"I ran and kept running. I sat outside in the park for a few hours, and afterward, I snuck into the house to look at Grandma one last time. I sat there beside her bed, in the darkness, listening to her breathing while her chest went up and down. At first, I was going to wake her and tell her the truth; let her call the police, even though I had run away when Jonovan suggested it.

"But then she started coughing in her sleep and she seemed to be struggling to breathe for a few seconds. She was way too sick to be burdened with the chaos that would have ensued if I'd told the truth. I was young but not dumb, and I already understood how most rape victims are treated; especially when they accuse men who are deemed too attractive to have to rape someone.

"The parents of those boys would have defended them, refused to believe that their sons would rape an ugly, anorexic girl whose mother was locked up in a psych ward. They would have made all sorts of accusations about me: That I had to be crazy like my mother. That I was a liar and starving for attention. That their sons all had girlfriends and would have no reason to lay a finger on me.

"Cherie and Bianca would've lied, if for no other reason than to cover their own asses. They'd lured me into the entire thing, and then watched when a drunk and high Herman took the first turn. It all happened so fast, but I swear that I remember Bianca helping to hold one of my legs open so they could hurt me."

Marcella let go of my hand and started rubbing it. "How many of them were there?"

"Six, maybe seven. It was at the party. I thought it was going to be at someone's house — that maybe even the parents would be there to supervise — but it was in an old, abandoned building in Southeast. They started fires in large metal trash cans for lights and the music was played from a battery-operated boom box. They had cases and cases of beer that some college students had purchased and a lot of illegal drugs.

"I wanted to go shortly after we arrived. The entire thing spelled trouble. The ironic thing was that I was worried about the police showing up and my being arrested on drug or alcohol charges because of the party law. My future possibly being ruined for being guilty by association, or being in the wrong place at the wrong time. That part about being in the wrong place rang true, but the police never showed up to break up the party. People didn't have to knock one another over to dash out broken windows or busted doors to get away from them. The only one who ended up running for her life was me."

"The statute of limitations has run out, but that doesn't mean we can't confront them, together." Marcella seemed so sincere when she said that. "They need to know how this affected you and at least face the fact that someone else knows."

"Marcella, that can't happen. In order for me to confront them, I'd have to admit to being Caprice Tatum, and that shit is out of the question."

She raised an eyebrow. "Then how do you

plan to get retribution?"

I started to tell her about the videos I already had of Michael, Glaze, and Duchess. I was still contemplating the best way to use them, but I was most certainly going to do so. I also started to tell her that Herman was next on my list, but she would've only tried to convince me not to do it.

"Caprice?"

"I'm not quite sure, with two exceptions. I'm not going to physically harm anyone, and they can never know why their lives are suddenly falling apart. They should assume that it's karma. We all know she's a bad bitch!"

"What do you mean by their lives suddenly falling apart?"

I shrugged. "Some people create their own storms, then get all upset and in their feelings when it starts to rain. Like I said, I haven't drawn any conclusions about it yet. Maybe that's why I'm here; for you to prevent me from doing anything at all."

Marcella smiled. I'd only said that to deflect her questions. There was not a chance in hell that I wasn't going to get them back, one way or another.

"That's a positive outlook, Caprice. It's really not healthy for you to wish negative things on others, or to be the catalyst for their struggles. Karma does work both ways. Whatever is thrown out into the universe comes back, regardless of who is doing the throwing. You need to learn to accept that they won't ever apologize, mainly because you never plan to give them the opportunity to do so."

"Even if I told them who I am, they wouldn't apologize. That would mean admitting what they did. I wonder if they ever discuss it with each other anymore, or if they've attempted to block it all out. Maybe they blamed it on the alcohol and drugs, and reasoned that it was a mistake. But it wasn't a fucking mistake. A mistake is making an oversight on a question on your final exam. A mistake is making salmon patties with a packet of crab cake seasoning because they looked the same. A mistake is putting an empty soda can in the regular trash instead of the recycling bin. But holding me down and raping me, or helping others to rape me, was not a mistake."

"I agree," Marcella replied. "It wasn't a mistake. It was a crime. But there's this amazing and *true* quote by Maya Angelou. 'Hate. It has caused a lot of problems in this world, but it has not solved one yet.' "

"That may be your truth, and her truth, but I can't overcome my hatred toward them, and I need to come up with some sort of solution so I can move on with my life. I'm almost forty and, to the naked eye, I have it all. But that's not the case. By the way, she also says, 'If we lose love and self respect for each other, this is how we finally die.' I can't say that Bianca or Cherie ever really loved or respected me, but I believed that they did up until that night, and by the time that night ended, I felt like a part of me was dead."

"Then it's time for you to resurrect it." Marcella got up and walked over to close a blind. The sun was shifting and beaming right in on the sofa. She pulled the string and then stood there, with her back to me as she asked, "So how's your love life?"

I let out a sound that I could not even describe with a word.

She turned around and then sat back in the armchair across from me as I sat up and put my feet on the floor. Then I stared at her. If I was going to tell it, I may as well go ahead and tell it all. Clearly, she knew that I was incapable of having a healthy, normal, loving relationship with a man.

"That bad, huh?"

"Depends on which way you look at it. I haven't had a string of bad relationships. I don't bother with having them at all."

"And why is that?"

"Whew, that's a list! Take your pick. Gold-digging men who would only want me for my fame and money. Men believing that they are the greater sex and therefore, can fuck the masses and expect women to only fuck them. Not believing in love because I've never truly seen it. Grandma never had a man around, Momma was raped and already bat-shit crazy before I came into the world, Daddy would rather run women than allow women to run him, and Hannah never found the look she was searching for. So what would I be basing such a situation on, even if I dared to go there?"

"That's the case with a lot of young ladies," Marcella replied. "But it makes no sense to just give up."

"You don't have on a wedding ring." Marcella seemed uncomfortable with that statement. "I'm not putting you down or anything, but I'm just saying. You're a psychiatrist, which hopefully means you don't have mental issues, and apparently you're single."

"I never discuss my personal life with clients."

I felt bad about what I'd said. She was right. I had no right to intrude on her personal life. Even though I was spilling my guts to her, it was my choice, and that was her profession.

"Mea culpa. My bad. In other words, mind my own fucking business."

"I didn't put it like that."

"But really, if I had to wrap the entire thing up and put a pretty red bow on it for you, I would say that falling in love to me would mean giving up power to another person."

"Power to do what?"

"Everything!" I sighed. "I once had a man tell me that he couldn't be in control of his life and be in love at the same time. I didn't understand what he meant then, but now I do. Also, the few times that I've *attempted* to date a man, it was always frustrating to me when it came to the intimacy. I wasn't ready and they weren't patient. You know what hurt the most?"

"What?"

"A man making me feel special one day and making me feel like a nobody the next. How do people switch up so fast? I see it all the time on the news with high-profile breakups and I've seen it in everyday life. One moment, a couple seems like they are perfect together and everyone is commenting on how loving and attentive they are, and how they wish they had that kind of love. Then wham! Next thing you know, they are calling each other all kinds of bitches and whores, they are taking out restraining orders and slanging accusations of cheating, abuse, violence, threats, diseases, and start snatching funds out bank accounts and hiding the jewelry."

"Interesting description but not far off base for some marriages."

"Oh, they do it sometimes without there even being a marriage. And that's another thing. I have some friends who dated men for less than six months, and when they decided they no longer wanted to be bothered with their trifling behinds, the men had the audacity to want to be paid to go away. Like they're owed something for their time. The Devil is a liar! I'm not putting myself in that situation."

"You said something about not wanting to be intimate. So you're not sexually active?"

I smirked. "Oh, that's a totally different concern. You may want to pour yourself a drink before I go there."

"I'm fine, but I can make you one if you need it," Marcella said.

"Give me whatever you have that's strong!"

CHAPTER TWENTY

I called the house to make sure Nikki was working with the label to get my upcoming tour schedule together. There were certain venues that I refused to perform in, either because I had some kind of beef with the managers or because I hated the acoustics. My ass could actually sing — unlike a lot of the lip-syncing broads — but some places had such fucked-up structure that I sounded ridiculous. I had a reputation to protect. Rarely did awesome performances go viral, other than people posting selfies of themselves with the stage in the background with me on it. But let a singer put on a bad show, have one bad night, and millions of people were spreading it all over social media. Mostly women, but that's not a surprise. Women putting other women down was like telling the world that they were more worried about the "competition" than their own progress. Silly, really, because how can you compete in a space that you don't even own any real estate in?

After she ran down the list for me, only one was unacceptable, so they were going to find another spot in Jacksonville, Florida, for me to "set it off." I was looking forward to touring, as always. That was when I felt most free and could talk shit to the masses through my lyrics and dance. Plus, the busier I was, the less time I had to concentrate on my pain.

"Sorry about that," I told Marcella as I hit the end button on my cell phone. "I still have to be Wicket after all of this, and during it, I guess."

"You're so talented, so beautiful. Did you ever think that you'd be so successful?"

I giggled. "Are you fucking serious? No, I never thought that any of this would happen — not when I was a child. I recognize that none of the good things in my life would have happened if I had not been through everything in the beginning. I am a living testament to the ideology that where there is no pain, there is no gain."

"Some people believe that pain is weakness leaving the body."

I let that sink in and nodded, taking a sip out of the double hit of cognac that Marcella had poured for me. "That makes a lot of sense. In some ways, my pain did make me stronger, and it put Hannah and Daddy into my life. I definitely can handle most normal problems better than the average person. My career is stressful, but I rarely feel any stress from it at all. When shit goes awry, I concentrate on resolutions instead of flipping out."

"Then that proves you can do the same thing when it comes to your personal life."

"Not so!" I said without hesitation. "Let me just keep it real." I swirled the ice cubes around in the glass. "Now that I have some liquid support. I'm not referring to you, but it's funny how everyone considers honesty a virtue, yet nobody wants to hear the truth."

"I want to hear the truth: your truth."

"I'm a sadist. I get off on inflicting pain on other people. To be more specific, I have these two pets." I looked in Marcella's eyes. They showed no signs of disgust, or even shock, so I added, "Their names are Glaze and Piece of Shit."

I could see that she had to suppress a laugh. "I'm assuming Piece of Shit is a man."

"You got it. When I was trying to come up with a name for him, that was the most derogatory one that came to mind."

"Well, it definitely sticks with you. And

who is Piece of Shit?"

"Doesn't matter, and there's no reason for you to need to know that. He's insignificant in my life. When I call, he comes . . . and then he *comes* again. We satisfy each other's need and then I fly him home coach. Same thing with Glaze. I don't beat their asses once or week, or some shit like that. That would draw too much attention. Everything's discreet."

Marcella glanced toward the porch, where my bodyguards were chilling with a pitcher of her lemonade and some glass jars to drink it out of. She'd even thrown in some chicken bacon ranch wraps for them.

"What about them? Do they know about Piece of Shit and, what was it, Glaze?"

"They know that I have a couple who I'm friends with who sometimes meets up with me in different cities to hang out. Since I have so few actual friends, it makes sense. They believe Glaze, who's a woman by the way . . ."

"I figured as much."

"They think she's a friend of mine from back in the day, that we used to take dance lessons together when I first started singing as a teen. She has the looks and the body for it."

"That's a good cover story."

"Marcella, I'm a beast when it comes to making shit up. Some people actually believe that Daddy adopted me after my parents were killed at Jonestown."

"Wow, that's over the top!"

"My life is over the top, but money talks and bullshit walks, and that's the backstory that Daddy and I came up with together. There were a lot of people, especially kids, who went unidentified, and that's rare in a mass-death situation. We couldn't say they died in a plane crash. Some nosy-ass reporter would've tried to confirm that by now. Same thing with a car accident.

"Anyway, KAD is under the impression that she's my friend and that Piece of Shit is her husband. They don't ask any questions, and I get them rooms under Natia, which means "hidden" in Samoan, and Eric Dotson. They ride in the limo with me to some concerts and I make KAD ride separately, so my friends and I can have some privacy."

"And you beat them?"

"Among other things. I also make them fuck each other in front of me. It gets me off, watching them do whatever I instruct them to do."

"Just seeing them makes you climax, or do you masturbate?"

314

"Damn right I masturbate. I'm a master of that, and I do it nearly every day." I paused and wondered if I should tell her about the things I did with my bodyguards. I decided against it. I was revealing enough for her to get the point. "I've tried to have intercourse with a few men throughout my life, but things always fell apart when the shit got real."

"The thought of having sex reminds you of the rape?"

"The thought of having sex reminds me of the *one* time that I was too weak to protect myself, the *first* time that I was betrayed by friends I believed I could trust, and the *last* time I will ever allow a man to physically hurt me."

"Caprice, we can work on this. Things can change, but only if you want them to change."

"Therein lies the five-million-dollar question. I'm not sure that I want to change. But there is this one guy."

"Oh, yeah? What's his name?"

"Jonovan Davis."

"The mascot from your high school?" Marcella grinned. "You have feelings for him, don't you?"

"I'm not so sure about feelings. More so some type of curiosity. He was a nice guy then, and he seems like a nice guy now. He's caring for his father, who has Alzheimer's."

"He's still in Atlanta?"

"Yes. He actually showed up at my place to interview me for his music-themed magazine."

"He's goal-oriented, he likes music, he showed compassion toward you before you became famous, and your voice changed the second you brought him up."

I was stunned. "My voice didn't change."

"You're not the one listening to you — I am — and a spark of happiness leaped into your tone when you mentioned him. It's also written all over your face."

I tried to wipe whatever expression she was reading off my face. "He's taken."

"He told you that?"

"Didn't have to. I ran into him at one of Bianca's events and he had a date with him. He did say it was casual, though."

"You can't expect a man to go without dating or intimacy before you even come into the picture. What were you doing at Bianca's event, and what kind of event was she having?"

"She's an interior designer and she had an event to thank her clients and also to show off Cherie's clothing designs. Jonovan was there because he was covering some of the attendees. At first I thought he was there as a friend of theirs and that upset me."

Marcella was about to say something when a light knock came at the front door. She got up to answer it and Kagiso entered.

"You guys must be getting impatient out there," Marcella said with a chuckle.

Kagiso looked like a doe caught in a headlight. "Just checking on Wicket to make sure everything's all right. This is going on for longer than usual."

"I'll be out in a few minutes," I said. "Are you all really worried about me, or did the food run out and you want to go get something greasy?"

He laughed. "Antonio's the grease king, but yeah, he's out there rubbing his stomach."

I shook my head and stood up. "We can get going."

Marcella glanced over her shoulder at me. "Are you sure? We were talking about um . . . you know who. Did you want to take that further?"

I walked up to her. "It's probably pointless, but I'll consider taking it *further.*" She was referring to me pursuing Jonovan but didn't want to come out and say it. I knew what she meant, though. "Maybe I'll call *you know who,* and feel him out."

Marcella actually hugged me and I started trembling. I'm sure she felt it. I was not big on human contact, only with hugging Daddy, or Hannah when she was still alive. I missed her so much. One day, I was going to have to let her truly go as well. Even though I had convinced myself that time heals all wounds, that was still an open cut on my heart.

"I'll see you later," she said, moving back and gazing into my eyes. "You can call me anytime, day or night. If I'm preoccupied, I'll call you right back. I promise."

I smiled at the concept that I might actually have a new friend. It had been so long. She knew about most of my crazy shit and was still willing to talk to me.

"That means a lot to me. Thank you."

Kagiso cleared his throat. "Antonio might pass out in a minute if you don't get him a fried chicken wing, or a taco, or something."

All three of us chuckled as I followed Kagiso out.

"What do you want to do for your birthday?" Nikki was sitting at the kitchen counter on a stool running her fingers swiftly across the keyboard of her laptop. "I'm getting requests for media passes for your party."

"I'm doing the same damn thing that I do for every other birthday. Spending it with Daddy or spending it alone if he's not around. And he's not going to be in the country on the eighteenth, so that means I'm flying solo."

Nikki smirked and kept typing. "Boss Lady, it would be great if you had a party for your big four-O. I put the ballroom at the Georgian Terrace on hold, just in case."

"So what you're basically saying is that you've started planning a birthday bash for me, and now you're trying to be slick and get me to do it because it's a press opp."

"I know you don't care about the media but yes, I have done some preplanning and, *if you want,* I can make it lovely. All you'll have to do is throw on a sexy outfit, a pair of fly shoes, and show up as the queen that you are."

I was making a chopped salad for dinner. I didn't like what the chef had prepared: Chilean sea bass with fried brussels sprouts and yellow squash. I loved the vegetables, but the sea bass killed it for me. It was often one of the most expensive entrées at fancier restaurants but, to me, it had no flavor. It was so light that it was invisible to my taste buds. No matter what they sautéed, marinated, or sprinkled it in, it did nothing for me. So I was making a salad of mixed greens, goat cheese, red onions, grapes, and Granny Smith apples with low-fat raspberry vinaigrette dressing.

"Flattery usually gets you everywhere with me, Nikki, but I'm not caving on this. Why should I spend a bunch of money to impress people who I don't give a fuck about and who don't give a fuck about me?"

"You do concerts all the time."

"Yeah, but I get paid to perform, and I don't do phony well. The last thing I want is a bunch of people touching up on me at a party. At concerts, I go onstage, do the damn thing, and bounce. Go to my dressing room, shower, and get the hell out of there."

Nikki laughed. "And you have that routine down pat."

"Damn right. I'm the modern-day Houdini, except instead of escaping, my ass pulls disappearing acts."

"I remember that time when we were in Phoenix and this reporter was checking for you less than ten minutes after the show and you were already ghost."

"Yes, girl! The shit, shower, and shave military policy didn't have anything on me that night. They usually get fifteen minutes, but I did my thing in nine and a half and was out in the car in ten."

Nikki chuckled, got up and took a bowl out the cabinet. "Let me have some of that salad. It looks good."

I pretended to block the salad bowl. "Didn't you eat that amazing sea bass for dinner?"

"I didn't want to hurt Simon's feelings, but that joint didn't have any taste."

"I keep telling you that," I said as I made a few more chops with the salad scissors and then put some in her bowl. "One of us needs to tell him that he needs to take that out of his recipe box."

"You're the boss."

"And you're supposed to be the extension of me, so handle that."

Nikki sat back down by her laptop and started typing. A few seconds later, she said, "Damn, you're right. They do only get fifteen minutes to shit, shower, and shave in the military."

"I don't know why you think I make shit up. I wouldn't have said it if it wasn't true."

"I know, I know. It's just that you're like a walking encyclopedia. Sometimes when you start dropping knowledge, it trips me out."

"When I was younger, I didn't have much else to do other than read a bunch of shit. The Internet wasn't even around, so I read book after book and, as I grew older, I still enjoyed trivia questions."

Nikki took a bite of her salad while she continued reading. She smiled. "They have this one site where men are debating on the order that they should shit, shower, and shave. Some say they shave before they shower and —"

"I hope no one is saying they shower before they shit. If they do that, then they're just mega nasty. That goes double for women. What sense does it make to come out the shower smelling and feeling pure and fresh and then take a dump and have shit kernels all in your crack?"

Nikki almost choked on her food. "This is such a lovely conversation to have over dinner."

"Isn't it, though?" I sat down on the stool next to her with my salad. "Back to your party idea. That's a negative for me, so stop fantasizing about it. And cancel any *preplans* you've made."

Nikki sighed in disappointment. "It was worth a try. I just want you to be happy."

"What makes you think I'm not?"

"When I go hang out with friends, I feel bad leaving you here. Some of the places in Atlanta are really hot. You need to check them out."

Nikki was on point with one thing. I couldn't simply go "hang out" anywhere without it being a big production. The paparazzi in Atlanta were nowhere near as bad as New York City and Los Angeles, but it wasn't toned all the way down like Birmingham, Alabama, either. I had to fly private — not because I was *bougie* — but because the commotion it would cause walking through the terminal would have been insane. Many times I longed to be able to run out to a convenience store to get a hot dog or a pack of sanitary napkins. I longed to walk through a grocery store, aisle by aisle, and see what new food products were on the market that I might want to try. I yearned to go for a walk down the street and take in the fresh air without people rushing up on me to ask for an autograph. But the life of Wicket was the hell that I had created and there was no turning back.

CHAPTER TWENTY-ONE

Monday, September 3, 2012
1:38 p.m.
Atlanta, Georgia

People look upon Mondays in different ways. Those like me could not care less. We work seven days a week if that is what it takes and there is little difference between the weekends and weekdays, with the exception of some of those who work with us, or for us, considering Saturdays and Sundays are times to get some errands out of the way, make special plans with loved ones, and laze around watching Netflix or *Law & Order, Criminal Minds, Hoarders,* or *The First 48* marathons.

Then there are those who feel like the weekends are their Holy Grail. They aren't a cup, dish, plate or stone in the biblical sense, but some do believe that weekends off from work are designed to provide them with happiness, eternal youth, and an abundance of food. They hate their jobs, so it feels like being let out of prison for the weekend. They get an opportunity to relieve some stress by taking morning jobs, playing basketball or softball in leagues, taking the kids to the neighborhood park or other child-themed places, and lie in bed late after a lengthy night of sex. Some curl up with books or the video game controllers, hit up the shopping malls. Then there is the food aspect of it. They can grill out, go have long, relaxed meals at restaurants — instead of adhering to breaks and lunch hours — or they can have friends or relatives over to laze around with them. But when Sundays start winding down, the stress of what happens on Monday mornings starts winding back up. Lunches have to be packed for the kids and/or leftover lunches for themselves because they don't want to spend more money on their lunch than they actually make on their lunch hour. Clothes and/or uniforms have to be washed and ironed and hung in closets for the week. They may have to run out and fill up their gas tanks that were depleted over the weekend to make sure they don't have to leave ten minutes earlier in the morning. In larger cities, they prepare to go to battle with the dins of other people who will be on the roads trying to get to work on time, for fear of being called on the carpet by their supervisors or docked of their pay. Or even worse, fired if this has happened before or sometimes fired if it is only the first time.

Last, there are those who love their careers. They thrive on their work and can't wait until Monday mornings arrive. They hate having to shut down their offices or businesses for the weekends. They find it to be a ridiculous concept because their motto is "I'll sleep when I'm dead." The weekends actually bring them a great degree of stress. They can't relax. Why the hell should they when money was out there to be made? They are the ones who look uncomfortable lingering by the bar with a beer in their hands while the rest of their buddies are joking and laughing and relaxed, completely appreciating their mini-sabbaticals from the office. They spend time with family and loved ones more out of obligation than a true desire to do so. While everyone is sitting around talking about the latest movies, or gossiping about who did what at their offices the past five days, they are worrying about how they can make up for lost time once Monday gets there, and it can't get there fast enough for them.

Based on Bianca's descriptions of her

husband, and my own observations over the past few months, Herman Hudson fell into the last category. Bianca definitely fell into the first. If Herman could've seen patients or performed surgeries every Saturday and Sunday, he probably would have. But orthopedic surgery was rarely an emergency or life-threatening intervention so sans a few people who didn't want to take their sick leave off work — most embrace taking it — people preferred to have their surgeries performed during the week.

On any given Monday, Herman generally did in-and-out surgeries in his fancy-*schmancy* clinic in the Buckhead area of Atlanta in the mornings, followed by a lunch break from noon to one, and consultations in the afternoon. If he could've done away with a lunch hour for his staff, he probably would have, but they had rights. He didn't take Mondays or Wednesdays off like many of his peers. The theory of having a three-day weekend or a two-day, one-day, two-day split week was beyond his comprehension. He hadn't busted his ass getting a four-year undergraduate degree, a four-year medical degree, and spending five years in a hospital as a resident to not swallow up every dollar he could make. He'd decided on orthopedic surgery because they tended to be one of the highest-paid specialties, averaging about a half million a year in take-home pay, comparable to a cardiologist.

I had been joking with Bianca when I kept talking about him playing with feet all day. I was amazed that she had not corrected me that day at the restaurant. I was very aware that an orthopedic surgeon was not a podiatrist. That while they could treat hammertoes and club feet, they also treated patients with cerebral palsy, severe arthritis, fractures, sprains, spinal issues, and many other things. Herman was brilliant, and that was nothing new. He had been very smart back in school, especially in math. He was to be the one who explained what the teacher had said in class to the rest of us.

But Herman was also evil. I clearly remembered him being the ringleader homecoming night. He thought that shit was funny and cute. Now I was going to show him how you could be trudging along in life, with everything seemingly golden one minute, and then a single incident could change it forever.

Herman's first consultation patient after lunch on this particular Monday was Louis Abbey — real name — a fifty-two-year-old Caucasian man who was complaining of back pain. Louis Abbey was about to do both of us a huge favor. It took me a minute to find the perfect person for what I had in mind. He and I had never spoken personally. In fact, I had put up a Chinese wall between us. An insurmountable barrier, especially to the passage of information and communication. I had utilized a business associate who I knew I could trust — because he loved money and knew that the better job he did, the more I would come back to him — to initiate the process. It trickled down to at least five or six more people before someone approached Louis with the plan.

Louis was a recovered drug addict but still had a serious gambling problem. He would often leave his wife at home alone, even though their four kids were grown, and head to Cherokee, North Carolina, to try his luck at Harrah's. He was *never* lucky, and the decent wage that he made working construction was quickly swallowed up upon his arrival. His wife, Ivy, was on depression medication at that point, struggling to believe that the man who had once promised to love and protect her was now putting their home and hopes of retirement at risk. Ivy was a schoolteacher, and everything had started to affect her ability to deal with the students. I only knew all of this because I had them both watched carefully before I pulled the final trigger on Plan B. I needed to make sure that Louis would not cave under pressure when the proverbial shit hit the fan. The only concern that I had was whether he had shared what he was about to do with his wife. From what I had heard, unlike her husband, she had morals, and sometimes people with morals thought it was better to do what was right instead of doing what was easy. Either way, her life was about to change, and I hoped she could handle it. No one was forcing her husband to participate. He had been paid well and would be paid again after he filed a multimillion-dollar lawsuit against Herman.

Obviously, I wasn't there in the office that day, or in the exam room, but things must have gone as planned. By the next morning, Herman's face and name were plastered all over both the news and Internet. It was a breaking news item about a prominent Atlanta orthopedic surgeon who had been accused of sexually molesting another man during a consultation. The fact that Herman was black and Louis was white meant the racist media outlets went on the warpath, digging deeper into Herman's business, interviewing staff, friends, neighbors, and other patients. It was a chance for several people to get fifteen minutes of fame that they never would've gotten otherwise. I was banking on that and it paid off in a serious way less than a week later.

Opportunists will always embrace an opportunity. There is an old proverb that goes: "Dear Optimist, Pessimist, and Realist: Thank you. While you guys were arguing about the glass of water, I drank it. — The Opportunist."

I did not know the number who would come marching, but I was convinced they would come and boy, did they. At last count, there were at least eight other patients, both male and female, who claimed that Herman had done something to them when there was no nurse present in the examination room. Then one of the nurses decided to hop on the gravy train and accused him of sexually harassing her for years.

Herman was arrested, charged, and his bail was set at a million dollars. He was looking at hundreds of thousands of dollars in legal fees for the criminal charges alone. Then there would be all the civil suits. People claiming that he had destroyed them, and Louis would be leading the pack. He had already been set up with an attorney to file his case before he ever stepped a toe in Herman's office. He would be the main plaintiff in a class-action lawsuit and the attorney, also acquired via a Chinese wall, would have a slate of clients that he would make a third off of and, like most class-action cases, he would walk away with more wealth than all the rest. It was a win-win for everyone except for Herman . . . and Bianca.

For a second, I almost felt like I had gone too far. Then I came to the conclusion, "Fuck nah!"

■ ■ ■ ■

Part Four:
The Bridge

■ ■ ■ ■

Anger is an acid that can do more harm
to the vessel in which it is stored than to
anything on which it is poured.

— Mark Twain

CHAPTER TWENTY-TWO

Tuesday, September 18, 2012
2:37 p.m.
35,000 Feet Over the Atlantic Ocean
I couldn't believe that I was actually doing what I was doing.

"How does it feel to be forty?"

Jonovan was sitting beside me on my private jet. We were both sunk into the tan leather seats, sharing a bottle of Duhart-Milon red Bordeaux.

"Honestly, it doesn't feel any different, other than realizing that my life is probably at least halfway over at this point."

"That's a dismal way to look at it. I have a few more months before I hit the hill, but I'm actually kind of excited about it."

"Why's that?"

"Maybe females embrace age differently than men. While it may seem like you are not what you used to be, I'm simply glad that I'm not *a used to be.* Make sense?"

I analyzed what he said. "Maybe I'm drunk but no, it doesn't make sense to me."

He leaned up in his seat. "I'm glad to still be alive. A black man in society, past or present, considers it a blessing to live forty years. They're so many things working against us."

"I agree with that to a degree, but I also see a lot of black men using that single fact as an excuse. Yes, racism is still alive and there are clear-cut and obvious disadvantages, but there are also a lot of advantages that did not exist before. A lot of people are still under the impression that more black men are in prison than in college, and that's not accurate."

"True enough, but there is definitely a disproportionate amount in prison, and in the graveyard."

"Don't get me wrong; we live in a very sick and depraved world. But even with what I've been through, I'd still like to believe that most people are good and simply trying to do what they can with their dash."

"Their dash?"

"The time between the day they are born and the day they die; what's reflected on their tombstones."

"You're a deep woman."

Jonovan and I grinned at each other.

"Thanks for inviting me to share your birthday with you. I must admit that you took me by surprise."

"I took myself by surprise!" I finished off my glass of wine. "It's so out of character for me. I'm not sure what came over me."

"Whatever it was, I hope the trend continues."

I blushed. "I even left my assistant and bodyguards at home, so we could get to know each other better."

Being alone with Jonovan had not been an easy thing to pull off. I'd had to pull another fast one. If I ever needed to find another career, I would've made one hell of a spy. I was a fantastic liar, and conniving and manipulation could've been my middle names. I'd convinced KAD that since we were going to Daddy's private island off the coast of Norway, the armed guards there would be sufficient to protect me. They were there around the clock to protect the property itself. I told Daddy that KAD was going and was hoping he didn't try to verify it. There was no reason for him to think I was lying, and the staff on the island had no reason to blow the whistle. I had learned that most people get caught doing things because they act guilty. They overthink every word that comes out of their mouths and overreact to the point where people get suspicious. Some people even overanalyze the fact that they overanalyze. It wasn't that serious in my case. Worst-case scenario would have been reminding everyone that I was grown and needed my space.

"I still feel like we have crossed paths before."

"Another time, another place. Maybe in a prior life, but it most certainly wasn't in this one," I lied. "Like I told you before, I've never met a stranger."

"You keep referring to that, but you seem like a recluse."

"Since you cover a lot of people in the entertainment field, that should be self-explanatory. Most creativity happens in solitary confinement and most celebrities can't trust anybody."

He chuckled. "You have a point."

"It's a fact. Some people amaze me. If they put as much effort into *being* a good person as they do *pretending* to be a good person, they'd actually *be* a good person."

"Never thought of it that way, but you have yet another point."

The pilot's voice came over the cabin speakers: "Ms. Wicket, we are beginning our descent and should be landing within the next twenty minutes."

I'd decided not to bring a flight attendant with us, either. Even if I had banished her to the back of the plane, she may have still been able to overhear us.

"I've never been to Norway," Jonovan said. "I heard it's lovely."

"We won't be around a lot of other people, just the staff, but the island itself is breathtaking. Plus, it's still summer solstice."

"What does that mean?"

"That you can see the sun around the clock, even at midnight."

"Wow, like in Alaska?"

"Yeah. You've been there?"

"Nope, never. It's going to be so strange to see the sun at night."

"It's strange and then there are the times of the year when it's polar night and it is dark throughout the day . . . like in some of those horror movies."

"Those things are about to play out. They put one of those out at least once every other year."

I giggled. "You sound like you know that because you've seen them."

Jonovan tried to suppress a laugh, but he couldn't. "Okay, okay, I confess. I have a thing for cheesy movies and bad horror flicks. Sometimes watching other people make stupid choices, or die with the benefit of special effects, can make the time go by."

"Speaking of making the time go by, how are things going with the woman you're dating?"

The grin disappeared off Jonovan's face. "I wouldn't be here with you if I was in a serious relationship. I'm not that kind of man."

"Who said I'm trying to get with you romantically?" My low self-esteem was about to jump out the closet like a skeleton. "Don't assume that I asked you to come with me because I want to have sex. I'm not that easy."

He had no idea! My hairbrush had a better shot than he did of getting into my panties!

"That's where you're mistaken about me. I can get sex anywhere, and I realize that a woman like you is not going to be down for games. You asked me to come and spend your birthday with you on a private island, and while I am hoping that we can sneak in a romantic moment here or there because of the surroundings, I don't have any expectations of this going anywhere. Dating someone doesn't mean that I'm having sex with them, and the woman you saw me with is not the only one who I spend time with."

That made me even more upset, even

though I am sure his intentions were the opposite. He realized it and tried to make it sound better.

"That's not to say that I have a romantic interest in any of them. It means that I'm a man who is still waiting for that special person to settle down with. I can't find her without exploring the possibilities."

"There's that term: 'settle down.' Why do men make it seem like they are walking into the gallows when it comes to being with one woman?"

"My father said it best one day when he was talking to me and some of my friends in college. He said that most men don't have an issue with saying yes to one woman. They have an issue with saying no to all their other options."

"Is that your philosophy?" I asked with a smirk. "You're keeping your options open?"

"You make it sound like a criminal act. People should take their time to find the person who complements them in every aspect of their lives instead of trying to pretend like the differences won't matter in the long run. Women tend to fall quick and hard and then wake up one day and realize that they have nothing in common with the man lying next to them, except for great sex."

"I'll give you an amen on that and add in a high five and a foot stomp with it. There are a lot of transformers running amuck on the dating scene. I hear the stories about bitch-assness and fuckery all the time."

"Not bitch-assness and fuckery?"

"Yes, that's the typical behavior of community dick and water cooler dick men."

"You are hilarious." Jonovan poured himself some more wine. "You're definitely going to have to break those terms down for me."

"No hay problema but *no es bueno."*

"Let me find out that you speak Spanish?"

"A little. Enough to know what the hell people are talking about when I'm touring. I also know enough French, German, Italian, and Japanese to get by."

"So what did you just say?"

"I said *no hay problema,* which means no problem, and *no es bueno,* which means it is not good."

"Gotcha!"

"So bitch-ass behavior is when a man acts effeminate, like a little bitch, when it comes to handling his responsibilities as a man. Throwing tantrums, trying to place the blame on the woman for their own spineless behavior, and running away instead of staying and facing the music when the shit hits the fan."

"Okay, that was enlightening. What is fuckery?"

"Fuckery is when every day begins and ends in drama because a man can't keep a dick in his pants. Instead of just staying single and doing him, he has to string a bunch of women along, pit them against one another like two dogs in a fight, and he causes a bunch of confusion and ruins several lives simultaneously, sometimes the lives of their own children. The men who think they're setting a good example for their kids by seeing their mothers crying themselves to sleep each night, with or without bruises, and then falling in way over in the morning in time to share a bowl of sugar-laden cereal with them before they leave for school, stressed out and angry."

"Wow, you sure have a low opinion of men!"

"Not all men, but you asked me to explain the terminology, so I am. You want me to stop?"

"No, but let me get some more wine." Jonovan downed that glass and poured another as I went on.

"Now the difference between community dick and water cooler dick is rather simple. Community dick is a man who sleeps with a bunch of women in the same vicinity, or a group of women within the same social circle. Like Leon blowing out Amy's back in the morning and blowing out Marigold's back that night."

"Marigold?" Jonovan laughed. "So community dick would be a dude who's sleeping with two best friends?"

"Or cousins, or sisters. Possibly even a mother and daughter combo." I poured some more wine as well. I was tipsy, so I was talking mad shit at that point. "Water cooler dick is a man who, like the name implies, is fucking a lot of broads at his place of employment. Let me backtrack for a hot minute and add that most community dicks don't have jobs. Their careers are making dozens of babies, claiming only some of them, and hitting up their various women for money."

"Hmm, okay."

"Now water cooler dick has chicks all confused. Their first mistake is lusting after people at work. The men have it made because the fact that they work together gives them a legitimate reason to keep their sexcapades on the down low. They convince each and every one of them that they are the one, but they're full of so much bullshit in their colons that it's amazing that it's not trickling out their mouths when they speak."

"This is fascinating," Jonovan said with much sarcasm. "You're funny."

"The drunk mind speaks the sober heart."

"So I've heard."

"The women who are sexing the same man in the workplace end up dealing with foolishness while clocking dollars and sometimes end up scrapping in the lunchroom over the man while he is in the broom closet eating another chick's snatch for lunch."

"Damn, the visual on that one!"

"I'm sure you've seen it all," I said with a giggle. "But you get my point."

"Yes, and thanks for breaking that down for me. Can I ask you a question?"

"Sure."

"Why do you hate men?"

"I don't hate men, but I do understand them. I believe that most men are capable of love. However, I don't believe they understand the parameters of being in love. They're given a blueprint for excuses to justify their actions, but is there ever truly a justification for damaging someone else's spirit? And just because a woman accepts their behavior and lets them get away with it, that doesn't make it right. A woman's ability to accept pain doesn't mean that she deserves it."

"I really like you," Jonovan blurted out. "I enjoy listening to you speak, and watching your lips move. I don't mean that in a sensual way, either, and it's not a pickup line. I'm happier when you're around and when you open up to me. I'm glad you feel comfortable doing it. When you told me what happened to you when you were a child in Guyana, that meant a lot to me and, as promised, I haven't mentioned it to anyone else, nor will I."

We sat there in silence, staring at each other. I was not a trusting person, but maybe that could change. Marcella had kind of gotten to me during our last visit. That was why I had called Jonovan. An excursion to a private island off the coast of Norway was a bit over the top for a first date, but that was the life I was living. There was no reason to downplay my lifestyle to prevent him from being intimidated. If we did hook up, it would all become a part of his life as well. But could it ever work? I'd seen a lot of men who were extremely successful in their own right cave under the pressure of having a celebrity wife, and vice versa. The one big difference between some of my counterparts and me was that being famous was not a factor for me. I loved to create, sing and dance, and perform in front of crowds but, after that, I craved solitude.

I kept staring at Jonovan. I could tell he was starting to feel uncomfortable and possibly even regret what he had expressed to me. The true question wasn't whether he could handle being with me, it was whether I could handle a relationship, period.

"Did I say something wrong?" he finally asked.

"No. I'm sorry. My mind was wandering."

"That's just what a guy aims for. Telling a woman that he's feeling her and discovering that her mind was someplace else while he was saying it."

"I heard every word you said, and my thoughts pertained to it."

"In that case, a penny for your thoughts."

I sighed and closed my eyes for a brief moment. Then I looked him in the eyes. "This entire thing is out of my element. I can't even remember the last time I've been on a date. Pathetic but true. You're a nice man, and I enjoy being in your company as well. But I need to take this slow."

"I understand and I've got nothing but time."

"It was asking a lot of you to come with me and leave your father."

"I have a home aide there with him. He

has to be watched around the clock, whether I'm in town or not, and I still have to work. I can't always be there with him."

"I still appreciate you coming."

"I wouldn't have missed this for anything."

Jonovan and I had a blast on Daddy's island. It could accommodate up to fifty guests spanned out over the nine buildings. Being that it was only the two of us and the staff, we were able to go from structure to structure and continued to have deep conversations with each other. I felt so bad about not admitting that I was Caprice, but that was not an option . . . never could be.

We had a nice dinner for my birthday in the dining room by candlelight. The chef on the island prepared an excellent meal of meatballs with brown gravy, herbed potatoes, creamed cabbage, and cucumber salad. He made an apple cake and rhubarb pudding for dessert and we switched from wine to Christiania Vodka, native to Norway.

We listened to jazz music throughout our meal and then slow-danced for about an hour to a mixture of old-school love ballads and recent freakier and mostly sexually explicit music. Our bodies meshed well together, and Jonovan had no idea that it was the first time that I had been so close to a man, dancing like that, in decades.

We most certainly did not have sex that night, but we did fall asleep together in a hammock by the ocean . . . with the sun out.

CHAPTER TWENTY-THREE

Tuesday, November 6, 2012
11:19 a.m.
Atlanta, Georgia

"Are you sure you want to go?" Antonio asked. "They're going to mob you in a clothing boutique."

We were on our way to Cherie's couture joint. It amused me when I heard a lot of chicks on YouTube — another pastime of mine because I was alone a lot — bragging about how they were sporting couture this or couture that and then posting links to where they could be purchased. That was true "hood rat" mentality, because a real couture experience is when fashions are designed to meet the specific requirements and measurements of clients. The word "couture" means sewing, not fashion, like they believe on the street. A video and a link where you can choose a size between 2 and 24 or XS and XXXL was couture? *Get the fuck out of here!*

Cherie was the real deal, though. Her store was called Ascending Trends, and I actually liked a lot of her designs. I had strung her along for months, like Bianca, and made it seem like I was ready to actually let her be my stylist. Nikki had called her the day before to set up an appointment, which meant that I should've had an exclusive window with her. But I was no dummy. I had been around the block a time or two. Once when I was on tour, I asked one of my backup dancers to set up a hair appointment in this small hick town we were staying on the outskirts of on our way to a major venue. When I got there, a lot of people "just happened to drop by" after work to see him, or make an appointment for the following week in person. I'd never seen so many chicks whose hair was recently done and already on fleek show up in a salon. He finally admitted that he had "mentioned it to a few people" and they ended up asking me to take photos and I even had Diederik go out to the limo and scrounge up some headshots for me to autograph for them.

I loved the fact that my fans loved me, so on the rare occasions when I was bombarded by them off the cuff, I didn't mind. I wasn't actually stuck-up like so much of

351

the media portrayed me to be since I rarely did interviews. I was motherfucking cautious because, as I stated before, opportunists will come out the woodwork and guzzle down that glass of water while others are still debating about what to do about it.

So Cherie was guaranteed to have mentioned my impending visit to at least some of her clients, especially the reality show broads who would jump at the chance to take photos that they could tweet or update their statuses with. They were all over the place, so it was not a big deal for someone to take a photo with them, but it was a big damn deal for them to take one with me. I was prepared and looking cute and sexy for the onslaught of nonsense. My hair and nails were real, though. No need to fuck with perfection with weaves and gel tips. I took good care of myself, outside of the occasional cutting back in the day, in spots not visible to anyone, and it showed. Some women are naturally beautiful and others look tore up from the floor up without all of their "gear" in place. I wasn't tripping on them; whatever worked to land men. I wasn't checking to land a man — just make my millions.

A lot of the men who complained about being gold diggers truly had a lot of nerve.

They would go around flashing their fancy cars, expensive watches, earrings, and chains, and brag about their mansions and hefty income and then turn around and get mad when women only wanted them for their money instead of their average dicks. An even swap wasn't a swindle, so the men got their trophies and the women got their bank to pay for their weaves, nails, clothes, and whips. It all panned out.

I was glad that Jonovan was not like the other men who I'd run across in my life. We had been spending a lot of quality time together, when time permitted, and I was really starting to fall for him. I could tell that he had already fallen for me but was afraid to admit it since he knew that I had such a low opinion of the majority of men. I'm sure that it was also tripping him out that a woman like me would seemingly be sweating a man like him. I would call him day and night, ask him to come over, and I had even been over to his place a few times to help him take care of his father. One time I even did household chores, including cleaning the toilets. I hadn't cleaned toilets since 1987, when Caprice ran away from Grandma's house. I was beginning to understand what the term "nose wide-open" meant. I was beginning to focus a lot of my attention on Jonovan, sometimes opting to be in his presence over being in the studio completing my album. But being around him was also helping me with my songwriting. I was able to relate some of my lyrics to real-life experiences for a change.

I was also still having my sessions with Marcella. I had managed to open up to her more and more. I didn't tell her what I had done to Herman. There is a huge difference between values, morals, and ethics. Values are rules that people attempt to adhere to. Morals are the basis on which people judge or evaluate other people. Ethics are professional standards. If I had told Marcella about how I had set up Herman, she would have followed her professional ethics and revealed it. No damn doubt about it.

But I did tell her about what I had done to Michael. Speaking of which, that was another reason why I knew Ascending Trends would be crowded that Tuesday morning. I had put Plan A out into the universe a few days earlier. I decided to pace myself and let that shit with Herman have a couple of months to marinate before I fucked up the world according to Cherie and Michael. I had edited the footage myself, cropping out heads and other identifying aspects of Glaze and Mrs. Teasedale, but leaving no doubt that it was Michael Vinson in every single frame. Then I had used a remote, untraceable router — the shit you could order offline was ridiculous — to post it on Porn4U.com. MediaTake-Out and WorldstarHipHop had a field day with it. Worldstar had about ten million views the first day. It was off the mother-fucking chain.

Michael had always wanted to be famous. Well, now he was. He was famous for stockpiling pussy on a sofa and eating and banging them both out, not to mention the other shit that went down that day. Cherie had to be embarrassed. One could only imagine the tags she received on social media, linking her to the video, or the phone calls and texts she received. I am sure people were talking mad shit about his cheating being the reason why he had never proposed.

In fact, Cherie hadn't even opened up her store since the leak, but when Nikki called to make an appointment, all that changed. She stood to make hundreds of thousands of dollars off me — both with my direct purchases and from the women who would want to look like me and would ask her to make them similar outfits. Cherie was hurt, she was disappointed, but she wasn't foolish

355

enough to miss out on landing me as a client. And the fact that I was actually coming to her so she could show off was an added bonus.

All of that had been running through my head prior to Antonio's question.

"Yeah, it's going to be a mess," Nikki added.

"It'll be fine. I have an appointment, so there really shouldn't be a lot of people around."

Nikki was sitting beside me on the rear seat of the SUV. Antonio was up front with the driver and Kagiso and Diederik were following us in a Mercedes CLS 550.

"You know better than that," she said. "That chick has probably called or texted everyone she knows to tell them you're coming. A chance to meet Wicket? *Girllllllllll,* it's going to be a madhouse!"

"If it gets too bad, I'll simply say unto her, 'Bye, Felicia.' "

We both giggled.

Antonio asked, "Isn't she the one whose dude was outed in a video last week? I saw something about it on MediaTakeOut."

"Really? What happened?" I replied, feigning ignorance.

"Oh snap!" Nikki exclaimed. "I hadn't even put that together." She turned to me.

356

"Her boyfriend has a sex tape with two women where he's doing them both at the same time."

"My motherfucking hero," Antonio remarked. I saw him give the driver a fist dap. Apparently, the driver had seen the shit, too. *Perfect!*

"That's a damn shame." I tried to pretend like I was bothered by it. "She must be so hurt. I've met him before and he seemed to be so into her."

"That video is on point," Nikki said. "You want me to pull it up on my iPad so you can see it before we get there?"

I suppressed a laugh. "Sure, why not? Seems like everyone else in this whip has seen it. I feel left out."

Once we arrived at Ascending Trends, a group of both men and women were hanging around outside like they were simply kicking it. *Who shoots the breeze in front of a clothing store?* You would've thought Cherie was serving free Starbucks coffee up in that mickey.

Some were obvious as we pulled up, and whipped out there camera phones, pointing them directly at the back door of the SUV. Others tried to act like they didn't know what was going down. Diederik and Kagiso got out the Benz first and went inside to make sure I could have a clear walkway into the place. Then Diederik came out and Antonio got out the front to help him make a path on the sidewalk for me. I had just finished off the video, making comments the entire time like I was shocked and appalled about the entire thing. In the back of my mind, I was commending Glaze once again for doing the damn thing.

Nikki and I were escorted out the back and I spent a good two to three minutes posing for photos, but no one was allowed to take one with me. All they were able to do was snap away and jockey for positions to take selfies with me in the background. After I grew tired of it, I walked inside.

"Wicket, I'm so glad you could come!" Cherie exclaimed, dressed to the nines at that time of the morning. She had on a red satin dress with a big bow on the side. It was smoking hot. I had to give it to her. "I have some champagne waiting for you back in the viewing area." She paused to make sure everyone was listening and then announced, "Cristal."

I wanted to gag. Cristal, at about two hundred a pop, was cheap to me. If she had been talking some vintage Krug Brut, then she would've been saying something.

I faked a smile. "Sounds good."

"I'm sorry they're so many people in here. A lot of people are hitting me up early for the holidays."

"Well, perfection takes time, so I understand. You're going to be real busy from the looks of it."

When she winked at me and flashed a phony smile, I lost it. I was about to initiate Plan C. I actually went there for a reason and wanted an audience. Nikki and Antonio mentioning the video in the car and then showing it to me had been unpredicted, but it was right on time. Now my "act" would make a lot more sense. *Won't He do it?*

There were a good twenty-five or so people in the boutique. I glanced around and took them in. Some of the hairstyles were "unbeweavable."

"It's a blessing to be so popular, both in the local community and globally."

"I guess you're ever more famous, or should I say infamous, now?" I ran my fingers over a little black strapless number on a mannequin. "I just caught that porno of Michael on the way here. Over forty million views on that one site? He's the man, huh?"

Cherie looked like she wanted to drop dead right then and there. The others were being quiet, trying to catch every word. Antonio chuckled a bit.

"That entire thing was a misunderstanding," Cherie replied. "He was set up."

I squinted at her in disbelief. This bitch was going to try to make excuses for him. Shame on it all. "Set up?"

"Yes, it was an audition for a movie and things got out of hand."

"Well, shit, if he didn't land that role, then the role couldn't be landed. He ate more pussy up in that flick than ten men in a whorehouse."

Everyone laughed but Cherie and me.

"That's going to become a classic. The way he ate them both out on top of each other."

"It's already a classic," Kagiso said with a grin. He'd apparently seen it as well.

"Like I *said,* it was a misunderstanding." Cherie was getting heated. "Everyone falls, but they get up. I'm quite sure you're no saint."

If she only knew the half of it!

"No need to get those cute little lace panties of yours up in a bunch, and don't insult me again. I made time out of my *extremely* busy schedule to come check out your stuff. Now you want to disrespect me?"

"Wicket, you disrespected me first. I'm

360

not in the mood to discuss Michael. He's fine. *We'll* be fine."

"Wow, that's some loyalty for a man who's been with you for decades and still hasn't put a ring on your finger. He's purchased the cow and at least a dozen calves by now."

"I know that's right!" one chick with orange hair and blue contacts yelled out. "I ain't laying up with no man for more than a year without a proposal!"

Another one yelled out, "Not unless his first name is Sugar and his last name is Daddy!"

"My personal life is none of your business!" Cherie yelled at me and then eyed the other two women. "And it's none of yours, either!"

One of the few men who was in the store said, "Maybe he shouldn't have been banging out random broads in front of a camera then."

"He didn't know he was being taped!"

I smirked. "Oh, come on. While it *appears* that there may have been cameras shooting from various angles, there was a big-ass tripod and camera right there in front of the sofa. Sad! He has you making up excuses for him. Must be some great dick, because it's made you blind!"

Cherie reached her breaking point. "You

know what, *Wicket*? I don't give a damn how famous you are or how rich you are, you can get the fuck out my place!"

"Hold the fuck on," Nikki said, beating KAD to the punch. "You can't talk to her like that."

"I just did! And you can get the fuck out of here, too!"

Nikki glanced at me. "You want me to whip this bitch's ass? I already know you've got me on the bail money."

It took every morsel of self-control in my body, from the roots of my hair to the edges of my pedicured toenails, not to choke Cherie's ass out right there in the middle of her marble floor in front of all those people.

"No, Nikki, she's not worth it," I replied to her. "A tiger never loses sleep over the opinion of sheep." I stepped up closer to Cherie. "Be glad that I'm in a good mood today, unlike yourself. You didn't make me look bad by asking me to leave. You showed these people, who I'm sure will spread the word, that you're an extremely weak woman."

"Damn sure did," Orange Hair said, followed by a lip smack.

"What your man was doing on that video came very naturally to him. It wasn't the first time or the last. You need to make sure you use protection, because I wouldn't fuck him with some other broad's pussy."

"Damn!" a man exclaimed. "She went there."

"If you want to be a dummy and let that man bring you down and humiliate you in front of the world, and allow him to jeopardize everything you've worked hard for, do you. But don't get upset with those of us who refuse to succumb to the power of the dick and act foolish over it."

I started heading toward the door as people snapped photos and, without a doubt, video to post all over the place. This was one time when I didn't mind. In fact, I welcomed it. Having a showdown with me would only make tens of millions of more people want to see the sex tape.

I decided to say something profound as I left with KAD and Nikki. I turned, glared at Cherie. "I truly pity you. The worst thing about being lied to is realizing you weren't even worth the truth."

I heard Cherie yell out, "Bitch!" and almost lost it for real. Diederik grabbed my lower arm and told me to keep walking. If he hadn't been there, I would've slammed her head against that sidewalk until I cracked her skull open. Little did I pick up on the fact that that thought was actually a premonition of what was to come.

CHAPTER TWENTY-FOUR

Friday, November 9, 2012
11:12 p.m.
Atlanta, Georgia

I rushed into the house and up to my bedroom and slammed the door. Then I slid down to the floor on the opposite side and started crying. I couldn't believe that I had done that. It was never my intention to physically hurt someone, even Cherie. I wasn't sure if she was dead or alive, but I was praying for the better of the two scenarios. But what if she was in a coma, or if she'd have to have some limbs amputated. All kinds of thoughts ran through my head and none of them were good.

Diederik knocked on my door. "Where have you been? Kagiso said you disappeared on him at the restaurant."

At first, I refused to answer, but he wasn't going to leave me alone until I made something up.

"Wicket?" He was pounding on the door and trying the knob, but I had locked it. "Ladonna?"

"I'm fine," I managed to get out. "Just tired. Kagiso is overreacting. You guys treat me like a baby. Sometimes I need some space . . . not to mention privacy. I'm entitled to that."

Then I heard Antonio and Kagiso walking down the hall. "Is she all right?" Antonio asked Diederik.

"She says she needed space," he replied to him. "And that we don't give her any privacy."

Kagiso said, "Bullshit. She could have told me that she needed space instead of running off like that."

"Maybe she needs to go see that lady doctor again," Antonio remarked.

"Something's definitely going on here," Diederik said. "Kagiso, where do you think she went tonight?"

"Hell if I know. Like I said, she ditched me like some espionage movie. When I went to look for her in the bathroom, she was gone and no one saw her leave the place."

"Next time, you need to call the authorities right away," Antonio chimed in. "Anything could've happened. From now on, she doesn't go anywhere without at least two of us with her."

"And one of us always stands outside bathrooms from now on," Diederik said.

"Her father will kill us if anything happens to her." Kagiso was getting too melodramatic in his tone and, quite frankly, they were beginning to piss me off.

They were taken aback when I flung the door open, after drying my tears. "You all do realize that I can hear you talking about me, right?" I eyed each one of them with disdain. "I'm not a fucking baby. I'm your boss. You don't tell me what to do. I tell you what to do."

I brushed past them and headed downstairs to the great room to pour myself a drink. I was still trembling and worried about the consequences of my actions. When Antonio mentioned the police, that had been a reality check for me. What if red lights and sirens flooded my driveway at any second? There were freaking security cameras everywhere in Atlanta, not to mention the possibility that someone had caught the entire thing on a cell phone. I had been covered up, but anything was possible.

KAD was in the room with me, but keeping their mouths shut, while I crammed a glass with ice from the bin behind the bar and mixed some Diet Coke with Mount

Gay Rum. I took my drink and went and sat on the leather sectional.

Kagiso must have been the elected spokesperson after they exchanged glances. He sat down beside me, but didn't get too close. "We're only concerned about you. Surely, you know that much. You're our boss, but we also consider you to be a friend. And in my case, I'll even admit that my feelings go much deeper than that."

I stared into Kagiso's eyes and sighed.

"Man, this isn't the time for all that," Antonio stated sarcastically. "She's not digging you like that."

Kagiso snapped at him. "And how do you know that?"

"Because she's not checking for any of us like that. Not for some sort of relationship."

Diederik kept quiet. To say that it was an awkward moment wouldn't have cut it. Everyone in the room was aware that I had done some freaky shit with all three of them over the years. I'm sure that they had compared notes. Spending time with Jonovan had put them all in their feelings, I was sure. The ironic part was that he was the only one I had yet to share my wild side with. Not sure that would ever happen, either.

"Listen, I'm home now, safe and sound.

Can I have some privacy?" I asked. "I assure you that I'm not going anywhere else tonight. I'm going to finish my drink and go to bed."

Kagiso reluctantly got up and walked off in a huff. Antonio followed in silence. Diederik was the only one who wished me "good night" quietly.

I turned on the local nightly news to see if they said anything about Cherie being the victim of a brutal attack. Nothing. I truly did feel bad about what I had done. I had no right to hurt her like that, even after what she had helped the others do to me.

I ended up making three or four more drinks and my emotions took over. I realized that if I were ever going to have closure, I had to go back to the beginning. I had to go back to the source of all my pain. The one person who had victimized me first and had caused my entire life to spiral out of control.

"What's wrong, Ladonna?" Daddy snatched up his cell phone in Buenos Aires. "What's happened?"

I was quiet on the other end, sans my breathing. It was 4:00 a.m. in Atlanta, which made it 6:00 a.m. in Argentina. He knew that I never called at that time of the morning so it had to be an emergency.

"Ladonna? Baby, what is it?"

"Daddy, I need you," I finally whispered. "Can I explain when you get here?"

"I can have my jet fueled in an hour and be there by six o'clock this evening."

"Thank you."

"But do you need anything right now? Where are your bodyguards?"

"I'm safe. It's not that. I did something that —"

"Don't say another word over the phone. See you in twelve hours."

He hung up the phone and it dawned on me that he was afraid that I was about to confess to a crime over a phone line. Damn shame that he was right. *A crime!* I'd never done such a thing; not to that degree.

My next call was to Marcella; not to tell her about what I had done to Cherie but to ask if she could arrange for me to sneak into the hospital to see my mother. I wanted to see her, but I couldn't risk being seen. Between her and Daddy's money and resources, I needed to make it happen somehow. Until I faced my mother, everything else that I was doing was for naught.

Marcella's reaction was similar to my father's after getting a call way over in the morning. She agreed to stop by my house about three. I didn't even care anymore

370

about going to the cabin. I would tell all my servants to leave, except for Nikki and my bodyguards. That way, there would be nothing for anyone to go to the press about. I didn't trust my household staff, confidentiality agreements or not. Matter of fact, once Daddy arrived, I was going to have him make KAD leave the premises as well. They wouldn't be bold enough to break bad with him over it. No one was that foolish, not if they wanted to have a job any longer. While I was technically the boss, and the queen of the castle, no one overlooked the fact that Richard Sterling was the king!

Daddy got into town right when he said he would and by seven, he was sitting across from me at the mixing board in my studio with a half glass of his favorite whiskey, Dalmore 62. Even though everyone else had vacated the property, as he'd instructed, I still felt more comfortable being in a soundproof space. He took a drag of his cigar and waited for me to spill my guts.

"I didn't mean to hurt her!"

"Her?"

"Cherie."

He set his glass down. "Two questions. Is she alive and are there any witnesses that I need to pay off?"

"I don't believe I killed her. She was still breathing when I left and, as far as I know, there were no witnesses."

Daddy closed his eyes for a brief second and sighed. "Atlanta was a bad idea. That was obvious to me from the start. I should've stopped this a long time ago. Tomorrow morning, we're headed back to New York; *all* of us."

"But let me explain. I was —"

Daddy held his palm up. "Let me stop you right there, Ladonna. What we've always feared about your condition has obviously come to pass and I'll do whatever it takes to make sure this goes away, but it ends right here and now. You're not mentally stable enough to be anywhere near those people."

"I lost control. I realize that, but it was because she called me a bitch the other day and something within me . . ."

"Snapped?" He took another drag of his cigar and tapped the ashes off the tip into a dish. "You snapped and you could've killed somebody. For all you know, you may have killed somebody."

He made a quick phone call and then hung up.

"I have someone checking on Cherie. She'll be discreet."

"Can I finish telling you what happened

372

last night? Please!"

"If it'll prevent you from ever, ever telling someone else, then go ahead. Whatever you did, I love you unconditionally and it won't change that."

"I know. I also know that you're the only person still breathing who I could ever fully trust."

He leaned back in the swivel leather chair he was sitting in. "So what happened last night?"

"Believe it or not, I was out on a date." I blushed, and his face didn't change at all. "I've been seeing Jonovan for a couple of months."

Daddy raised an eyebrow.

"No, we haven't gone there yet, and he doesn't know about my issues with intimacy."

Daddy actually wasn't aware of my sexual behavior either, not totally. He was aware that I freaked out whenever things transgressed too far with a man, and that I would shut it all down with a quickness. That I would break things off before they ever truly got going and make up an excuse why I didn't want to continue spending time with them. He didn't have a clue about my sadistic activities, though. I would've died if he ever found out, not because I felt that he would judge me. Like he'd just reminded me, his love for me was unconditional. I was too ashamed to admit that I was doing such things and, besides, the fact that I was beating people would only lend credence to his theory of me being a violent person. Having pets and them voluntarily allowing me to harm them had probably been the main reason why I hadn't "snapped" sooner. I hadn't had any "sessions" with them since that night in Hilton Head, so maybe that was part of the reason.

I voiced what I was thinking out loud. "I'm all fucked-up. Maybe I truly am bat-shit crazy like my mother."

Daddy shook his head. "Your mother is a paranoid schizophrenic with a bipolar disorder."

"Yes, and both of those disorders are genetic."

"What you have is caused by childhood trauma. Two different things. Do you hear voices in your head?"

"No."

"Do you constantly feel like people are plotting against you?"

"Well, no. But I do have mood swings, so maybe I'm bipolar."

"You're not, Ladonna. I had you tested for everything as a teenager and since those are genetic, you would've shown traits back then. They scanned your brain and none of that is the case." He sighed. "But intermittent explosive disorder is definitely nothing to play with. I've done all that I can to protect you, but you coming here was not a wise decision. That's become quite apparent."

His phone rang. He listened for a brief moment and then hung up.

"She's at Emory Hospital, but she's alive and expected to recovery. She has several broken ribs and she almost lost her left eye, but they'll be able to reattach it."

I gasped and put my right hand over my mouth to stifle a scream.

"New York, tomorrow!" Daddy said. "Nikki can stay behind and close up the house, put it on the market."

There was no sense in debating with him, when he was right. I needed to leave Atlanta before I did something even worse to Bianca. After all, I hated her the most. The inevitable was the inevitable.

"Okay, I'll go back, but we can't leave tomorrow. Maybe the next day. There's another reason why I asked you to come here. I already ran this by Marcella earlier today and she's agreed to help me."

Daddy eyed me suspiciously. "Help you

do what?"

"Talk to Momma!"

CHAPTER TWENTY-FIVE

Sunday, November 11, 2012
7:12 a.m.
Smyrna, Georgia

The Broadmore Institute was on the outskirts of Atlanta. Momma had started out in an overcrowded, no-one-gave-a-damn psychiatric hospital. I had assumed she was still in that place until Daddy informed me that he'd had her moved a long time ago.

I was upset. I felt like she deserved the worst treatment that she could get. He reminded me that she had been born with mental issues, which led to her developing various substance addictions, which was culminated with being raped by her own uncle in the back of a car, which resulted in me. He felt like basic human kindness — and the fact that paying for it was a nonissue for him — dictated that he pay for her care.

Because he was doing that, and had made

an additional huge donation to the place, getting in to see her was like shooting fish in a barrel instead of going through a lot of red tape and swearing people to secrecy. No one knew why Richard Sterling was paying for her care, and her confinement had happened so long ago, in another institution, that Daddy had simply paid to have her records doctored so that there was no mention of cutting up her daughter's face. They knew that she was crazy and needed to be treated but that was all.

"She's never told them about me?" I asked as we pulled up into the rear lot early on Sunday morning, when both staff and visitors would be at a minimum. "Why do they think we're coming here?"

"I told Dr. Broadmore that you wanted to meet Denise. He knows that you're my daughter. He thinks that since you moved here, you're curious about meeting the woman who I've paid for all this time."

"And who do they think Momma is to you?"

He shrugged. "I've never offered up an explanation. I'm sure they speculated about a lot of different scenarios, but who cares? That's not their place to be concerned with the who and why, just the money."

"Maybe she doesn't even remember she

has a daughter," I said, halfway disappointed.

"Actually, paranoid schizophrenics tend to have excellent memory. If she has mentioned it, they probably didn't believe her."

Marcella was waiting for us when we walked in the back door, escorted by a security officer. Then all three of us were taken to a room that was nothing but four walls and a table with four chairs. I paced the floor impatiently while I waited for a male nurse to go get Momma.

Once he walked her in, Daddy told him to leave and wait outside. He did as told without saying a word.

Momma stared at me. I stared at her. Marcella and Daddy stared at both of us.

Marcella broke the silence. "Denise, do you —"

"Caprice," Momma whispered.

I took a step back. "You know who I am?"

"Of course. A mother always recognizes her child." She ran her fingertips down her left cheek. "What happened? Why'd you let them do that to you?"

"Denise, maybe you should sit down," Marcella suggested.

Momma looked at Marcella and then at Daddy. "Who are you people?"

379

Daddy cleared his throat. "Actually, I'm her —"

"Lawyer," Marcella cut in. "Mr., um, Langford is Caprice's lawyer, and I'm her, uh, friend."

I furrowed up my brow, wondering what Marcella was doing, and she made a gesture toward Daddy to go along with her lies. Then it dawned on me why she had done it. If Momma slipped and said that Richard Sterling was my father, and also told people that her daughter had come to see her, all of the damn cats would be out of the bag.

Momma walked toward a chair but never took her eyes off me, to the point where she almost missed the chair as she sat down and would've landed on the floor. Daddy rushed over to help her and held the chair for her.

Momma didn't ask why I needed a lawyer, and I'm glad she didn't. I was already working over some scenarios in my mind in case she did. She was now in her late fifties but looked all of eighty. Her hair was brittle, her skin was dry, and she had several missing teeth. All of a sudden, I cared.

"I thought you said they were taking good care of her in here?" I asked Daddy.

He looked her over as well and then replied, "I'll have her moved tomorrow."

I sat down across from her, trembling.

"Momma, do you ever regret what you did to me?"

"You mean your face?"

"Yes."

She continued to stare at the side of my face where the scar had once been. Then she shook her head vehemently. "No, no, no, I don't regret it. I did it to save you."

"Save me from who?" My voice was cracking. "Uncle Donald was already dead. He couldn't hurt any of us anymore."

"No, he's not dead. I see him all the time."

"What?"

Marcella and Daddy just stood there. They were both there more for moral support than anything else. Moral and emotional in case I lost it right then and there. It was difficult not to.

"Donald comes into my room every night and pulls down my panties and . . ." She lowered her eyes to the table. "He does nasty things to me."

I looked at Daddy, who kind of widened his eyes and nodded as if to say, "I told you so."

"Momma, Uncle Donald was killed in prison long before you ever came to this place."

She banged her left fist on the table. "That's a lie!" She looked around the room, moving her head back and forth while her head was tilted toward the ceiling. "Don't you hear them?"

"Hear who?"

Daddy interrupted. "Caprice, maybe we should go. This is pointless."

I held my palm up toward him. "Just one more minute."

"Who's up there?" I asked Momma, pointing at the ceiling.

"Donald, and Momma, and Elvis, and Abraham Lincoln, and Martin Luther, and Jesus." She looked at me. "Don't you hear Jesus?"

Marcella motioned to me that we should go.

"You promise you'll get her out of here tomorrow?" I asked Daddy.

"I promise."

I stood up. "Momma, I have to go now. You take care of yourself."

"You should've kept the scar. Now you have nothing to protect you." Momma let out a soft hiss. "They're going to hurt you. You're too pretty."

"Actually, they hurt me even though I had the scar," I informed her. "But I'm never going to let anyone else hurt me."

A grimace appeared on Momma's face. "Never say never, Caprice."

I fought back tears as I watched Momma sitting there, looking sickly and pitiful. It suddenly hit me, even though I knew it all along: she was a victim of her circumstances exactly like me. Except she was locked up in an institution and I was one of the greatest, biggest, and wealthiest entertainers in the world. She had definitely gotten the shorter end of the stick.

I walked around the table and touched her on the shoulder. "Good-bye, Momma."

She grabbed my hand and clutched it tight. Then she gazed up into my eyes. "Good friends never say good-bye. They simply say see you soon."

Daddy tapped on the door and the male nurse appeared within seconds to let us out.

As we were exiting, he told the nurse, "Tell Dr. Broadmore that I need to speak with him . . . *today.*"

"Is everything all right, sir?" the nurse asked.

"No, it's not, but I'll discuss it with him."

Marcella forced a smile toward the nurse, took one last look at Momma's back, and walked out after Daddy. I hesitated. Part of me wanted to rush over and throw my arms around her and break down. She was my mother, and as a child, like so many children who are abused, I loved her no matter what.

I still *loved* her, even though I had tried to pretend that I hated her the majority of my life.

I told Daddy that I wanted to catch a ride home with Marcella. It was still only about eight o'clock on a Sunday morning, so I doubted that anyone would see us together. Even if they did, so what? I was entitled to have a life and friends.

I settled into the passenger side of her BMW X3.

She didn't immediately pull off. "Are you okay?"

"No," I readily admitted.

"Tell me what you're feeling, right at this moment."

"I'm not altogether sure that I can." I clutched my hands together to try to keep myself from trembling. "I'm still taking it all in."

"Let me turn on a little heat," Marcella said, and put the vent on low. "Take your time, Caprice. I'm sure that was a traumatic experience for you, seeing your mother for the first time since she disfigured you."

"Did you hear what she said about opening myself up to be hurt now that the scar is gone?"

"Yes."

384

"Funny, huh?"

"Nothing funny about any of this."

"True, but I'm trying to ward off my tears."

"You can only do that but so long."

"She recognized me right away."

"That actually didn't surprise me. There have been instances where mothers have been separated from their children for fifty or sixty years and their maternal instincts still kick in."

"But Momma's insane!"

"Your mother has some serious mental disorders, but she's not clinically insane."

"Really?"

Marcella nodded. "If she was insane, she would've been in a straitjacket in a rubber room. Insanity is a state of madness. Your mother knows where she is and she knows what she did. She also knows what she's been through."

"But what about her saying that she was hearing people?"

"That's her schizophrenia. But that didn't stop her from remembering that she cut you."

"I can't believe that I feel sorry for her. She did this to me. All of this was her fault and —"

"It's *partially* her fault, but this all stems

back to someone you can never get revenge on: your uncle. He destroyed your mother's life, probably your grandmother's life and well, and your life."

"I wish I could get my fucking hands on him! I'd wring his neck!" I stated vehemently.

"Well, you can't . . . get your hands on him. Caprice, it's time for you to try to let all of this go. You're taking your medication and that's a good thing, but this entire concept of retaliating against your classmates is consuming your entire life at this point. Have you even finished your album? You've been working on it for months."

"I'm almost done. Just one more song left."

"And how long has there been just one more song left?"

I sighed. "Too long."

"Your father told me he's taking you back to New York."

I looked at her. "Do you think that's a good idea?"

"It's the *only* idea that makes sense. If you want, I can come there once a month, or we can do weekly sessions over the phone. I feel like we've made a connection, and you expressed that you've had issues being comfortable with therapists in the past."

"Maybe you can meet me in some of my tour cities? I'll cover all the expenses and your fees, of course. I'm trying to stop, you know, that stuff."

"Good. Everything has its time and place, but participating in all of that is not going to help you eventually connect to any men intimately."

"You're right." I paused. "What about Jonovan, though?"

She shrugged. "You have a dilemma, one that I anticipated would come up. How much have you told him?"

"Depends on if we are talking about lies or the truth."

"Are you sure you don't want to tell him that you're Caprice Tatum?"

Marcella finally put the SUV in gear and pulled out of the lot as we continued talking.

I shook my head. "I don't see how *anything* positive can come from that. And there's a trust factor. I can't risk him telling someone else. Caprice is dead. She died in 1987 and she's not coming back. Nor do I want her to come back. It's hard enough being Ladonna and Wicket."

"I understand. You're going to have to either get some closure with him before you leave, or figure out if you want to take it further."

"I'm leaving and he has his father. He can't uproot him like that, and we're not even at that point yet."

"I'm not sure what to tell you about trying to take on a serious relationship right now. I'm honestly on the fence. You deserve to be loved, but we still need to work on loving yourself. On the other hand, Jonovan might be able to make you want to do that very thing."

"Then I guess I need to discuss it with him."

"We're both on the same page with that one."

We rode in silence the rest of the way. Marcella must have realized that I needed to do some serious thinking, and that's exactly what I did.

CHAPTER TWENTY-SIX

Friday, February 8, 2013
8:36 p.m.
Miami, Florida

"Here we go," I said as I cut the ribbon in front of Wicket's Thicket for the grand opening. All the who's who of Miami were there, along with a lot of New York– and Los Angeles–based celebrities. I wouldn't call any of them my friends; I would say that I was friendly with them. "Welcome to Wicket's Thicket Miami!"

I had tagged the Miami part on because I already had plans to make it a chain. In fact, Daddy and I had either broken ground or started renovating buildings in Chicago, Los Angeles, and Las Vegas already. No Atlanta for obvious reasons.

Jonovan was standing right by my side. I had decided that I simply couldn't walk away from him. He meant too much to me, and he'd made it clear that I also meant too much to him. The grand opening was an opportunity to introduce him to a lot of people he could interview for *G-Clef*. An intro from me went a long way in convincing people to grant him interviews.

There was a level of comfort for me with Jonovan from the start. Before there was ever a Wicket, or even a Ladonna, Jonovan had genuinely cared for Caprice. No, we had never hooked up, but he had been my friend. Even though I was far from an expert at relationships — never had a bona fide one — it was embedded in my thought process that your soul mate should also be your best friend. Someone you feel like you can discuss anything with, without believing that they will judge you or throw things back up into your face later on. That was the one true danger of relationships, the way that I saw it. Not being cheated on. Not being ripped off for money. Not being manipulated. The true danger was the possibility of your pillow talk being exposed if things didn't work out.

Before I left for New York that prior November, I had gone to speak with Jonovan. I went over to his house and asked him to come out onto the porch for a moment. I didn't want to drag the conversation out. It was going to be difficult enough. It turned into a life-changing experience that I never saw coming.

"You sure you don't want to come in?" he asked, pointing at the door. "I was about to make a pot of hot chocolate."

"Wow, I haven't had hot chocolate since I was kid." I shook my head and put my hands in the pockets of my fleece jacket to keep them warm. "But, no, thank you. I can't stay long."

He looked around and noticed the CLS550 in the driveway, empty of other people. "No bodyguards? I'm impressed. Usually, they linger outside my house like the secret service when you're here."

"I insisted that I do this alone."

Jonovan looked concerned. "Do what alone?"

I took a deep breath. "Everyone's back at the house . . . packing."

"Oh, you're taking a trip? Concert or something?"

"My tour starts right after the New Year."

"So where are you headed?"

I lowered my eyes to avoid his. "There's no easy way to say this, and you might not even care, but I'm moving back to New York."

I kept my eyes down, but I could see him

cross his arms and lean against the door-frame from my peripheral vision. "I see."

We were both quiet for a long pause.

"I realize it's sudden." I gazed up into his eyes. "But I hope this doesn't mean that we can't still get to know each other better."

"And how are we supposed to do that?"

I shrugged. "I'll be honest. I don't think that I'll be coming back here. Atlanta isn't for me."

"Why isn't Atlanta for you?"

I didn't have any response that would make sense and, for the first time, a lie didn't formulate in my head at the speed of lightning.

He sighed. "Well, I guess it just is what it is. If you feel you need to go, then there's nothing I can do to stop you. I'm not sure how often I can travel, with Dad being sick and all. I definitely can't do it much."

"What if I could get someone to be here full-time, so you can come see me?"

I was sure that I had a pitiful look in my eyes by that point.

"It's not only about having someone else here. I have someone here most of the time. You know that. It's about leaving my father. My worst nightmare is his needing me and my not being here for him."

As soon as Jonovan said that, I completely

understood. I used to avoid spending a single night away from Grandma when she was sick. That was the other thing that I had ended up discussing with Marcella once we got back to my house. I had carried the guilt of leaving Grandma after being raped for my entire life. Writing her letters with no return addresses was not enough, and an excuse to avoid telling her the truth. I'd often wondered what she would have done if she had known. That was a question that would forever go unanswered, like so many others. I wished that I could've asked her if my mother was also my sister. Being truthful to myself, I had always believed Momma. I believed that my uncle had also raped his own sister and impregnated her with my mother. She really had no reason to make any of that up, and I was sure that it had been grounded in some kind of fact.

"I understand," I said. "Well, then I guess I'll see you soon." I remembered what Momma had said about saying good-bye.

I was about to leave when Jonovan grabbed my arm. "I want you to know that your past is safe with me. I'll never tell a soul."

"I know," I said, turning to face him. "You've kept your promise since our interview. I appreciate that."

He gazed deep into my eyes. "That's not the past I'm referring to. I had always hoped you'd come back one day. I was so worried about you."

I gasped. "I have no idea what you're talking about, but I should really get going. I'll call you."

Jonovan grabbed my hand and held it tight. "I don't blame you for trying to get them back. At first, I wasn't sure, but there were way too many coincidences. Way too many negative things falling upon people right after you came here."

I didn't deny anything, but I didn't admit to anything, either.

"I'm totally confused," I replied. "You're talking foolish."

"If you say so." He let my hand go. "Like I said, I'm glad you came back, even if you're about to run again. But please don't run from me. At least keep in touch and let me know that you're alive. Before . . . it was so hard. The not knowing."

I wondered how long it had been since he'd figured it out. So he was playing a game of deception with me while I was playing a game of deception with him. *What a fucked-up relationship!*

"We don't ever have to discuss it, Caprice. I only wanted you to know that I'm aware; I don't care. Well, I take that back. I do care; I always have. But nothing you've been through makes you any less of a woman to me. In fact, it makes you more of one."

A tear fell on my right cheek and I wrote it away quickly. "Please don't say that name again."

"I won't, if you so wish. But I need to tell you one other thing. I love you, Wicket . . . Ladonna . . . or whomever you choose to be tomorrow. I love you and I want to make this work. Please don't leave me."

"There's too much pain here."

"And an incredible amount of love."

"There are a lot of things you don't know about me," I whispered. "Bad things."

"I don't care. I don't want to lose you again. We're at least halfway through our lives. Let's not spend the rest of them alone. We've already lost twenty-five years."

I made up my mind right then and there that I wanted to be with Jonovan, for whatever it was worth, for whatever it meant.

"If you truly want to be with me, it can't be here . . . in Atlanta."

He sighed and took a deep breath.

"But maybe I had it all wrong before, with my suggestion."

"What do you mean?"

"I love you, too, Jonovan. Move to New

York with me . . . both you and your father. You can do your magazine from anywhere. Matter of fact, New York is the best place to thrive with a music magazine."

"I won't live off you," he said.

"Technically, we'd both be living off my daddy." I smiled for the first time in the entire conversation. "My apartment sold a couple of months ago, but he has dozens of places in the city. We only need one."

He frowned. "I'm not trying to live off him, either."

"So, make your magazine an amazing success so you can contribute to the bills." I was joking, but a man needed to feel like a man, so if he wanted to pony up something, I would let him do that. "It's a win-win for everyone."

"But my dad's used to being here."

"No disrespect, but does your father even know that he's in Atlanta? Will he even know the difference? As long as he has you there with him, and you can be there for him, that's all that matters, right?"

Jonovan grinned. "This is crazy. I can't believe that we're sitting here discussing this."

"Yeah, I never saw this coming, either, but that's how we know it's supposed to be."

Jonovan took me into his arms and laid a

huge kiss on me, tongue and all. Surprisingly, I relaxed and went with it, enjoying every second.

"Do you realize that was our first real kiss?" he asked as we moved apart a moment later. "And yet, I'm talking about moving with you?"

"It won't be our last kiss." I proved that by yanking him by the collar and kissing him again.

Something ignited inside me. I pulled him inside the front door. His father and his aide were in the back of the house, in the family room where they spent the majority of their time.

I moved backward, still kissing him, and started up the steps. He pushed me back on the third or fourth step and I spread my legs, welcoming him between them as he started kissing my neck and pressing his dick up against my pussy through my panties underneath my skirt.

I reached my hands to pull up the back of his sweater, up and over his head and tossed it aside. Then I ran my fingers up and down his back.

He picked me up with my ankles locked around his hips and hurriedly carried me upstairs to the master bedroom, kicking the door shut with his foot. We ripped each other's clothes off and within two minutes, Jonovan was deep inside me with a condom on.

I wrapped my ankles around his neck so he could go deeper and I had an orgasm almost immediately. He kept going until he was spent and I was curled up like a baby in his arms.

"That's the first time I've ever made love," I confessed, trying to regulate my breathing. "I'm glad it was you."

He kissed me on the forehead. "I only ever want it to be me."

I looked him in the eyes. "Are you going to pack?"

"Taking a big chance in life is very scary, but regret is even more scary. I'm not letting you go again. So yes, I'm going to pack."

The grand opening went over great in Miami. People raved over the decor, the food, the music, and everything in between. Of course, I was expected to perform at least one song, so I sang "Surge," the song that I had written for Jonovan. Well, actually, the first of many songs that he had inspired in me.

While I would never fully understand why I had to go through so much to get to a place of contentment, there had to have been a reason for it all. As long as I had the love of my life by my side, that was all that ultimately mattered.

■ ■ ■ ■

PART FIVE:
CODA

■ ■ ■ ■

One day you'll meet someone who
doesn't care about your past because
they want to be with you in your future.
— Unknown

Epilogue

Two years later and things were still going well between Jonovan and me. He had proposed, but I really didn't see the purpose in marriage. I was actually able to make love to him on a regular basis. Gone were the times when I could only relate intimacy to pain. His magazine truly took off, in an age when a lot of other industry periodicals were dying. I even did a monthly editorial piece, and he had other famous contributors as well.

I did give up my sadist behavior. I won't front; it was hard. Really hard. Piece of Shit took it harder than Glaze. I'd always had the sneaking suspicion that Glaze was doing her thing the entire time and I wasn't jealous or upset about it. It was all about role-playing, and the three of us using one another to satisfy our individual needs. I never got to know either one of them well enough to understand — or even care to understand — why they had chosen to be dominated. I had enough of a challenge trying to comprehend why I was doing what I was doing. Everyone has a past, and everyone is a culmination of everything they've ever experienced, witnessed, or been taught. Glaze and Piece of Shit had both been through something, but that was none of my business.

Piece of Shit had a breakdown over the phone when I told him it was over. I used a burner phone, of course, just in case he snapped and started recording the conversation. I could always deny it was me, if he decided to go to the media to pay me back for refusing to continue to whomp on that ass. He wasn't practicing the life with anyone else; that was clear. I told him that there were *plenty* of women who were about that life who would be more than happy to hook him up. I was really a self-taught amateur. I had read some books and watched some videos on the Internet. With such a recognizable face, it wasn't like I could attend BDSM clubs or seminars or register for one of their "no-holds-barred" — no pun intended — weekends at hotels where they rented out the entire block of rooms and had security posted everywhere so people could get in where they fit in.

Even if I could've pulled it off without being recognized by donning a mask, I was too afraid that someone might assume that they could fuck me, or even touch me, and I would've cut off some dude's dick in a flashback.

It was what it was, and when Piece of Shit had the nerve to try to issue a threat against me, I made it clear that I was not the one. I reminded him that Daddy had long money and if he didn't shut the fuck up, I would scour the earth to find him and make him take a dirt nap. That was enough to make him "find his center." I wished him well and instructed him never to contact me again . . . or else. I realized Piece of Shit was not exactly normal, but I didn't think he was a fool, either. Only a fool would come for me before I came for them. I never heard back from him.

Cherie fully recovered from her injuries. Between "the incident," and finding out that her man was a whore, I was satisfied that she had received what was coming to her. She was the laughingstock of women in her circle, and her client base fell off as well. No one cared to be associated with her. It was a negative blemish on their images.

Michael ended up going into the porn industry, and that didn't surprise me. He was really left with little choice at that point. The world had seen him in action; getting any work in a major motion picture, or network production, was even less of a possibility than it was before I leaked that tape. If his ass could have acted, he wouldn't have still been carrying that bit role in *New Jack City* like it was an Academy Award–winning performance. I watched that flick like three more times on DVD and still didn't spot his ass in it. I was beginning to wonder if whatever scene he was in had been left on the cutting-room floor. Both he and Cherie swore up and down he was in it.

So now he was banging out random broads while they made fake moans on camera. Porn didn't pay like it used to, especially not for men. Everyone was making homemade nookie films, and there were literally more than a million free porn movies on the Internet on any given day. But he made what he could and, quite frankly, I'm sure he was enjoying the hell out of it. He always played the alpha male in the films, proving that his manhood was directly connected to his dick time and time again.

Herman was still in jail and had to serve at least another two years before he would be eligible for probation. His practice and career were history, and I heard that Bianca stopped going to visit him early on and filed for divorce. I was hoping his pretty-boy ass was getting worked over while he was on lockdown. It would've served him right.

Bianca was still putting on a lot of pretenses, in spite of everyone talking about her like no tomorrow. She managed to keep her clients, for the most part. They felt sorry for her, and I had to give it to her — she did have a good eye when it came to interior design. It was such a shame that my once best friend was now my greatest enemy. And she didn't even know it. I decided to concentrate on my career and my relationship with Jonovan, but there was no guarantee that I wouldn't revisit doing something drastic to her in the future.

I was still seeing Marcella once a month in New York. I was still taking all my medications. Life was far from perfect, but it was good. I had released three albums in three years, so I was on a roll. The songs and their lyrics came leaking out of my pores, once I was able to release the majority of my anger. Of course, falling in love with Jonovan had something to do with it as well. Before I had been fantasizing about the love of my life when I penned songs; now I actually had one.

I was in love. I knew that for sure. But I

was still having an issue giving up that kind of power to another human being. Daddy liked Jonovan a lot, but he was skeptical about my ability to make it work. I'm sure he desired that for me but, like me, he was a realist. He was hitting his midseventies, so he was ready to start slowing down in regards to travel and exploring new business interests. It had long stopped being about making money and had become more about remaining active. I could tell that he was growing weary, but he had lived ten lifetimes in one.

Jonovan's father died in the spring of 2014. He took it extremely hard, but I was there for him every step of the way. I helped him pick out his father's casket and suit and sang "Tears in Heaven" by Eric Clapton, a song written about the tragic death of his own son, Conor, after he fell from a fifty-third-story window in New York in 1991. The funeral was well attended and it was when a lot of the media found out that we were dating. Up until then, since I wouldn't go to that many places, not that many people knew. It wasn't a secret, but I didn't feel the need to talk about my personal business, nor did I want others interfering with my happiness.

It would be a long road, but I was looking

forward to my next phase of life. I had made it through the most difficult phase, which was not about other people misunderstanding me but more about a lack of understanding of self. Thanks to Marcella, Jonovan, Daddy, and even the somewhat of a closure that I had gotten from my mother, I had more clarity than I had ever had before. The most valuable thing that I learned is that sometimes when things seem like they are falling apart, they might actually be falling into place.

I also felt like two people were watching carefully over me.

Thanks, Grandma!

Thanks, Hannah!

COMMENTARY BY ZANE

I believe everything happens for a reason. People change so you can learn to let go. Things go wrong so you can appreciate them when they're right. You believe lies so you can learn to trust no one but yourself, and sometimes good things fall apart so better things can fall together.
— Marilyn Monroe

I felt it appropriate to start off this commentary with a quote from Marilyn Monroe. Besides, it is an awesome quote and one that I can totally relate to, especially at this time in my life. When I started this book, I was at one place in my life journey, and by the time I sat down to complete it, I had evolved into a much different and stronger person. I am still a work in progress, but I have learned to let go of the things that have limited my purpose in life.

411

One thing that I did realize after finishing this novel during a very dark point in my life is that I am truly walking in my gift. Once I tightened up my inner circle and remained focused on my writing, everything became much clearer.

The main character in this novel — Caprice Tatum / Ladonna Sterling / Wicket — is by far the most complicated and confused character that I have ever undertaken to date. As always, I began to live and breathe her while I was locked away alone creating her story. There were times when she became so real to me that I became emotionally drained by dealing with her issues — even though they were all in my head — that I had to run out to a grocery store and snatch up some diet sodas and doughnuts. Lean meats, steamed vegetables, and water with lemon simply weren't going to cut it. There is much truth to the term "comfort food." I discovered that on my production sets, when frustration and the feeling of being overwhelmed were transformed to smiles and jokes once craft services passed out Popsicles, small cups of chicken noodle soup, or nachos with chili and cheese.

I only bring that up because Caprice comforted herself in other ways. By engaging in self-mutilation during her younger

years, lashing out at others in angry episodes, and being a dominatrix controlling
her pets. She couldn't let go of her past,
like so many people who carry a lot of bitterness and baggage to the point where they
block any blessings that may cross their
paths. Like her predecessors — Zoe from
Addicted and Jonquinette from *Nervous* —
Caprice's issues were to the extreme, but
that was only done to drive several points
home to others who may be dealing with
similar issues on a much smaller level. By
writing these kind of books, I want to let
people know that they can overcome their
challenges if people with the same ones —
times ten — can overcome theirs.

I continue to try to impress upon people
that it is okay to seek therapy and medication when needed. The stigma of weakness
surrounding seeing a psychiatrist, especially
in the African-American community, keeps
a lot of people drowning in misery for their
entire lives. During the writing of this book,
I also went through training to become a
rape, incest, and abuse counselor. Even
though I have been answering advice e-mails
— many from rape and incest victims —
since 1997, I was not completely aware of
the magnitude of people who have endured
such traumatic pasts.

According to various sources, one in four people have a mental disorder. ONE IN FOUR! On any given day, nearly ten million people are having suicidal thoughts, and suicide is the third leading cause of death. One in thirty people are suffering from post-traumatic stress disorder. Children with any kind of mental disorders are the least likely to receive treatment. A lot of that comes from parents being in denial. It is understandable because no one wants to accept that something may be wrong with their children, or that something may have happened to their children under their watch. Again, that was the case with both the main characters in the previous novels in this series — *Addicted* and *Nervous.* In *Vengeance,* Caprice experiences a "series" of destructive events that leave her completely broken. It has to make one wonder how much more she can possibly take. I won't list them here because several readers have told me at signings that they were mad at themselves for reading my commentary before reading the book, and learning too many of the spoilers because of it.

Therefore, I am simply going to say that this book is about tolerance of other people and their lifestyles. It is not only about learning to forgive others but also about self-forgiveness. It is about realizing, like the quote states in the beginning of this section, that everything truly does happen for a reason, and that sometimes things fall apart so even better things can come together. Caprice was on the threshing floor, a piece of wheat being pulled and tugged at by oxen, until the shaft was pulled away and only the purest and strongest part of the grain was left. She still has a ways to go, but she will get there. I didn't want to end the book with a fairy-tale ending, just a realistic one.

I hope that you enjoyed *Vengeance* as much as I enjoyed creating it. As always, I love and appreciate each and every one of you. Let your enemies become your footstools, your tests become your testimonies, and your messes become your messages. I speak from vast experience on that one.

Blessings,
Zane
facebook.com/AuthorZane
twitter.com/AuthorZane
instagram.com/PlanetZane
zinnapp.com/the-author-zane-zinnapp
eroticanoir.com
zaneromance.com

ABOUT THE AUTHOR

Zane is the *New York Times* bestselling author of *Afterburn, The Heat Seekers, Dear G-Spot, Gettin' Buck Wild, The Hot Box, Total Eclipse of the Heart, Nervous, Skyscraper, Love Is Never Painless, Shame on It All,* and *The Sisters of APF;* the ebook short stories *I'll be Home for Christmas* and *Everything Fades Away;* and editor for the Flava anthology series, including *Z-Rated* and *Busy Bodies.* Her television series, *Zane's Sex Chronicles* and *The Jump Off,* are featured on Cinemax, and her bestselling novel *Addicted* has been adapted for a major motion picture with Lionsgate Films. She is the publisher of Strebor Books, an imprint of Atria Books/ Simon & Schuster. Visit her online at Erotica Noir.com.